M⚙RTAL ENGINES

OTHER SCHOLASTIC BOOKS
BY PHILIP REEVE:

PHILIP REEVE

MORTAL ENGINES

SCHOLASTIC INC.

ISBN 978-1-338-20112-3

10 9 8 7 6   18 19 20 21 22

Printed in the U.S.A.   40
First Scholastic American paperback printing, June 2012

This edition first printing 2018

The text type was set in Rialto.
Book design by Steve Scott

For Sarah

CONTENTS

PART ONE

THE HUNTING GROUND

It was a dark, blustery afternoon in spring, and the city of London was chasing a small mining town across the dried-out bed of the old North Sea.

In happier times, London would never have bothered with such feeble prey. The great Traction City had once spent its days hunting far bigger towns than this, ranging north as far as the edges of the Ice Waste and south to the shores of the Mediterranean. But lately prey of any kind had started to grow scarce, and some of the larger cities had begun to look hungrily at London. For ten years now it had been hiding from them, skulking in a damp, mountainous western district that the Guild of Historians said had once been the island of Britain. For ten years it had eaten nothing but tiny farming towns and static settlements in those wet hills. Now, at last, the Lord Mayor had decided that the time was right to take his city back over the land bridge into the Great Hunting Ground.

It was barely halfway across when the lookouts on the high watchtowers spied the mining town, gnawing at the salt flats twenty miles ahead. To the people of London it seemed like a sign from the gods, and even the Lord Mayor (who didn't believe in gods or signs) thought it was a good beginning to the journey east, and issued the order to give chase.

The mining town saw the danger and turned tail, but already the huge caterpillar tracks under London were starting to roll faster and faster. Soon the city was lumbering in pursuit, a moving mountain of metal that rose in seven tiers like the layers of a wedding cake, the lower levels wreathed in engine smoke, the villas of the rich gleaming white on the higher decks, and above it all the cross on top of St. Paul's Cathedral glinting gold, two thousand feet above the ruined earth.

❈

Tom was cleaning the exhibits in the London Museum's Natural History section when it started. He felt the telltale tremor in the metal floor, and looked up to find the model whales and dolphins that hung from the gallery roof swinging on their cables with soft creaking sounds.

He wasn't alarmed. He had lived in London for all of his fifteen years, and he was used to its movements. He knew that the city was changing course and putting on speed. A prickle of excitement ran through him, the ancient thrill of the hunt that all Londoners·shared. There must be prey in sight! Dropping his brushes and dusters he pressed his hand to the wall, sensing the vibrations that came rippling up from the huge engine rooms down in the Gut. Yes, there it was — the deep throb of the auxiliary motors cutting in, *boom, boom, boom,* like a big drum beating inside his bones.

The door at the far end of the gallery slammed open and Chudleigh Pomeroy came storming in, his toupee askew and his round face red with indignation. "What in the name of Quirke . . . ?" he blustered, gawping at the gyrating whales and the stuffed birds jigging and twitching in their cases as if they were shaking off their long captivity and getting ready to take wing again. "Apprentice Natsworthy! What's going on here?"

"It's a chase, sir," said Tom, wondering how the Deputy Head of the Guild of Historians had managed to live aboard London for so long and still not recognize its heartbeat. "It must be something good," he explained. "They've brought all the auxiliaries on line. That hasn't happened for ages. Maybe London's luck has turned!"

"Pah!" snorted Pomeroy, wincing as the glass in the display cases started to whine and shiver in sympathy with the beat of the engines. Above his head the biggest of the models — a thing called a blue whale that had become extinct thousands of years ago — was jerking back and forth on its hawsers like a plank-swing. "That's as may be, Natsworthy," he said. "I just wish the Guild of Engineers would fit some decent shock absorbers in this building. Some of these specimens are very delicate. It won't do. It won't do at all." He tugged a spotted handkerchief out of the folds of his long black robes and dabbed his face with it.

"Please, sir," asked Tom, "could I run down to the observation platforms and watch the chase, just for half an hour? It's been years since there was a really good one. . . ."

Pomeroy looked shocked. "Certainly not, Apprentice! Look at all the dust that this wretched chase is shaking down! All the exhibits will have to be cleaned again and checked for damage."

"Oh, but that's not fair!" cried Tom. "I've just dusted this whole gallery!"

He knew at once that he had made a mistake. Old Chudleigh Pomeroy wasn't bad, as Guildsmen went, but he didn't like being answered back by a mere Third Class Apprentice. He drew himself up to his full height (which was only slightly more than his full width) and frowned so sternly that his Guild-mark almost vanished between his bushy eyebrows. "Life isn't fair, Natsworthy," he boomed. "Any more cheek from you and you'll be on Gutduty as soon as this chase is over!"

Of all the horrible chores a Third Class Apprentice had to perform, Gut-duty was the one Tom hated most. He quickly shut up, staring meekly down at the beautifully buffed toes of the Chief Curator's boots.

"You were told to work in this department until seven o'clock, and you will work until seven o'clock," Pomeroy went on. "Meanwhile, I shall consult the other curators about this dreadful, dreadful shaking. . . ."

He hurried off, still muttering. Tom watched him go, then picked up his gear and went miserably back to work. Usually he didn't mind cleaning, especially not in this gallery, with its amiable, moth-eaten animals and the Blue Whale smiling its big blue smile. If he grew bored, he simply took refuge in a daydream in which he was a hero who rescued beautiful girls from air-pirates, saved London from the Anti-Traction League, and lived happily ever after. But how could he daydream, with the rest of the city enjoying the first proper chase for ages?

He waited for twenty minutes, but Chudleigh Pomeroy did not return. There was nobody else about. It was a Wednesday, which meant the Museum was closed to the public, and most of the senior Guildsmen and First and Second Class Apprentices

6

would be having the day off. What harm could it do if he slipped outside for ten minutes, just to see what was happening? He hid his bag of cleaning stuff behind a handy yak and hurried through the shadows of dancing dolphins to the door.

Out in the corridor all the argon lamps were dancing, too, spilling their light up the metal walls. Two black-robed Guildsmen hurried past, and Tom heard the reedy voice of old Dr. Arkengarth whine, "Vibrations! Vibrations! It's playing merry hell with my twenty-fifth century ceramics. . . ." He waited until they had vanished around a bend in the corridor, then slipped quickly out and down the nearest stairway. He cut through the Twenty-First Century gallery, past the big plastic statues of Pluto and Mickey, animal-headed gods of lost America. He ran across the main hall and down galleries full of things that had somehow survived through all the millennia since the Ancients destroyed themselves in that terrible flurry of orbit-to-earth atomics and tailored-virus bombs called the Sixty Minute War. Two minutes later he slipped out through a side entrance into the noise and bustle of Tottenham Court Road.

The London Museum stood at the very hub of Tier Two, in a busy district called Bloomsbury, and the underbelly of Tier One hung like a rusty sky a few feet above the rooftops. Tom didn't worry about being spotted as he pushed his way along the dark, crowded street toward the public Goggle-screen outside the Tottenham Court Road elevator station. Joining the crowd in front of it he had his first glimpse of the distant prey: a watery, blue-gray blur captured by cameras down on Tier Six. "The town is called Salthook," boomed the voice of the announcer. "A mining platform of nine hundred inhabitants. She is currently moving at eighty miles per hour, heading due east, but the Guild of Navigators predicts London will catch her before sundown. There are sure to be many more towns awaiting us beyond the land bridge: clear proof of just how wise our beloved Lord Mayor was when he decided to bring London east again. . . ."

Tom had never felt his city move at such an astonishing speed, and he longed to be down at the observation deck, feeling the wind on his face. He was probably already in trouble with Mr. Pomeroy. What difference could it make if he stole a few more minutes?

He set off at a run, and soon reached Bloomsbury Park, out in the open air on the tier's brim. It had been a proper park once, with trees and duck ponds, but because of the recent shortage of prey it had been given over to food production and its lawns grubbed up to make way for cabbage plots and algae-pans. The observation platforms were still there, though, raised balconies jutting out from the edge of the tier, where Londoners could go to watch the passing view. Tom hurried toward the nearest. An even bigger crowd had gathered there, including quite a few people in the black of the Historians' Guild, and Tom tried to look inconspicuous as he pushed his way through to the front and peered over the railings. Salthook was only five miles ahead, traveling flat out with black smoke spewing from its exhaust stacks.

"Natsworthy!" called a braying voice, and his heart sank. He looked around and found that he was standing next to Melliphant, a burly First Class Apprentice, who grinned at him and said, "Isn't it wonderful? A fat little salt-mining platform, with C20 land-engines! Just what London needs!"

Herbert Melliphant was the worst sort of bully, the sort who didn't just hit you and stick your head down the lavatory, but made it his business to find out all your secrets and the things that upset you most and taunt you with them. He enjoyed picking on Tom, who was small and shy and had no friends to stick up for him — and Tom could not get back at him, because Melliphant's family had paid to make him a First Class Apprentice, while Tom, who had no family, was a mere Third. He knew Melliphant was only bothering to talk to him because he was hoping to impress a pretty young Historian named Clytie Potts, who was standing just behind. Tom nodded and turned his back, concentrating on the chase.

"Look!" shouted Clytie Potts.

The gap between London and its prey was narrowing fast, and a dark shape had lifted clear of Salthook. Soon there was another and another. Airships! The crowds on London's observation platforms cheered, and Melliphant said, "Ah, air-merchants. They know the town is doomed, you see, so they are making sure they get away before we eat it. If they don't, we can claim their cargoes along with everything else aboard!"

Tom was glad to see that Clytie Potts looked thoroughly bored by Melliphant: She was a year above him and must already know this stuff, because she had passed her Guild exams and had the Historian's mark tattooed on her forehead. "Look!" she said again, catching Tom's glance and grinning. "Oh, look at them go! Aren't they beautiful!"

Tom pushed his untidy hair out of his eyes and watched as the airships rose up and up and vanished into the slate-gray clouds. For a moment he found himself longing to go with them, up into the sunlight. If only his poor parents had not left him to the care of the Guild, to be trained as a Historian! He wished he could be cabin boy aboard a sky-clipper and see all the cities of the world: Puerto Angeles adrift on the blue Pacific and Arkangel skating on iron runners across the frozen northern seas, the great ziggurat-towns of the Nuevo-Mayans and the unmoving strongholds of the Anti-Traction League . . .

But that was just a daydream, better saved for some dull Museum afternoon. A fresh outbreak of cheering warned him that the chase was nearing its end, and he forgot the airships and turned his attention back to Salthook.

The little town was so close that he could see the antlike shapes of people running about on its upper tiers. How frightened they must be, with London bearing down on them and nowhere to hide! But he knew he mustn't feel sorry for them: It was natural that cities ate towns, just as the towns ate smaller towns, and smaller towns snapped up the miserable static settlements. That was Municipal Darwinism, and it was the way the world had worked for a thousand years, ever since the great engineer Nikolas Quirke had turned London into the first Traction City.

"London! London!" Tom shouted, adding his voice to the cheers and shouts of everybody else on the platform, and a moment later they were rewarded by the sight of one of Salthook's wheels breaking loose. The town slewed to a halt, smokestacks snapping off and crashing down into the panicked streets, and then London's lower tiers blocked it from view and Tom felt the deckplates shiver as the city's huge hydraulic Jaws came slamming shut.

There was frantic cheering from observation platforms all over the city. Loudspeakers on the tier-support pillars started to play "London Pride," and somebody Tom had never even seen before hugged him tight and shouted in his ear, "A catch! A catch!" He didn't mind; at that moment he loved everybody on the platform, even Melliphant. "A catch!" he yelled back, struggling free, and felt the deckplates trembling again. Somewhere below him the city's great steel teeth were gripping Salthook, lifting it and dragging it backward into the Gut.

". . . and perhaps Apprentice Natsworthy would like to come as well," Clytie Potts was saying. Tom had no idea what she was talking about, but as he turned she touched his arm and smiled. "There'll be celebrations in Kensington Gardens tonight," she explained. "Dancing and fireworks! Do you want to come?"

People didn't usually invite Third Class Apprentices to parties — especially not people as pretty and popular as Clytie — and Tom wondered at first if she was making fun of him. But Melliphant obviously didn't think so, for he tugged her away and said, "We don't want Natsworthy's sort there."

"Why not?" asked the girl.

"Well, you know," huffed Melliphant, his square face turning almost as red as Mr. Pomeroy's. "He's just a Third. A skivvy. He'll never get his Guild-mark. He'll just end up as a curator's assistant. Won't you, Natsworthy?" he asked, leering at Tom. "It's a pity your dad didn't leave you enough money for a proper apprenticeship. . . ."

"That's none of your business!" shouted Tom angrily. His elation at the catch had evaporated and he was on edge again, wondering what punishments would be in store when Pomeroy found out that he had sneaked away. He was in no mood for Melliphant's taunts.

"Still, that's what comes of living in a slum on the lower tiers,

I suppose," smirked Melliphant, turning back to Clytie Potts. "Natsworthy's mum and dad lived down on Four, see, and when the Big Tilt happened they both got squashed flat as a couple of raspberry pancakes: *splat!*"

Tom didn't mean to hit him; it just happened. Before he knew what he was doing his hand had curled into a tight fist and he lashed out. "Ow!" wailed Melliphant, so startled that he fell over backward. Someone cheered, and Clytie stifled a giggle. Tom just stood staring at his trembling fist and wondering how he had done it.

But Melliphant was much bigger and tougher than Tom, and he was already back on his feet. Clytie tried to restrain him, but some other Historians were cheering him on and a group of boys in the green tunics of Apprentice Navigators clustered close behind and chanted, "Fight! Fight! Fight!"

Tom knew he stood no more chance against Melliphant than Salthook had stood against London. He took a step backward, but the crowd was hemming him in. Then Melliphant's fist hit him on the side of the face and Melliphant's knee crashed up hard between his legs and he was bent double and stumbling away with his eyes full of tears. Something as big and softly yielding as a sofa stood in his way, and as he rammed his head against it, it said, "Ooof!"

He looked up into a round, red, bushy-eyebrowed face under an unconvincing wig; a face that grew even redder when it recognized him.

"Natsworthy!" boomed Chudleigh Pomeroy. "What in Quirke's name do you think you're playing at?"

2

VALENTINE

And so Tom found himself being sent off to do Gut-duty while all the other apprentices were busy celebrating the capture of Salthook. After a long, embarrassing lecture in Pomeroy's office ("Disobedience, Natsworthy . . . Striking a senior Apprentice . . . What would your poor parents have thought?") he trudged over to Tottenham Court Road station and waited for a down elevator.

When it came, it was crowded. The seats in the upper compartment were packed with arrogant-looking men and women from the Guild of Engineers, the most powerful of the four Great Guilds that ran London. They gave Tom the creeps, with their bald heads and those long white rubber coats they wore, so he stayed standing in the lower section, where the stern face of the Lord Mayor stared down at him from posters saying, *Movement is Life — Help the Guild of Engineers keep London moving!* Down and down went the elevator, stopping at all the familiar stations — Bakerloo, High Holborn, Low Holborn, Bethnal Green — and at every stop another crowd of people surged into the car, squashing

13

him against the back wall until it was almost a relief to reach the bottom and step out into the noise and bustle of the Gut.

The Gut was where London dismantled the towns it caught: a stinking sprawl of yards and factories between the Jaws and the central engine rooms. Tom loathed it. It was always noisy, and it was staffed by workers from the lower tiers, who were dirty and frightening, and convicts from the Deep Gut Prisons, who were worse. The heat down there always gave him a headache, and the sulfurous air made him sneeze, and the flicker of the argon globes that lit the walkways hurt his eyes. But the Guild of Historians always made sure some of its staff were on hand when a town was being digested, and tonight he would have to join them and go about reminding the tough old foremen of the Gut that any books and antiques aboard the new catch were the rightful property of his Guild and that history was just as important as bricks and iron and coal.

He fought his way out of the elevator terminus and hurried toward the Guild of Historians' warehouse, through tubular corridors lined with green ceramic tiles and across metal catwalks high above the fiery gulfs of the Digestion Yards. Far below him he could see Salthook being torn to pieces. It looked tiny now, dwarfed by the vastness of London. Big yellow dismantling machines were crawling around it on tracks and swinging above it on cranes and clambering over it on hydraulic spider-legs. Its wheels and axles had already been taken off, and work was starting on the chassis. Circular saws as big as Ferris wheels bit into the deckplates, throwing up plumes of sparks. Great blasts of heat came billowing from furnaces and smelters, and before he had gone twenty paces Tom could feel the sweat starting to soak through the armpits of his black uniform tunic.

But when he finally reached the warehouse, things started to look a bit brighter. Salthook had not had a museum or a library, and the small heaps that had been salvaged from the town's junk shops were already being packed into crates for their journey up to Tier Two. If he was lucky he might be allowed to finish early and catch the end of the celebrations! He wondered which Guildsman was in charge tonight. If it was old Arkengarth or Dr. Weymouth he was doomed — they always made you work your whole shift whether there was anything to do or not. If it was Potty Pewtertide or Miss Plym he might be all right. . . .

But as he hurried toward the supervisor's office he began to realize that someone much more important than any of them was on Gut-duty tonight. There was a bug parked outside the office, a sleek black bug with the Guild's emblem painted on its engine cowling, much too flash for any of the usual staff. Two men in the livery of high-ranking Guild staff stood waiting beside it. They were rough-looking types, in spite of their plush clothes, and Tom knew at once who they were — Pewsey and Gench, the reformed air-pirates who had been the Head Historian's faithful servants for twenty years and who piloted the 13th Floor Elevator whenever he flew off on an expedition. *Valentine is here!* Tom thought, and tried not to stare as he hurried past them up the steps.

Thaddeus Valentine was Tom's hero: a former scavenger who had risen to become London's most famous archaeologist — and also its Head Historian, much to the envy and disgust of people like Pomeroy. Tom kept a picture of him tacked to the dormitory wall above his bunk, and he had read his books, *Adventures of a Practical Historian* and *America Deserta — Across the Dead Continent with Gun, Camera, and Airship,* until he knew them by heart. The proudest moment of his life had been when he was twelve and Valentine had come down to present the apprentices' end-of-year prizes, including the one Tom had won for an essay on identifying fake antiquities. He still remembered every word of the speech the great man had made: "*Never forget, Apprentices, that we Historians are the most important Guild in our city. We don't make as much money as the Merchants, but we create knowledge, which is worth a great deal more. We may not be responsible for steering London, like the Navigators, but where would the Navigators be if we hadn't preserved the ancient maps and charts? And as for the Guild of Engineers, just remember that every machine they have ever developed is based on some fragment of old-tech — ancient high technology that our museum-keepers have preserved or our archaeologists have dug up.*"

All Tom had been able to manage by way of reply was a mumbled, "Thank you, sir," before he scurried back to his seat, so it never occurred to him that Valentine would remember him. But when he opened the door of the supervisor's office, the great man looked up from his desk and grinned.

"It's Natsworthy, isn't it? The apprentice who's so good at spotting fakes? I'll have to watch my step tonight, or you'll find me out!"

It wasn't much of a joke, but it broke through the awkwardness that usually existed between an apprentice and a senior Guildsman, and Tom relaxed enough to stop hovering on the threshold and step right inside, holding out his note from

Pomeroy. Valentine jumped to his feet and came striding over to take it. He was a tall, handsome man of nearly forty with a mane of silver-flecked black hair and a trim black beard. His gray mariner's eyes twinkled with humor, and on his forehead a third eye — the Guild-mark of the Historian, the blue eye that looks backward into time — seemed to wink as he raised a quizzical eyebrow.

"Fighting, eh? And what did Apprentice Melliphant do to deserve a black eye?"

"He was saying stuff about my mum and dad, sir," mumbled Tom.

"I see." The explorer nodded, watching the boy's face. Instead of telling him off he asked, "Are you the son of David and Rebecca Natsworthy?"

"Yes, sir," admitted Tom. "But I was only six when the Big Tilt happened. . . . I mean, I don't really remember them."

Valentine nodded again, and his eyes were sad and kind. "They were good Historians, Thomas. I hope you'll follow in their footsteps."

"Oh, yes, sir!" said Tom. "I mean — I hope so, too!" He thought of his poor mum and dad, killed when part of Cheapside collapsed onto the tier below. Nobody had ever spoken like that about them before, and he felt his eyes filling with tears. He felt as if he could tell Valentine anything, anything at all, and he was just on the point of saying how much he missed his parents and how lonely and boring it was being a Third Class Apprentice, when a wolf walked into the office.

It was a very large wolf, and white, and it appeared through the door that led out into the stockroom. As soon as it saw Tom it came running toward him, baring its yellow fangs. "Aaaah!" he shrieked, leaping onto a chair. "A wolf!"

"Oh, do behave!" a girl's voice said, and a moment later the girl herself was there, bending over the beast and tickling the soft white ruff of fur under its chin. The fierce amber eyes closed happily, and Tom heard its tail whisking against her clothes. "Don't worry," she laughed, smiling up at him. "He's a lamb. I mean, he's a wolf, really, but he's as *gentle* as a lamb."

"Tom," said Valentine, his eyes twinkling with amusement, "meet my daughter, Katherine, and Dog."

"Dog?" Tom came down off his chair, feeling foolish and still a little scared. He had thought the brute must have escaped from the zoo in Circle Park.

"It's a long story," said Valentine. "Katherine lived on the raft-city of Puerto Angeles until she was five. Then her mother died, and she was sent to live with me. I brought Dog back for her as a present from my expedition to the Ice Wastes, but Katherine couldn't speak very much Anglish in those days and she'd never heard of wolves, so when she first saw him she said, 'Dog!,' and it sort of stuck."

"He's perfectly tame," the girl promised, still smiling up at Tom. "Father found him when he was just a cub. He had to shoot the mother, but he hadn't the heart to finish poor Dog off. He likes it best if you tickle his tummy. Dog, I mean, not Father." She laughed. She had a lot of long, dark hair, and her father's gray eyes and the same quick, dazzling smile, and she was dressed in the narrow silk trousers and flowing tunic that were all the rage in High London that summer. Tom gazed at her in wonder.

18

He had seen pictures of Valentine's daughter, but he had never realized how beautiful she was.

"Look," she said, "he likes you!"

Dog had ambled over to sniff at the hem of Tom's tunic. His tail swished from side to side and a wet, pink tongue rasped over Tom's fingers.

"If Dog likes people," said Katherine, "I usually find I like them, too. So come along, Father; introduce us properly!"

Valentine laughed. "Well, Kate, this is Tom Natsworthy, who has been sent down here to help, and if your wolf has finished with him, I think we will have to let him get to work." He put a kindly hand on Tom's shoulder. "There's not much to be done; we'll just take a last look around the Yards and then . . ." He glanced at the note from Pomeroy, then tore it up into little pieces and dropped them into the red recycling bin beside his desk. "Then you can go."

Tom was not sure what surprised him more — that Valentine was letting him off, or that he was coming down to the Yards in person. Senior Guildsmen usually preferred to sit in the comfort of the office and let the apprentices do the hard work down in the heat and fumes, but here was Valentine pulling off his black robes, clipping a pen into the pocket of his waistcoat, pausing to grin at Tom from the doorway.

"Come along then," he said. "The sooner we start, the sooner you can be off to join the fun in Kensington Gardens. . . ."

❋

Down they went and down, with Dog and Katherine following, down past the warehouse and on down twisting spirals of metal stairs to the Digestion Yards, where Salthook was growing smaller by the minute. All that remained of it now was a steel skeleton, and the machines were ripping even that apart, dragging deckplates and girders away to the furnaces to be melted down. Meanwhile, mountains of brick and slate and timber and salt and coal were trundling off on conveyor belts toward the heart of the Gut, and skips of furniture and provisions were being wheeled clear by the salvage gangs.

The salvagemen were the true rulers of this part of London, and they knew it. They swaggered along the narrow walkways with the agility of tomcats, their bare chests shiny with sweat and their eyes hidden by tinted goggles. Tom had always been frightened of them, but Valentine hailed them with an easy charm and asked them if they had seen anything amongst the spoils that might be of interest to the Museum. Sometimes he stopped to joke with them, or ask them how their families were doing — and he was always careful to introduce them to "My colleague, Mr. Natsworthy." Tom felt himself swell with pride. Valentine was treating him like a grown-up, and so the salvagemen treated him the same way, touching the peaks of their greasy caps and grinning as they introduced themselves. They all seemed to be called Len or Smudger.

"Take no notice of what they say about these chaps up at the Museum," warned Valentine as one of the Lens led them to a skip where some antiques had been stowed. "Just because they live down in the nether boroughs and don't pronounce their Hs doesn't mean they're fools. That's why I like to come down in person when the Yards are working. I've often seen salvagemen and scavengers turn up artifacts that Historians might have missed. . . ."

"Yes, sir . . ." agreed Tom, glancing at Katherine. He longed to do something that would impress the Head Historian and his beautiful daughter. If only he could find some wonderful fragment of old-tech amongst all this junk, something that would make them remember him after they had gone back to the luxury of High London. Otherwise, after this wander around the Yards, he might never see them again!

Hoping to amaze them, he hurried to the skip and looked inside. After all, old-tech *did* turn up from time to time in small-town antique shops, or on old ladies' mantelpieces. Imagine being the one to rediscover some legendary secret, like heavier-than-air flying machines, or pot noodles! Even if it wasn't something that the Guild of Engineers could use it might still end up in the Museum, labeled and preserved in a display case with a notice saying, "*Discovered by Mr. T. Natsworthy*." He peered hopefully at the heap of salvage in the skip: shards of plastic, lamp stands, a flattened toy ground-car. . . . A small metal box caught his eye. When he pulled it out and opened it his own face blinked back at him, reflected in a silvery plastic disc. "Mr. Valentine! Look! A seedy!"

Valentine reached into the box and lifted out the disc, tilting it so that rainbow light darted across its surface. "Quite right," he said. "The Ancients used these in their computers, as a way of storing information."

"Could it be important?" asked Tom.

Valentine shook his head. "I'm sorry, Thomas. The people of the old days may only have lived in static settlements, but their electronic machines were far beyond anything London's Engineers have been able to build. Even if there is still something stored on this disc we have no way of reading it. But it's a good find. Keep hold of it, just in case."

He turned away as Tom put the seedy back in its box and slid it into his pocket. But Katherine must have sensed Tom's disappointment, because she touched his hand and said, "It's lovely, Tom. Anything that has survived all those thousands of years is lovely, whether it's any use to the horrible old Guild of Engineers or not. I've got a necklace made of old computer discs. . . ." She smiled at him. She was as lovely as one of the girls in his daydreams, but kinder and funnier, and he knew that from now on the heroines he rescued in his imagination would all be Katherine Valentine.

There was nothing else of interest in the skip; Salthook had been a practical sort of town, too busy gnawing at the old seabed to bother about digging up the past. But instead of going straight back to the warehouse Valentine led his companions up another staircase and along a narrow catwalk to the Incomers' Station, where the former inhabitants were queuing to give their names to the Clerk of Admissions and be taken up to new homes in the hostels and workhouses of London. "Even when I'm not on duty," he explained, "I always make a point of going down to see the scavengers when we make a catch, before they have a chance to sell their finds at the Tier Five antique markets and melt back into the Out-Country."

There were always some scavengers aboard a catch — townless wanderers who roamed the Hunting Ground on foot, scratching up pieces of old-tech. Salthook was no exception; at the end of a long queue of dejected townsfolk stood a group more ragged than the rest, with long, tattered coats that hung down to their

22

ankles and goggles and dust-masks slung about their grubby necks.

Like most Londoners, Tom was horrified by the idea that people still actually lived on the bare earth. He hung back with Katherine and Dog, but Valentine went over to speak with the scavengers. They came clustering around him, all except one, a tall, thin one in a black coat — a girl, Tom thought, although he could not be sure, because she wore a black scarf wrapped across her face like the turban of a desert nomad. He stood near her and watched while Valentine introduced himself to the other scavengers and asked, "So — have any of you found anything the Historians' Guild might wish to purchase?"

Some of the men nodded, some shook their heads, some rummaged in their bulging packs. The girl in the black head-scarf slid one hand inside her coat and said, "I have something for you, Valentine."

She spoke so softly that only Tom and Katherine heard her, and as they turned to look she suddenly sprang forward, whipping out a long, thin-bladed knife.

3

THE WASTE CHUTE

There was no time to think: Katherine screamed, Dog growled, the girl hesitated for a moment, and Tom saw his chance and threw himself forward, grabbing her arm as she drove the knife at Valentine's heart. She hissed, writhing, and the knife dropped to the deck as she twisted free and darted away along the catwalk. "Stop her!" bellowed Valentine, starting forward, but the other refugees had seen the knife and were milling about in fright, barring his way. Several of the scavengers had pulled out firearms and an armored policeman came lumbering through the crowd like a huge blue beetle, shouting, "No guns allowed in London!"

Glancing over the scavengers' heads, Tom glimpsed a dark silhouette against the distant glare of furnaces. The girl was at the far end of the catwalk, climbing nimbly up a ladder to a higher level. He ran after her and snatched at her ankle as she reached the top. He missed by a few inches, and at the same moment a dart hissed past him, striking sparks from the rungs. He looked back. Two more policemen were thrusting through the crowd with crossbows raised. Beyond them he could see Katherine and her father watching him. "Don't shoot!" he shouted. "I can catch her!"

He flung himself at the ladder and scrambled eagerly upward, determined to be the one to capture the would-be assassin. He could feel his heart pounding with excitement. After all those dull years spent dreaming of adventures, suddenly he was having one! He had saved Mr. Valentine's life! He was a hero!

The girl was already heading along the maze of high-level catwalks that led toward the furnace district. Hoping that Katherine could still see him, Tom set off in pursuit. The catwalk forked and narrowed, the handrails only a yard apart. Below him the work of the Digestion Yards went on regardless; no one down there had noticed the drama being played out above their heads. He plunged through deep shadows and warm, blinding clouds of steam with the girl always a few feet ahead. A low duct caught her head-scarf and ripped it off. Her long hair was coppery in the dim glow of the furnaces, but Tom still couldn't see her face. He wondered if she was pretty: a beautiful assassin from the Anti-Traction League.

He ducked past the dangling head-scarf and ran on, gasping for breath, fumbling his collar open. Down a giddy spiral of iron stairs and out onto the floor of the Digestion Yards, flashing through the shadows of conveyor belts and huge spherical gas tanks. A gang of convict laborers looked up in amazement as the girl raced by. "Stop her!" yelled Tom. They just stood gawping as he passed, but when he looked back he saw that one of the Apprentice Engineers who had been supervising them had broken off his work to join the chase. Tom immediately regretted shouting out. He wasn't going to give up his victory to some stupid Engineer! He put on an extra spurt of speed, so that he should be the one who caught her.

Ahead, the way was barred by a circular hole in the deck-plate, ringed by rusty handrails — a waste chute, scorched and blackened where clinker from the furnaces had been tipped down. The girl broke her pace for a moment, wondering what way to turn. When she went on, Tom had narrowed her lead. His out-stretched fingers grabbed her pack; the strap broke and she stopped and spun to face him, lit by the red glare of the smelters.

She was no older than Tom, and she was hideous. A terrible scar ran down her face from forehead to jaw, making it look like a portrait that had been furiously crossed out. Her mouth was wrenched sideways in a permanent sneer, her nose was a smashed stump, and her single eye stared at him out of the wreckage, as gray and chill as a winter sea.

"Why didn't you let me kill him?" she hissed.

He was so shocked that he couldn't move or speak, could only stand there as the girl reached down for her fallen pack and turned to run on. But behind him, police whistles were blowing, and crossbow darts came sparking against the metal deckplates and the overhead ducts. The girl dropped the pack and fell sideways, gasping a filthy curse. Tom hadn't even imagined that girls knew such words. "Don't shoot!" he yelled, waving toward the policemen. They were lumbering down the spiral stair beyond the gas tanks, shooting as they came, as if they didn't much care that Tom was in the way. "Don't shoot!"

The girl scrambled up, and he saw that a crossbow dart had gone through her leg just above the knee. She clutched at it, blood welling out between her fingers. Her breath came in sobs as she backed up against the handrail, lifting herself awkwardly over it. Behind her, the waste chute gaped like an open mouth.

"NO!" shouted Tom, seeing what she meant to do. He didn't feel like a hero anymore — he just felt sorry for this poor, hideous girl, and guilty at being the one who had trapped her here. He held out his hand to her, willing her not to jump. "I couldn't let you hurt Mr. Valentine!" he said, shouting to make her hear him above the din of the Gut. "He's a good man, a kind, brave, wonderful . . ."

The girl lunged forward, shoving her awful noseless face toward him. "Look at me!" she said, her voice all twisted by her twisted mouth. "Look what your brave, kind Valentine did to me!"

"What do you mean?"

"Ask him!" she screamed. "Ask him what he did to Hester Shaw!"

The police were closer now; Tom could feel their footsteps drumming on the deck. The girl glanced past him, then heaved her wounded leg over the handrail, crying out at the pain. "No!" pleaded Tom again, but too late. Her ragged greatcoat snapped and fluttered and she was gone. He flung himself forward and peered down the shadowed chute. A cool blast of air came up at him, mingled with the smell of mud and crushed vegetation; the smell of the speeding earth beneath the city.

"No!"

She had jumped! She had jumped right out of the city to her death! *Hester Shaw.* He would have to remember that name, and say a prayer for her to one of London's many gods.

Shapes loomed out of the drifting smoke. The policemen were advancing cautiously, like watchful crabs, and Valentine was with them, running ahead. In the shadows under a gas tank Tom saw

27

the young Engineer looking on, shocked. Tom tried to smile at him, but his face felt frozen, and the next moment another thick swag of smoke had folded over him, blotting out everything.

"Tom! Are you all right?" Valentine ran up, barely winded by the long chase. "Where is she? Where is the girl?"

"Dead," Tom said lamely.

Valentine stood beside him at the handrail and peered over. The shadows of the drifting smoke moved over his face like cobwebs. There was a strange light in his eyes, and his face was tight and white and frightened. "Did you see her, Tom? Did she have a scar?"

"Yes," said Tom, wondering how Valentine could know that. "It was horrible! Her eye was gone, and her nose . . ." Then he remembered the terrible thing the girl had told him. "And she said . . ." But he wasn't sure if he should tell Mr. Valentine what she had said — it was a lie, insane. "She said her name was Hester Shaw."

"Great Quirke!" hissed Valentine, and Tom flinched backward, wishing he had never mentioned it. But when he looked up again Valentine was smiling kindly at him, his eyes full of sorrow. "Don't worry, Tom," he said. "I'm sorry. . . ."

Tom felt a big, gentle hand on his shoulder and then — he was never sure quite how it happened — a twist, a shove, and he was pitching over the handrail and falling, just as Hester Shaw had fallen, flailing wildly for a hold on the smooth metal at the brim of the waste chute. *He pushed me!* he thought, and it was more amazement that he felt than fear as the black throat swallowed him down into the dark.

4

THE OUT-COUNTRY

Silence. Silence. He couldn't understand it. Even when London wasn't moving there was usually some sort of noise in the dormitory: the whirr of ventilators, the hum and rattle of distant elevator shafts, the snores of other apprentices in the neighboring bunks. But now — silence. His head ached. In fact, *all* of him ached. His bunk felt strange, too, and when he moved his hands there was something cold and slimy that oozed between his fingers like . . .

MUD! He sat up, gasping. He wasn't in the Third Class dormitory at all. He was lying on a great humpbacked mound of mud, on the edge of a deep trench, and in the thin, pearl-gray light of dawn he could see the girl with the ruined face sitting nearby. His horrible dream of sliding down that fire-blackened chute had been true: He had fallen out of London, and he was alone with Hester Shaw on the bare earth!

He moaned in terror, and the girl glanced quickly around at him and then away. "You're alive, then," she said. "I thought you'd died." She sounded as if she didn't much care either way.

Tom scrambled up onto all fours, so that only his knees and his toes and the palms of his hands were touching the mud. His arms were bare, and when he looked down he saw that his bruised body was naked to the waist. His tunic lay on the mud nearby, but he couldn't find his shirt at all, until he crawled closer to the scarred girl and realized that she was busily tearing it into strips that she was using to bandage her wounded leg.

"Hey!" he said. "That's one of my best shirts!"

"So?" she replied without looking up. "It's one of my best legs."

He pulled his tunic on. It was tattered and filthy from his fall down the waste chute, full of rents that let the chill Out-Country air through. He hugged himself, shivering. *Valentine pushed me! He pushed me and I fell down the shaft into the Out-Country! He pushed me. . . . No, he can't have. It must have been a mistake. I slipped, and he tried to grab me, that's what must have happened.*

Hester Shaw finished her bandaging and stood up, grunting at the pain as she pulled her filthy, blood-stiffened breeches on over the wound. Then she threw what was left of Tom's shirt back at him, a useless rag. "You should have let me kill him," she said, and turned away, setting off with a kind of furious limp up the long curve of the mud.

Tom watched her go, too shocked and bewildered to move. It was only when she vanished over the top of the slope that he realized he didn't want to be left alone here; he would prefer any company, even hers, to the silence.

He flung the torn shirt away and ran after her, slithering in the thick, clagging mud, stubbing his toes on fragments of rock and torn-up roots. The deep, sheer-walled trench yawned on his left, and as he reached the crest of the rise he realized that it was just one of a hundred identical trenches: the huge track-marks of London stretching ruler-straight into the distance. Far, far ahead he saw his city, dark against the brightening eastern sky, wrapped in the smoke of its own engines. He felt the cold tug of home-sickness. Everyone he had ever known was aboard that dwindling mountain, everyone except Hester, who was stomping angrily after it, dragging her injured leg behind her.

"Stop!" he shouted, half running, half wading to catch her up. "Hester! Miss Shaw!"

"Leave me alone!" she snapped.

"But where are you going?"

"I've got to get back into London, haven't I?" she said. "Two years it took me to find it, trudging across the Out-Country on foot, jumping aboard little townlets in the hope it would be London that scoffed them. And when I finally get there and find Valentine, come down to strut round the Yards just like the scavengers told me he would, what happens? Some idiot stops me from cutting his heart out like he deserves." She stopped walking and turned to face Tom. "If you hadn't shoved your oar in he'd be dead, and I'd have fallen down and died beside him and I'd be at peace by now!"

Tom stared at her, and before he could stop himself his eyes filled with stinging tears. He hated himself for looking like a fool in front of Hester Shaw, but he couldn't help it; the shock of what had happened to him and the thought of being abandoned out here overwhelmed him, and the hot tears flooded down his face and cut white runnels through the mud on his cheeks.

Hester, who had been on the point of turning away, stopped

31

and watched, as if she wasn't sure what was happening to him. "You're crying!" she said at last, quite gently, sounding surprised.

"Sorry," he sniffed.

"I never cry. I can't. I didn't even cry when Valentine murdered my mum and dad."

"What?" Tom's voice was all wobbly from weeping. "Mr. Valentine would never do something like that! Katherine said he couldn't even bring himself to shoot a wolf cub. You're lying!"

"How come you're here, then?" she asked, mocking him. "He shoved you out after me, didn't he? Just because you'd seen me."

"You're lying!" said Tom again. But he remembered those big hands thrusting him forward; remembered falling, and the strange light that had shone in the archaeologist's eyes.

"Well?" asked Hester.

"He pushed me!" murmured Tom, amazed.

Hester Shaw just shrugged, as if to say, *See? See what he's really like?* Then she turned away and started walking again.

Tom hurried along at her side. "I'll come with you! I've got to get back to London, too! I'll help you!"

"You?" She gave a hissing laugh and spat on the mud at his feet. "I thought you were Valentine's man. Now you want to help me kill him?"

Tom shook his head. He didn't know what he wanted. Part of him still clung to the hope that it was all a misunderstanding and Valentine was good and kind and brave. He certainly didn't want to see him murdered and poor Katherine left without a father. . . . But he *had* to catch up with London somehow, and he couldn't do it alone. And anyway, he felt responsible for Hester Shaw. It was his fault that she had been wounded, after all. "I'll help you walk," he said. "You're injured. You need me."

"I don't need anybody," she said fiercely.

"We'll go after London together," Tom promised. "I'm a member of the Guild of Historians. They'll listen to me. I'll tell Mr. Pomeroy. If Valentine really did the things you said then the law will deal with him!"

"The *law*?" she scoffed. "Valentine is the law in London. Isn't he the Lord Mayor's favorite? Isn't he the Head Historian? No, he'll kill me unless I kill him first. Kill you, too, probably. *Ssshinnng!*" She mimed drawing a sword and driving it through Tom's chest.

The sun was rising, lifting wreaths of steam from the wet mud. London was still moving, visibly smaller since the last time he looked. The city usually stopped for a few days when it had eaten, and some part of Tom's brain that was not quite numb wondered idly, *Where on earth is it going?*

But just then the girl stumbled and fell, her bad leg crumpling under her. Tom scrambled to help her up. She didn't thank him, but she didn't push him away, either. He pulled her arm around his shoulders and hauled her up, and they set off together along the mud ridge, following London's tracks into the east.

5

THE LORD MAYOR

A hundred miles ahead the sunrise shone on Circle Park, the elegant loop of lawns and flower beds that encircled Tier One. It gleamed in ornamental lakes and on pathways glistening with dew, and it glittered on the white metal spires of Clio House, Valentine's villa, that stood among dark cedars at the park's edge like some gigantic conch shell abandoned by a freak high tide.

In her bedroom on the top floor Katherine awoke and lay watching the sunbeams filter through the tortoiseshell shutters on her window. She knew she was unhappy, but at first she did not know why.

Then she remembered the previous evening: the attack in the Gut and how that poor, sweet young apprentice had chased after the assassin and got himself killed. She had gone running after Father, but by the time she reached the waste chute it was all over; a young Apprentice Engineer was stumbling away, his shocked face as white as his rubber coat, and beyond him she found Father, looking pale and angry, surrounded by policemen. She had never seen him look like that before, nor heard the harsh, unnatural voice in which he snapped at her to go straight home.

Part of her just wanted to curl up and go back to sleep, but she had to see him and make sure he was all right. She flung back the quilt and got up, pulling on the clothes from last night that lay all crumpled on the floor, still smelling of furnaces.

Outside her bedroom door a hallway sloped gently downward, round-roofed, curling about on itself like the inside of an ammonite. She hurried down it, pausing to pay her respects before the statue of Clio, goddess of History, who stood in a niche outside the door to the dining room. In other niches lay treasures that her father had brought back from his expeditions: potsherds, fragments of computer keyboards, and the rusting metal skulls of Stalkers, those strange, half-mechanical soldiers from a forgotten war. Their cracked glass eyes stared balefully at Katherine as she hurried by.

Father was drinking coffee in the atrium, the big open space at the center of the house. He was still in his dressing gown, his long face serious as he paced up and down between the potted ferns. A glance at his eyes was enough to tell Katherine that he had not slept at all. "Father?" she asked. "What's happened?"

"Oh, Kate!" He came and hugged her tight. "What a night!"

"That poor boy," Katherine whispered. "Poor Tom! I suppose they didn't . . . *find* anything?"

Valentine shook his head. "The assassin dragged him with her when she jumped. They were both drowned in the mud of the Out-Country, or crushed beneath the tracks."

"Oh," whispered Katherine, and sat down on the edge of a table, not even noticing Dog when he came padding in to rest his great head on her knee. *Poor Tom!* she thought. He had been so sweet, so eager to please. She had really liked him. She had even thought of asking Father about bringing him up to work at Clio House so she and Dog could get to know him better. And now he was dead, his soul fled down to the Sunless Country and his body lying cold in the cold mud, somewhere in the city's wake.

"The Lord Mayor isn't happy," said Valentine, glancing at the clock. "An assassin loose in the Gut on London's first day back in the Hunting Ground. He is coming down here in person to discuss it. Will you sit with me while I wait for him? You can have some of my breakfast if you like. There is coffee on the table — rolls — butter. I have no appetite at all."

Katherine had no appetite, either, but she glanced at the food and noticed a battered leather pack lying on the far side of the table. It was the pack the girl assassin had dropped in the Gut last night, and its contents were spread out around it like exhibits in a strange museum: a metal water bottle, a first-aid kit, some string, a few strips of dried meat that looked tougher than the tongues of old boots, and a stained and crumpled sheet of paper with a photograph stapled to it. Katherine picked it up. It was an identity form, issued in a town called Strole, filthy and faded and coming apart along the creases. Before she could study the writing her eye was drawn to the photograph. She gasped. "Father! Her face!"

Valentine turned, saw her holding the paper, and snatched it from her hand with an angry cry. "No, Kate! That is not for your eyes! It is not for anybody's eyes. . . ."

He pulled out his lighter and carefully lit a corner of the form, folding it into the ashtray on his desk as it burned. Then he went back to his pacing, and Katherine sat and watched him. In the ten years since she arrived in London Katherine had come to think of him as her best friend as well as her father. They liked the same things, and laughed at the same jokes, and never kept secrets from each other — but she could see that he was keeping something from her about this girl. She had never seen him so worried by anything. "Who is she, Father?" she asked. "Do you know her from one of your expeditions? She is so young, and so . . . Whatever happened to her *face?*"

There were footsteps, a knock at the door, and Pewsey burst into the room. "Lord Mayor's on his way, Chief."

"Already?" gasped Valentine.

"'Fraid so. Gench just saw him coming across the park in his bug. Said he didn't look pleased."

Valentine didn't look pleased, either. He grabbed his robes from the chair-back where they had been flung and started trying to make himself presentable. Katherine stepped forward to help, but he waved her away, so she kissed him quickly on the cheek and hurried out with Dog trotting behind her. Through the big oval windows of the drawing room she could see a white official bug pulling in through the gates of Clio House. A squad of soldiers ran ahead of it, dressed in the bright red armor of the Beefeaters, the Lord Mayor's personal bodyguard. They took up positions around the garden like ugly lawn ornaments as Gench and one of the other servants hurried forward to open the bug's glastic lid. The Lord Mayor stepped out and came striding toward the house.

Magnus Crome had been ruler of London for nearly twenty years, but he still didn't look like a Lord Mayor. The Lord Mayors in Katherine's history books were chubby, merry, red-faced men, but Crome was as thin as an old crow, and twice as gloomy. He didn't even wear the scarlet robes that had been the pride and joy of other mayors, but still dressed in his long, white rubber coat and wore the red wheel of the Guild of Engineers upon his brow. Those earlier Lord Mayors had had their Guild-marks removed to show that they were serving the whole of London, but things had changed when Crome seized power — and even if some people said it was unfair for one man to be master of the Engineers *and* Lord Mayor, they still admitted that Crome made a good job of running the city.

Katherine didn't like him. She had never liked him, even though he had been so good to her father, and she was not in any mood to meet him this morning. As soon as she heard the front door iris open she hurried back into the corridor and started up it, calling softly for Dog to follow her. She stopped as soon as she was around the first bend, hidden in a shallow alcove, resting the tips of her fingers on the wolf's head to keep him still. She could tell that some terrible trouble had overtaken her father, and she was not going to let him keep the truth from her as if she were still a little girl.

A few seconds later she saw Gench arrive at the door to the atrium, clutching his hat in his hands. "This way, yer worshipful honor," he mumbled, bowing. "Mind yer step, yer Mayorness."

Close behind came Crome. He paused for a moment, his head flicking from side to side in an oddly reptilian way, and Katherine felt his gaze sweep the corridor like a wind from the Ice Wastes. She squeezed herself tighter into the alcove and prayed to Quirke and Clio that he would not see her. For a moment she could hear his breathing and the faint squeaks and creakings of his rubber coat. Then Gench led him into the atrium, and the danger was past.

With one hand firmly on Dog's collar she crept back to the door and listened. She could hear Father's voice and imagined him standing beside the ornamental fountain while his men showed Crome to a seat. He started to make some polite comment about the weather, but the cold, thin voice of the Lord Mayor interrupted him. "I have been reading your report of last night's escapade, Valentine. You assured me that the whole family had been dealt with."

Katherine flinched away from the door as though it had burned her. How dare the old man talk to Father like that! She did not want to hear any more, but curiosity got the better of her and she set her ear against the wood again.

". . . a ghost from my past," Father was saying. "I can't imagine how she escaped. And Quirke alone knows where she learned to be so agile and cunning. But she is dead now. So is the boy who caught her, poor Natsworthy. . . ."

"You are sure of that?"

"They fell out of the city, Crome."

"That means nothing. We are traveling over soft ground; they may have survived. You should have sent men down to check. Remember, we don't know how much the girl knew of her mother's work. If she were to tell another city that we have MEDUSA, before we are ready to use it . . ."

"I know, I know," said Valentine irritably, and Katherine heard a chair creak as he flung himself down in it. "I'll take the 13th Floor Elevator back and see if I can find the bodies. . . ."

"No," ordered Crome. "I have other plans for you and your

39

airship. I want you to fly ahead and see what lies between London and its goal."

"Crome, that is a job for a Planning Committee scout-ship, not the *Elevator*. . . ."

"No," snapped Crome again. "I don't want too many people to know where we are taking the city. They will find out when the time is ripe. Besides, I have a task in mind that only you can be trusted with."

"And the girl?" asked Valentine.

"Don't worry about her," said the Lord Mayor. "I have an agent who can be relied on to track her down and finish the job you failed to do. Concentrate on preparing your airship, Valentine."

The meeting was at an end. Katherine heard the Lord Mayor getting ready to leave, and hurried away up the corridor before the door opened, her mind whirling faster than one of the tumble dryers in the London Museum's Hall of Ancient Technology.

Back in her room she sat down to wonder about the things she had heard. She had hoped to solve a mystery, but instead it had grown deeper. All she was sure of was that Father had a secret. He had never kept anything from her before. He always told her everything, and asked her opinion, and wanted her advice, but now he was whispering with the Lord Mayor about the girl being *"a ghost from his past"* and some agent being sent back to look for her and do . . . what? Could Tom and the assassin really still be alive? And why was the Lord Mayor packing Father off on a reconnaissance flight amid such secrecy? And why didn't he want to say where London was going? And what, what on earth was MEDUSA?

6

SPEEDWELL

All that day they struggled onward, trudging along in the scar that London had clawed through the soft earth of the Hunting Ground. The city was never out of their sight, but it grew smaller and smaller, more and more distant, pulling away from them toward the east, and Tom realized that it might soon be lost forever beyond the horizon. Loneliness wrenched at him. He had never much enjoyed his life as an Apprentice Historian (Third Class), but now his years in the Museum felt like a beautiful, golden dream. He found himself missing fussy old Dr. Arkengarth and pompous Chudleigh Pomeroy. He missed his bunk in the drafty dormitory and the long hours of work, and he missed Katherine Valentine, although he had known her for only a few minutes. Sometimes, if he closed his eyes, he could see her face quite clearly, her kind gray eyes and her lovely smile. He was sure that she didn't know what sort of man her father was. . . .

"Watch where you're going!" snapped Hester Shaw, and he opened his eyes and realized that he had almost led her over the brink of one of the gaping track-marks.

On they went, and on, and Tom started to think that what he

missed most about his city was the food. It had never been much, the stuff they served in the Guild canteen, but it was better than nothing, and nothing was what he had now. When he asked Hester Shaw what they were supposed to live on out here she just said, "I bet you wish you hadn't lost my pack for me now, London boy. I had some good dried dog meat in my pack."

In the early afternoon they came across a few dull, grayish bushes that London's tracks had not quite buried, and Hester tore some leaves off and mashed them to a pulp between two stones. "They'd be better cooked," she said as they ate the horrid vegetable goo. "I had the makings of a fire in my pack."

Later, she caught a frog in one of the deep pools that were already forming in the chevroned track-prints. She didn't offer Tom any, and he tried not to watch while she ate it.

He still did not know what to make of her. She was silent mostly, and glared so fiercely at him when he tried to talk to her that he quickly learned to walk in silence, too. But sometimes, quite suddenly, she would start talking. "The land's rising," she might say. "That means London'll go slower. It would waste fuel, going full speed on an uphill stretch." Then, an hour or two later, "My mum used to say Traction Cities are stupid. She said there was a reason for them a thousand years ago when there were all those earthquakes and volcanoes and the glaciers pushing south. Now they just keep rolling around and eating each other 'cos people are too stupid to stop them."

Tom liked it when she talked, even though he did think that her mum sounded like a dangerous Anti-Tractionist. But when he tried to keep the conversation going she would go quiet again, and her hand would go up to hide her face. It was as if there were two

Hesters sharing the same thin body: one a grim avenger who thought only of killing Valentine, the other a quick, clever, likable girl whom he sometimes sensed peeking out at him from behind that scarred mask. He wondered if she was slightly mad. It would be enough to send anyone mad, seeing your parents murdered.

"How did it happen?" he asked her gently. "I mean, your mum and dad, are you sure it was Valentine who —?"

"Shut up and walk," she said.

But long after dark, as they huddled in a hollow of the mud to escape the chill night wind, she suddenly started telling him her story.

"I was born on the bare earth," she said, "but it wasn't like this. I lived on Oak Island, in the far west. It used to be a part of the Hunting Ground once, but the earthquakes drowned all the land around and made an island of it, too far offshore for any hungry city to attack, and too rocky for the amphibious towns to get at. It was lovely: green hills and great outcrops of stone and the streams running through tangly oak woods, all gray with lichen — the trees shaggy with it, like old dogs."

Tom shuddered. Every Londoner knew that only savages lived on the bare earth. "I prefer a nice firm deck-plate under me," he said, but Hester didn't seem to hear him; the words kept spilling out of her twisted mouth as if she had no choice in the matter.

"There was a town there called Dunroamin'. It was mobile once, but the people got sick of running all the time from bigger towns, so they floated it across to Oak Island and took its wheels and engines off and dug it into a hillside. It's been sitting there a hundred years or more, and you'd never know it used to move at all."

"But that's awful!" Tom gasped. "It's downright Anti-Tractionist!"

"My mum and dad lived down the road a way," she went on, talking straight over him. "They had a house on the edge of the moor, where the sea comes in. Dad was a farmer, and Mum was a Historian like you — only a lot cleverer than you, of course. She flew off each summer in her airship, digging for old-tech, but in the autumn she'd come home. I used to go up to her study in the attic on winter's nights and eat cheese on toast and she'd tell me about her adventures.

"And then one night, seven years ago, I woke up late and there were voices up in the attic arguing. So I went up the ladder and looked, and Valentine was there. I knew him, because he was Mum's friend and used to drop in on us when he was passing. Only he wasn't being very friendly that night. 'Give me the machine, Pandora,' he kept saying. 'Give me MEDUSA.' He didn't see me watching him. I was at the top of the ladder, looking into the attic, too scared to go up and too scared to go back. Valentine had his back to me and Mum stood facing him, holding this machine, and she said, 'Damn you, Thaddeus, I found it, it's *mine!*'

"And then Valentine drew his sword and he . . . and he . . ."

She paused for breath. She wanted to stop, but she was riding a wave of memory and it was carrying her backward to that night, that room, and the blood that had spattered her mother's star charts like the map of a new constellation.

"And then he turned round and saw me watching, and he came at me and I dived back so his sword only cut my face, and I fell back down the ladder. He must have thought he'd killed me. I heard him go to Mum's desk and start rustling through the papers there, and I got up and ran. Dad was lying on the kitchen floor; he was dead, too. Even the dogs were dead.

"I ran out of the house and saw Valentine's great black ship moored at the end of the garden with his men waiting. They came after me, but I escaped. I ran down to the boathouse and shoved off in Dad's skiff. I think I meant to go round to Dunroamin' and get help — I was only little, and I thought a doctor could help Mum and Dad. But I was so weak with the pain and all the blood . . . I untied the boat somehow, and the current swept it out, and the next thing I knew I was waking up on the shores of the Hunting Ground.

"I lived in the Out-Country after that. At first I didn't remember much. It was as if when he cut my head open some of my memories spilled out, and the rest got muddled about. But slowly I started remembering, and one day I remembered Valentine and what he'd done. That's when I decided to come and find him. Kill him the same way he killed my mum and dad."

"What was this machine?" asked Tom, in the long silence. "This MEDUSA thing?"

Hester shrugged. (It was too dark to see her by this time, but he heard her shrug, the hunch of her shoulders inside her filthy coat.) "Something my mum found. Old-tech. It didn't look important. Like a metal soccer ball, all bashed and dented. But that's what he killed her for."

"Seven years ago," whispered Tom. "That's when Mr. Valentine got made head of the Guild. They said he'd found something in the Out-Country and Crome was so pleased that he promoted him, straight over the heads of Chudleigh Pomeroy and all the rest. But I never heard what it was he'd found. And I never heard of a MEDUSA before."

Hester said nothing at all. After a few minutes she began to snore.

Tom sat awake for a long time, turning her story over and over in his mind. He thought of the daydreams that had kept him going through long, tedious days in the Museum. He had dreamed of being trapped in the Out-Country with a beautiful girl, on the trail of some murderous criminal, but he had never imagined it would be so wet and cold, or that his legs would ache so, or that the murderer would be London's greatest hero. And as for the beautiful girl . . .

He looked at the blunt wreck of Hester Shaw's face in the faint moonlight, scowling even in her sleep. He understood her better now. She hated Valentine, but she hated herself even more, for being so ugly, and for being still alive when her parents were dead. He remembered how he had felt when the Big Tilt happened, and he came home and found his house flattened and Mum and Dad gone. He had thought that it was all his fault somehow. He had felt full of guilt, because he had not been there to die with them.

I must help her, he thought. *I won't let her kill Mr. Valentine, but I'll find a way to get the truth out. If it is the truth. Maybe tomorrow London will have slowed down a bit and Hester's leg will be better. We'll be back in the city by sundown, and somebody will listen to us. . . .*

❀

But next morning they woke to find that the city was even farther ahead, and Hester's leg was worse. She moaned with pain at almost every step now; her face was the color of old snow, and fresh blood was soaking through her bandages and running down into her boot. Tom cursed himself for throwing those rags of shirt away, and for making Hester lose her pack, and her first-aid kit. . . .

In the middle of the morning, through shifting veils of rain, they saw something ahead of them. A pile of slag and clinker lay spilled across the track-marks, where London had vented it the day before. Drawn up beside it was a strange little town, and as they got closer Hester and Tom could see that people were scrambling up and down the spoil-heap, sifting out collops of melted metal and fragments of unburnt fuel.

The sight gave them hope and they pressed forward faster. By early afternoon they were walking under the shadow of the townlet's huge wheels, and Tom was staring up in amazement at its single tier. It was smaller than a lot of the houses in London, and it appeared to have been built out of wood by somebody whose idea of good carpentry was to bang a couple of nails in and hope for the best. Behind the shedlike town hall rose the huge, crooked chimneys of an experimental engine array.

"Welcome!" shouted a tall, white-bearded man, picking his way down the clinker-heap, grubby brown robes flapping. "Welcome to Speedwell. I am Orme Wreyland, Mayor. Do you speak Anglish?"

Hester hung back suspiciously, but Tom thought the old man looked friendly enough. He stepped forward and said, "Please, sir, we need some food, and a doctor to look at my friend's leg. . . ."

"I'm not your friend," hissed Hester Shaw. "And there's nothing wrong with my leg." But she was white and trembling and her face shone with sweat.

"No doctor in Speedwell anyway," laughed Wreyland. "Not

one. And as for food . . . Well, times are hard. Do you have anything you can trade?"

Tom patted the pockets of his tunic. He had a little money, but he didn't see what use London money would be to Orme Wreyland. Then he touched something hard. It was the seedy he had found in the Gut. He pulled it out and looked wistfully at it for a moment before he handed it to the old man. He had been planning to make a present of it to Katherine Valentine one day, but now food was more important.

"Pretty! Very pretty!" admitted Orme Wreyland, tilting the disc and admiring the rippling rainbows. "Not a lot of use, but worth a few nights' shelter and a bit of food. It's not very good food, mind, but it's better than nothing. . . ."

❋

He was right: It *wasn't* very good, but Tom and Hester ate greedily anyway and then held out their bowls for more.

"It's made from algae, mostly," explained Orme Wreyland as his wife slopped out second helpings of the bluish muck. "We grow it in vats down under the main engine room. Nasty stuff, but it keeps body and soul together when pickings is thin, and between you and me, pickings has never been thinner. That's why we were so glad to come across this mound of trash we're scraping through."

Tom nodded, leaning back in his chair and looking around the Wreylands' quarters. It was a tiny, cheese-shaped room, and not at all what he would have expected of a mayoral residence — but then Orme Wreyland was not exactly what he would have expected of a mayor. The shabby old man seemed to rule over a town composed mainly of his own family: sons and daughters, grandchildren, nieces, nephews, and the husbands and wives that they had met on passing towns.

But Wreyland was not a happy man. "It's no fun, running a traction town," he kept saying. "No, no fun at all, not anymore. There was a time when a little place like Speedwell could go about its business quite safely, being too small for any other town to bother eating. But not now. Not with prey so scarce. Everyone we see wants to eat us. We even found ourselves running from a city the other day. One of those big Frankish-speaking *Villes Mobiles* it was. I ask you, what good would a place like Speedwell be to a monster like that? We'd barely take the edge off its appetite. But they chased us, anyway."

"Your town must be very fast," said Tom.

"Oh, yes," agreed Wreyland, beaming, and his wife put in, "Hundred miles an hour, top speed. That's Wreyland's doing. He's a wizard with those big engines of his."

"Could you help us?" asked Tom, leaning forward in his seat. "We need to get to London, as quickly as possible. I'm sure you could catch it up, and there might be more spoil-heaps along the way. . . ."

"Bless you, lad," said Wreyland, shaking his head. "What London drops isn't worth going far for, not these days. Everything's recycled now that prey's so short. Why, I remember the days when cities' waste-heaps used to dot the Hunting Ground like mountains. Oh, there was good pickings then! But not anymore. Besides," he added with a shudder, "I wouldn't take my town too close to London, or any other city. You can't trust them these days. They'd turn around and snaffle us, like as not. Chomp! No, no."

Tom nodded, trying not to show his disappointment. He

glanced across at Hester, but her head was hanging down and she seemed to be asleep, or unconscious. He hoped it was just the effects of her long walk and her full stomach, but as he started up to check that she was all right Wreyland said, "I tell you what, though, lad; we'll take you to the cluster!"

"To the what?"

"To the trading-cluster! It's a gathering of small towns, a couple of days' run southeast of here. We were going anyway."

"There'll be lots of towns at the cluster," Mrs. Wreyland agreed. "And even if none of them is prepared to take you and your friend to London, you'll soon find an air-trader who will. Bound to be air-traders at a cluster."

"I . . ." said Tom, and stopped. He wasn't feeling very well. The room seemed to waver, then started to roll like the picture on a badly tuned Goggle-screen. He looked at Hester and saw that she had slipped off her seat onto the floor. The Wreylands' household gods grinned at him from their shrine on the wall, and one of them seemed to be saying in Orme Wreyland's voice, "Sure to be airships there, Tom, always airships at a trading-cluster . . ."

"Would you like some more algae, dear?" inquired Mrs. Wreyland as he fell to his knees. From a long, long way away he heard her saying, "It took an awfully long time to take effect, didn't it, Ormey?" and Wreyland replying, "We'll have to put more in next time, my sweet." Then the swirling patterns on the carpet reached up and twined around him and pulled him down into a sleep that was as soft as cotton wool, and filled with dreams of Katherine.

7

HIGH LONDON

Above Tier One, above the busy shops of Mayfair and Piccadilly, above Quirke Circus, where the statue of London's savior stands proudly on its fluted steel column, Top Tier hangs over the city like an iron crown, supported by vast pillars. It is the smallest, highest, and most important of the seven Tiers, and, though only three buildings stand there, they are the three greatest buildings in London. To sternward rise the towers of the Guildhall, where the greater and lesser Guilds all have their offices and meet in council once a month. Opposite it is the building where the *real* decisions are made: the black glass claw of the Engineerium. Between them stands St. Paul's, the ancient Christian temple that Quirke re-erected up here when he turned London into a Traction City. It is a sad sight now, covered in scaffolding and shored up with props, for it was never meant to move, and London's journeys have shaken the old stonework terribly. But soon it will be open to the public again: The Guild of Engineers has promised to restore it, and if you listen closely you can hear the drills and hammers of their men at work inside.

Magnus Crome hears them as his bug goes purring through

the old cathedral's shadow to the Engineerium. They make him smile a faint, secret smile.

Inside the Engineerium the sunlight is kept at bay behind black windows. A cold neon glow washes the metal walls, and the air smells of antiseptic, which Crome thinks is a welcome relief from the stench of flowers and new-mown grass that hangs over High London on this warm spring day. A young apprentice leaps to attention as he stalks into the lobby and bows her bald head when he barks, "Take me to Doctor Twix."

A monorail car is waiting. The apprentice helps the Lord Mayor into it and it takes him sweeping up in a slow spiral through the heart of the Engineerium. He passes floor after floor of offices and conference rooms and laboratories, and glimpses the shapes of strange machines through walls of frosted glass. Everywhere he looks he sees his Engineers at work, tinkering with fragments of old-tech, performing experiments on rats and dogs, or guiding groups of shaven-headed children who are up on a day trip from the Guild's nurseries in the Deep Gut. He feels safe and satisfied, here in the clean, bright inner sanctum of his Guild. It makes him remember why he loves London so much, and why he has devoted his whole career to finding ways to keep it moving.

When Crome was a young apprentice, many years ago, he read gloomy forecasts which said that prey was running out and Traction Cities were doomed. He has made it his life's work to prove them wrong. Clawing his way to the top of his Guild and then on to the Lord Mayor's throne was just the start. His fierce recycling and anti-waste laws were merely a stopgap. Now he is almost ready to unveil his real plan.

But first he must be certain that the Shaw girl can make no more trouble.

The car comes sighing to a halt outside one of the upper laboratories. A squat, white-coated barrel of a woman stands waiting at the entrance, hopping nervously from foot to foot. Evadne Twix is one of the best Engineers in London. She may look like someone's dotty auntie and decorate her laboratory with pictures of flowers and puppies (a clear breach of Guild rules), but when it comes to her work she is utterly ruthless. "Hello, Lord Mayor," she simpers, bowing. "How lovely to see you! Have you come to visit my babies?"

"I want to see Shrike," he snaps, brushing past, and she dances along in his wake like a leaf in the slipstream of a passing city.

Through her laboratory they go, past startled, bowing Engineers, past glittering racks of glassware — and past tables where rusting metal skeletons are being painstakingly repaired. Dr. Twix's team has spent years studying the Stalkers, the Resurrected Men whose remains turn up sometimes in the Out-Country — and lately they have had more than just remains to work on.

"You have completed your researches on Shrike?" asks Crome as he strides along. "You are certain he is of no further use to us?"

"Oh, I've learned everything we can, Lord Mayor," twitters the doctor. "He's a fascinating piece of work, but really far more complicated than is good for him; he has almost developed his own personality. And as for his strange fixation with this girl . . . I shall make sure my new models are much simpler. Do you wish me to have him dismantled?"

"No." Crome stops at a small, round door and touches a stud

that sends it whirling open. "I intend to keep my promise to Shrike. And I have a job for him."

Beyond the door hang shadows and a smell of oil. A tall shape stands motionless against a far wall. As the Lord Mayor steps into the room, two round, green eyes snap on like headlights.

"Mr. Shrike!" says Crome, sounding almost cheery. "How are we today? I hope you were not asleep?"

"I DO NOT SLEEP," replies a voice from the darkness. It is a horrible voice, sharp as the squeal of rusty cogs. Even Dr. Twix, who knows it well, shudders inside her rubber coat. "DO YOU WISH TO EXAMINE ME AGAIN?"

"No, Shrike," Crome says. "Do you remember what you warned me of when you first came to me, a year and a half ago? About the Shaw girl?"

"I TOLD YOU THAT SHE IS ALIVE, AND ON HER WAY TO LONDON."

"Well, it seems you were right. She turned up just as you said she would."

"WHERE IS SHE? BRING HER TO ME!"

"Impossible, I'm afraid. She jumped down a waste chute, back into the Out-Country."

There is a slow hiss, like steam escaping. "I MUST GO AFTER HER."

Crome smiles. "I was hoping you'd say that. One of my Guild's Goshawk 90 reconnaissance airships has been made ready for you. The pilots will retrace the city's tracks until you find where the girl fell. If she and her companion are dead, all well and good. If they are alive, kill them. Bring their bodies to me."

"AND THEN?" asks the voice.

"And then, Shrike," Crome replies, "I will give you your heart's desire."

It was a strange time for London. The city was still traveling at quite a high speed, as if there were a catch in sight, but there was no other town to be seen on the gray, muddy plains of the north-western Hunting Ground, and everybody was wondering what the Lord Mayor could be planning. "We can't just go driving on like this," Katherine heard one of her servants mutter. "There are big cities farther east, and they'll scoff us up and spit out the bones!" But Mrs. Mallow, the housekeeper, whispered back, "Don't you know nothing, Sukey Blinder? Ain't Mr. Valentine himself being sent off on a hexpedition to spy out the land ahead? Him and Magnus Crome have got their eye on some vast great prize, you can be sure of it!"

Some vast great prize, perhaps, but nobody knew what, and when Valentine came home at lunchtime from another meeting with the Guild of Engineers, Katherine asked him, "Why do they have to send you off on a reconnaissance flight? That's a job for a Navigator, not the best archaeologist in the world. It's not fair!"

Valentine sighed patiently. "The Lord Mayor trusts me, Kate. And I will soon be back. Three weeks. A month. No more. Now, come down to the hangar with me, and we'll see what Pewsey and Gench have been doing to that airship of mine."

❉

In the long millennia since the Sixty Minute War, airship technology had reached levels that even the Ancients had never dreamed of. Valentine had the 13th Floor Elevator specially constructed, using some of the money that Crome had paid him for the old-tech he found on his trip to America, twenty years before. He said she was the finest airship ever built, and Katherine saw no reason to doubt him. Of course he didn't keep her down at the Tier Five air-harbor with the common merchantmen, but at a private air-quay a few hundred yards from Clio House.

Katherine and her father walked toward it through the sunlit park. The hangar and the metal apron in front of it were busy with people and bugs as Pewsey and Gench set about loading the *Elevator* with provisions for the coming flight. Dog went hurrying ahead to sniff at the stacks of crates and drums: tinned meat, lifting gas, medicines, airship-puncture repair kits, sun lotion, gas masks, flameproof suits, guns, rain-capes, cold-weather coats, mapmaking equipment, portable stoves, spare socks, plastic cups, three inflatable dinghies, and a carton labeled "Pink's Patent Out-Country Mud-Shoes — *Nobody Sinks with Pink's!*"

In the shadows of the hangar the great airship waited, her sleek, black armored envelope screened by tarpaulins. As usual, Katherine felt a rising thrill at the thought of that huge vessel lifting Father up into the sky — and a sadness, too, that he was leaving her, and a fear that he might not return. "Oh, I wish I could go with you!" she said.

"Not this time, Kate," her father told her. "One day, perhaps."

"Is it because I'm a girl?" she asked. "But that doesn't matter. I mean, in Ancient times women were allowed to do all the same things men did, and anyway, the air-trade is full of women pilots. You had one yourself, on the American trip, I remember seeing pictures of her. . . ."

"It's not that, Kate," he said, hugging her. "It's just that it may be dangerous. Anyway, I don't want you to start turning into an old ragamuffin adventurer like me; I want you to stay here and finish school and become a fine, beautiful High London lady.

And most of all I want you to stop Dog from peeing over all my crates of soup. . . ."

When Dog had been dragged away and scolded they sat down together in the shadow of the hangar and Katherine said, "So will you tell me where you are going, that is so important and dangerous?"

"I am not supposed to say," said Valentine, glancing down at her out of the corner of his eye.

"Oh, come on!" she laughed. "We're best friends, aren't we? You know I'd never tell anybody else. And I'm desperate to know where London is going to! Everyone at school keeps asking. We've been traveling east at top speed for days and days. We didn't even stop when we ate Salthook. . . ."

"Well, Kate," he admitted, "the fact is, Crome has asked me to take a look into Shan Guo."

Shan Guo was the leading nation of the Anti-Traction League, the barbarian alliance that controlled the old Indian subcontinent and what was left of China, protected from hungry cities by a great chain of mountains and swamps that marked the eastern limits of the Hunting Ground. Katherine had studied it in Geography. There was only one pass through those mountains, and it was protected by the dreadful fortress-city of Batmunkh Gompa, the Shield-Wall, beneath whose guns a hundred cities had come to grief in the first few centuries of Traction. "But why there?" she asked. "London can't be going there!"

"I didn't say it was," replied Valentine. "But one day we may have to go to Shan Guo and breach the League's defenses. You know how short prey has become. Cities are starting to starve, and turn on one another."

Katherine shivered. "But there must be some other solution," she protested. "Can't we talk to the Lord Mayors of other cities and work something out?"

He laughed gently. "I'm afraid Municipal Darwinism doesn't work like that, Kate. It's a town-eat-town world. But you mustn't worry. Crome is a great man, and he will find a way."

She nodded unhappily. Her father's eyes had that haunted, hunted look again. He had still not confided in her about the girl assassin, and now she could tell that he was keeping something else from her, something about this expedition and the Lord Mayor's plans for London. Was it all connected somehow? She could not ask him directly about the things she had overheard in the atrium without admitting that she had spied on him, but just to see what he would say she asked, "Does this have something to do with that awful girl? Was *she* from Shan Guo?"

"No," said Valentine quickly, and she saw the color drain from his face. "She is dead, Kate, and there is no reason to worry about her anymore. Come on." He stood up quickly. "We have a few days more together before I set off, so let's make the most of them. We'll sit by the fire and eat buttered toast and talk about old times, and not think about . . . about that poor disfigured girl."

As they walked back hand in hand across the park a shadow slid over them — a Goshawk 90 departing from the Engineerium. "You see?" said Katherine. "The Guild of Engineers has airships of its own. I think it's horrid of Magnus Crome, sending you away from me."

But her father just shaded his eyes to watch as the white airship circled Top Tier and flew quickly toward the west.

8

THE TRADING CLUSTER

Tom was dreaming of Katherine. She was walking arm in arm with him through the familiar rooms of the Museum, only there were no curators or Guildsmen about, nobody to say, "Polish the floor, Natsworthy," or "Dust the forty-third century glassware." He was showing her around the place as if he owned it, and she was smiling at him as he explained the details of the replica airships and the great cutaway model of London. Through it all a strange, moaning music sounded, and it wasn't until they reached the Natural History gallery that they realized it was the blue whale, singing to them.

The dream faded, but the weird notes of the whale's song lingered. He was lying on a quivering wooden deck. Wooden walls rose on either side, with morning sunlight glinting through the gaps between the planks, and overhead a mad confusion of pipes and ducts and tubes crawled over the ceiling. It was Speedwell's plumbing, and its burblings and grumbles were what he had mistaken for the song of the whale.

He rolled over and looked around the tiny room. Hester was

sitting against the far wall. She nodded when she saw that he was awake.

"Where am I?" he groaned.

"I didn't know anybody really said that," she said. "I thought that was just in books. 'Where am I?' How interesting."

"No, really," Tom protested, looking around at the rough walls and the narrow metal door. "Is this still Speedwell? What happened?"

"The food, of course," she replied.

"You mean Wreyland drugged us? But why?" He got up and made his way to the door across the pitching deck.

"Don't bother," Hester warned him, "it's locked." He tried it anyway. She was right. Next he stumbled over to peer through a crack in the wall. Beyond it he could see a narrow wooden walkway that flickered like a Goggle-screen picture as the shadow of one of Speedwell's wheels flashed across it. The Out-Country was rushing past, looking much rockier and steeper than when last he saw it.

"We've been heading south by southeast since first light," explained Hester wearily, before he could ask. "Probably longer, but I was asleep, too."

"Where are they taking us?"

"How should I know?"

Tom sat down in a heap with his back to the shuddering wall. "That's it then!" he said. "London must be hundreds of miles away! I'll never get home now!"

Hester said nothing. Her face was white, making the scars stand out even more than usual, and blood had soaked into the planking around her injured leg.

60

An hour crawled by, and then another. Sometimes people went hurrying along the walkway outside, their shadows blocking out the skinny shafts of sunlight. The plumbing burbled to itself. At last Tom heard the sound of a padlock being undone. A hatch down low on the door popped open and a face peered in. "Everybody all right?" it asked.

"All right?" shouted Tom. "Of course we're not all right!" He scrambled toward the door. Wreyland was on hands and knees outside, crouching down so he could see through the hatch (which Tom suspected was really a cat-flap). Behind him were the booted feet of some of his men, standing guard. "What have you done this for?" Tom asked. "We haven't done you any harm!"

The old mayor looked embarrassed. "That's true, dear boy, but times are hard, you see, cruel hard these days. No fun, running a traction town. We have to take what we can get. So we took you. We're going to sell you as slaves, you see. That's how it is. There'll be some slaving towns at the cluster, and we're going to sell you. It has to be done. We need spare parts for our engines, if we're to keep a step ahead of the bigger towns. . . ."

"Sell us?" Tom had heard of cities that used slaves to work their engine rooms, but it had always seemed like something distant and exotic that would never affect him. "I've got to catch London! You can't sell me!"

"Oh, I'm sure you'll fetch a good price," Wreyland said, as if it were something Tom should be pleased about. "A handsome, healthy lad like you. We'll make sure you go to a good owner. I don't know about your friend, of course: She looks half dead, and she was no oil painting to start with. But maybe we can sell you off together; 'buy one, get one free' sort of thing." He pushed

61

two bowls through the flap, round metal bowls such as a dog would eat from. One contained water, the other more of the blueish algae. "Eat up!" he said cheerfully. "We want you looking nice and well fed for the auction. We'll be at the cluster by sundown, and sell you in the morning."

"But . . ." Tom protested.

"Yes, I know, and I'm terribly sorry about it, but what can I do?" said Wreyland sadly. "Times are hard, you know."

The hatch slammed shut. "What about my seedy?" shouted Tom. There was no answer. He heard Wreyland's voice in the passage outside, talking to the guard, then nothing. He cupped his hands and drank some water, then took the bowl across to Hester. "We've got to get away!" he told her.

"How?"

Tom looked around their cell. The door was no use, locked and guarded as it was. He peered up at the plumbing until he had a crick in his neck, but although some of the pipes looked big enough for a person to crawl through he could see no way to get into them, or even to reach them. Anyway, he wouldn't have fancied crawling through whatever that thick fluid was that he could hear gurgling inside them. He turned his attention to the wall, feeling his way along the planks. At last he found one that felt slightly loose, and gradually, as he worked at it, it started to get looser still.

It was slow, hard, painful work. Tom's fingers filled with splinters and the sweat ran down his face and he had to stop each time someone passed along the walkway outside. Hester watched silently, until he started to feel cross with her for not helping.

But by evening, as the sky outside turned red and the racing townlet started to slow, he had made a gap just wide enough to get his head through.

He waited until he was sure there was no one about, then leaned out. Speedwell was passing through the shadows of some tall spines of rock, the town-gnawed cores of old mountains. Ahead lay a natural amphitheater, a shallow bowl between more rock-spires, and it was full of towns. Tom had never seen so many trading suburbs and traction villages gathered in one place before. "We're here!" he told Hester. "It's the trading cluster!"

Speedwell slowed and slowed, maneuvering into a space between a ragged little sail-powered village and a larger market town. Tom could hear the people on the new towns hailing Speedwell, asking where it had come from and what it had to trade. "Scrap metal," he heard Mrs. Wreyland bellow back, "and some wood, and a pretty seedy, and two fine, fresh, healthy young slaves!"

"Oh, Quirke!" muttered Tom, working away at enlarging the hole he had made.

"It'll never be big enough," said Hester, who always expected the worst and was usually right.

"You could try helping, instead of just sitting there!" Tom snapped back, but he regretted it at once, for he could see that she was very ill. He wondered what would happen if she was too weak to escape. He couldn't run off into the Out-Country alone and leave her here. But if he stayed, he would end up as a slave on one of these filthy little towns!

He tried not to think about it and concentrated on making

the hole bigger, while the sky outside grew dark and the moon rose. He could hear music and laughter drifting across the trading cluster and the sounds of gangways being run out as some of Wreyland's people went off to enjoy themselves aboard the other towns. He scrabbled and scratched at the hole, prising at the planks, scraping at them with a rusty nail, but it was no use. At last, desperate, he turned to Hester and hissed, "Please! Help!"

The girl stood up unsteadily and walked over to where he crouched. She looked sick, but not quite as bad as he'd feared. Perhaps she had been saving herself, harboring her last reserves of strength until it was dark enough to escape. She felt around the edges of the hole he had made and nodded. Then, leaning all her weight on Tom's shoulder, she swung her good foot up hard against the wall. Once, twice she kicked it, the wood around the hole splintering and yielding, and at the third kick a whole section of planking fell out, spilling across the walkway outside.

"I could have done that!" said Tom, staring at the ragged hole and wondering why he hadn't thought of it.

"But you didn't, did you?" said Hester, and tried to smile. It was the first time he had seen her smile: an ugly, crooked thing, but very welcome; it made him feel that she was starting to like him and didn't just regard him as an annoyance.

"Come on then," she said, "if you're coming."

❊

Hundreds of miles away across the moonlit mud, Shrike spots something. He signals to the Engineer pilots, who nod and grumble as they steer the Goshawk 90 down to land. "What now? How much longer are we going to keep flying back and forth along these track-marks before he'll admit the kids are dead?" But they grumble quietly: They are terrified of Shrike.

The hatch opens and Shrike stalks out. His green eyes sweep from side to side until he finds what he is looking for. A rag of white fabric from a torn shirt, soggy with rain, half buried in the mud. "HESTER SHAW WAS HERE," he tells the Out-Country at large, and begins sniffing for her scent.

9

THE *JENNY HANIVER*

At first it looked as if their luck might hold. They scrambled quickly across the dimly lit walkway and down into the shadows under one of Speedwell's wheel arches. They could see the dark bulks of the other towns, with lights burning in their windows and a big bonfire on the top deck of one of them, a mining townlet on the far side of the cluster where a noisy party was in progress.

They crept along the outside edge of Speedwell to a place where a gangplank stretched across to the market town that was parked next door. It was unguarded, but brightly lit, and as they reached the far end and stepped onto the deck of the market town a voice somewhere behind them shouted, "Hey!" and then, louder, "Hey! Hey! Uncle Wreyland! Them slaves is 'scaping!"

They ran, or rather, Tom ran, and dragged Hester along beside him, hearing her whimper in pain at every step. Up a stairway, along a catwalk, past a shrine to Peripatetia, goddess of wandering towns, and they were in a market square lined with big iron cages, in some of which thin, miserable slaves were waiting to be sold off. Tom forced himself to slow down and tried to look inconspicuous, listening all the time for sounds of pursuit. There were none. Maybe the Wreylands had given up the chase, or maybe they weren't allowed to chase people onto other towns — Tom didn't know what the rules were in a trading cluster.

"Head for the bows," said Hester, letting go his arm and pulling the collar of her coat up to hide her face. "If we're lucky there'll be an air-harbor at the bows."

They were lucky. At the front of the town's top deck was a raised section where half a dozen small airships were tethered, their dark, gas-filled envelopes like sleeping whales. "Are we going to steal one?" Tom whispered.

"Not unless you know how to fly an airship," said Hester weakly. "There's an airman's café over there; we'll have to try and book passage like normal people."

The café was just an ancient, rusting airship gondola that had been bolted to the deck. A few metal tables stood in front beneath a stripey awning. Hurricane lamps were burning there and an old aviator slumped snoring in a chair. The only other customer was a sinister-looking woman in a long, red leather coat who sat in the shadows near the bar. In spite of the dark she wore sunglasses, the tiny lenses black as the wing cases of beetles. She turned to stare at Tom as he walked up to the counter.

A small man with a huge, drooping moustache was polishing glasses. He glanced up without much interest when Tom said, "I'm looking for a ship."

"Where to?"

"London," said Tom. "Me and my friend have to get back to London, and we have to leave tonight."

"London, is it?" The man's moustachios twitched like the tails of two squirrels that had been shoved up his nose and were starting to get a bit restless. "Only ships with a license from the London Merchant's Guild can dock there. We've got nuffink like that here. Stayns ain't that sort of town."

"Perhaps I may be of help?" suggested a soft, foreign-sounding voice at Tom's shoulder. The woman in the red coat had come silently to his side: a lean, handsome woman with badgery slashes of white in her short black hair. Reflections of the hurricane lamps danced in her sunglasses, and when she smiled Tom noticed that her teeth were stained red. "I haven't a license for London, but I am going to Airhaven. You could find a ship there that will take you the rest of the way. Have you some money?"

Tom hadn't thought about that part. He rummaged in his tunic and fished out two tattered banknotes with the face of Quirke on the front and Magnus Crome gazing sternly from the back. He had put them in his pocket the night he fell out of London, hoping to spend them at the catch-party in Kensington Gardens. Here, under the fizzing hurricane lamps of the air-harbor, they looked out of place, like toy money.

The woman seemed to think so, too. "Ah," she said. "Twenty Quirkes. But notes like that can only be spent in London. Not much use to a poor wandering skyfarer like me. Don't you have any gold? Or old-tech?"

Tom shrugged and mumbled something. Out of the corner of his eye he saw some newcomers pushing their way between the tables. "Look, Uncle Wreyland!" he heard one of them shout. "Here they are! We've got 'em!"

Tom looked around and saw Wreyland and a couple of his boys closing in, carrying heavy clubs. He grabbed Hester, who was leaning against the counter, barely conscious. One of the Speedwell men moved to cut off their escape, but the woman in the red coat barred his way and Tom heard her say, "These are my passengers. I was just arranging a fee."

"They're our slaves!" shouted Wreyland, pushing past her. "Tom Nitsworthy and his friend. Found 'em in the Out-Country, fair and square. Finders keepers . . ."

Tom hurried Hester across the metal deck, past stairways leading up to the quays where the airships moored. He could hear Wreyland's men splitting up, shouting to each other as they searched, then a grunt and a crash as if one of them had fallen over. *Good*, he thought, but he knew that the others would soon find him.

He dragged Hester up a short iron stairway to the quays. There were lights in some of the ships that hung at anchor there, and he had a vague idea about forcing his way aboard one of them and making them take him to London. But he had nothing that would serve as a weapon, and before he could look for one there were feet ringing on the ladder behind him and Wreyland's voice saying, "Please try and be reasonable, Mr. Nitsworthy! I don't want to have to hurt you. Fred!" he added. "I've got the rotters cornered. Fred?"

Tom felt the hope drain out of him. There was no escape now. He stood there meekly as Wreyland stepped forward into the light from the portholes of a nearby airship, hefting his club. Hester slumped against a dockside winch and moaned.

"It's only fair," said Wreyland, as if he thought she was complaining. "I don't like this slaving lark any more than you do, but times are hard, and we *did* catch you, there's no denying it. . . ."

Suddenly, faster than Tom would have thought possible, Hester moved. She dragged a metal lever out of the winch and swung it at Wreyland. His club went whirling out of his hand and hit the deck with a glockenspiel sound, and the metal bar struck him a glancing blow on the side of his head. "Ow!" he wailed, crumpling to the floor. Hester lurched forward and raised the bar again, but before she could bring it down on the old man's skull Tom grabbed her arm. "Stop! You'll kill him!"

"So?" She swung toward him, snaggleteeth bared, looking like a demented monkey. "So?"

"He's right, my dear," said a gentle voice. "There is no need to finish him."

Out of the shadows stepped the woman from the bar, her red coat swirling around her ankles as she walked toward them. "I think we should get aboard my ship before the rest of his people come looking for you."

"You said we didn't have enough money," Tom reminded her.

"You don't, Mr. Nitsworthy," said the aviatrix. "But I can hardly stand by and watch you be taken away to be sold as slaves, can I? I was a slave myself once, and I wouldn't recommend it." She had taken off her glasses. Her eyes were dark and almond-shaped, and fine webs of laughter lines crinkled at their corners when she smiled. "Besides," she added, "you intrigue me. Why is a Londoner wandering about in the Hunting Ground, getting into trouble?" She held out her hand to Tom, a long, brown hand with the thin machinery of bones and tendons clearly visible, sliding under papery skin.

"How do we know you won't betray us like Wreyland did?" he demanded.

"You don't, of course!" she laughed. "You will just have to trust me."

After Valentine and the Wreylands, Tom didn't think he would ever be able to trust anybody again, but this strange foreigner was the only hope he had. "All right," he said. "But Wreyland got my name wrong; it's Natsworthy."

"And mine is Fang," said the woman. "Miss Anna Fang." She still had her hand outstretched as if he were a scared animal she wanted to tame, and she was still smiling her alarming red smile. "My ship is on Air-quay Six."

So they went with her, and somewhere in the oily shadows under the quays they stepped over Wreyland's companions, who lay slumped against a stanchion with their heads lolling drunkenly. "Are they . . . ?" whispered Tom.

"Out cold," said Miss Fang. "I'm afraid I just don't know my own strength."

Tom wanted to stop and check that the men were all right, but she led him quickly past and up a ladder to Quay Six. The ship that hung at anchor there was not the elegant sky-clipper Tom had been expecting. In fact, it was little more than a shabby scarlet gasbag and a cluster of rusty engine-pods bolted to a wooden gondola.

"It's made of junk!" he gasped.

"Junk?" laughed Miss Fang. "Why, the Jenny Haniver is built from bits of the finest airships that ever flew! An envelope of silicon-silk from a Shan Guo clipper, twin Jeunet-Carot aero-engines off a Paris gunship, the reinforced gas-cells of a Spitzbergen war-balloon . . . It's amazing what you can find in the scrap-yards. . . ."

She led them up the gangplank into the cramped, spicey-smelling gondola. It was just a narrow wooden tube with a flight deck at the front and Miss Fang's quarters at the stern, a jumble of other little cabins in between. Tom had to keep ducking to avoid braining himself on overhead lockers and dangerous-looking bundles of cables that hung from instrument panels on the roof, but the aviatrix flitted around, mumbling in some strange foreign tongue as she set switches, pulled levers, and lit dim green electrics that filled the cabin with an aquarium glow. She laughed when she saw Tom's worried look. "That is Airsperanto, the common language of the sky. It's a lonely life on the Bird Roads, and I have a habit of talking to myself. . . ."

She pulled on a final lever and the creak and sigh of gas valves echoed through the gondola. There was a clang as the magnetic docking clamps released, and the radio crackled into life and snapped, "*Jenny Haniver*, this is the Stayns Harbor Board. You are not cleared for departure!"

But the *Jenny Haniver* was departing anyway. Tom felt his stomach turn over as she lifted into the midnight sky. He scrambled to a porthole and saw the market town falling away below. Then Speedwell came into view, and soon the whole cluster was spread out below him like a display of model towns in the Museum.

"*Jenny Haniver*," insisted the loudspeaker, "return to your berth at once! We have a request from the Speedwell town council that you give up your passengers, or they will be forced to —"

"Boring!" trilled Miss Fang, flicking the radio off. A home-made rocket battery on the roof of Speedwell town hall spat a fizzing flock of missiles after them. Three hissed harmlessly past, a fourth exploded off the starboard quarter, making the gondola swing like a pendulum, and the fifth came even closer. (Anna Fang raised an eyebrow at that one, while Tom and Hester ducked for cover like frightened rabbits.) Then they were out of range; the *Jenny Haniver* was climbing into the cold clear spaces of the night, and the trading cluster was just a distant smear of light beneath the clouds.

THE *13TH FLOOR ELEVATOR*

It rained that night on London, but by first light the sky was as clear and pale as still water, and the smoke from the city's engines rose straight up into the windless air. Wet decks shone silver in the sunrise and all the banners of Tier One hung limp and still against their flagpoles. It was a fine spring morning, the morning that Valentine had been hoping for and Katherine had been dreading. It was perfect flying weather.

Although it was so early, crowds had gathered all along the edge of Tier One to watch the 13*th Floor Elevator* lift off. As Gench drove Katherine and her father over to the air-quay she saw that Circle Park was crowded, too; it looked as if the whole of High London had come to cheer Valentine on his way. None of them knew where he was going, of course, but as London sped eastward the city's rumor mills had been grinding night and day: Everyone was sure that Valentine's expedition was connected with some huge prize that the Lord Mayor hoped to catch out in the central Hunting Ground.

Temporary stands had been erected for the Council and Guilds and, when she and Dog had wished Father good-bye in the bustling shadows of the hangar, Katherine went to take her place with the Historians, squeezed between Chudleigh Pomeroy and Dr. Arkengarth. All around her stood the great and good of London: the sober black robes of Father's Guild and the purple of the Guild of Merchants, somber Navigators in their neat green tunics and a row of Engineers robed and hooded in white rubber, looking like novelty erasers. Even Magnus Crome had risen to the occasion, and the Lord Mayor's ancient chain of office hung gleaming around his thin neck.

Katherine wished they had all just stayed at home. It was difficult saying good-bye to someone when you were part of a great cheering mob all waving flags and blowing kisses. She stroked Dog's knobbly head and told him, "Look, there's Father, going up the gangplank now. They'll start the engines in a moment."

"I just hope nothing goes wrong," muttered Dr. Arkengarth. "One hears stories about these airships suddenly going off bang for no reason."

"Perhaps we should stand a little farther back?" suggested Miss Plym, the Museum's twittery curator of furniture.

"Nonsense," Katherine told them crossly. "Nothing is going to go wrong."

"Yes, do shut up, Arkengarth, you silly old coot," agreed Chudleigh Pomeroy, surprising her. "Never fear, Miss Valentine. Your father has the finest airship and the best pilots in the world: Nothing can go wrong."

Katherine smiled gratefully at him, but she kept her fingers crossed just the same, and Dog caught something of her mood and started to whimper softly.

From inside the hangar came the sound of hatches slamming

shut and the rattle of boarding-ladders being dragged clear. An expectant hush fell over the stands. Along the tier's edge High London held its breath. Then, as the band struck up "Rule Londinium," Valentine's ground crew began dragging the 13th Floor Elevator out into the sunlight, a sleek, black dart whose armored envelope shone like silk. On the open platform at the stern of the control gondola Valentine stood waving. He saluted the ground crew and the flag-decked stands and then smiled straight at Katherine, picking her face out of all the others without a moment's hesitation.

She waved back frantically, and the crowd cheered themselves hoarse as the 13th Floor Elevator's engine-pods swiveled into take-off position. The ground crew cast off the mooring hawsers, the propellers began to turn, and blizzards of confetti eddied in the downdrafts as the huge machine lifted into the air. Some Apprentice Historians spread out a banner reading Happy Valentine's Day! and the cheers went on and on, as if the crowds thought it was their love alone that was keeping the explorer airborne. "Val-en-tine! Val-en-tine!"

But Valentine took no notice of the noise or the flags. He stood watching Katherine, one hand raised in farewell, until the airship was so high and far away that she could not make him out anymore.

At last, when the Elevator was just a speck in the eastern sky and the stands were emptying, she wiped away her tears, took Dog's lead, and turned to go home. She was already missing her father, but she had a plan now. While he was away she would make her own inquiries and find out who that mysterious girl had been, and why she scared him so.

11

AIRHAVEN

Once he had washed and slept and had something to eat, Tom began to decide that adventuring might not be so bad after all. By sunrise he was already starting to forget the misery of his trek across the mud and imprisonment in Speedwell. The view from the *Jenny Haniver*'s big forward windows as the airship flew between golden mountains of dawn-lit cloud was enough to make even the pain of Valentine's betrayal fade a little. At breakfast time, drinking hot chocolate with Miss Fang on the flight deck, he found that he was enjoying himself.

As soon as the *Jenny Haniver* was safely out of the range of Speedwell's rockets, the aviatrix had become all smiles and kindness. She locked her airship on course and set about finding Tom a warm fleece-lined coat and making up a bed for him in the hold, a space high up inside the airship's envelope, heaped with a cargo of sealskins from Spitzbergen. Then she led Hester into the medical bay and went to work on her injured leg. When Tom looked in on her after breakfast that morning the girl was sleeping soundly under a white blanket. "I gave her something for the pain," explained Miss Fang. "She will sleep for hours, but you need have no fear for her."

Tom stared at Hester's sleeping face. Somehow he had expected her to look better now that she had been washed and fed and had her leg fixed, but of course she was as hideous as ever.

"He has made a mess of her, your wicked Mr. Valentine," the aviatrix said, leading him back to the flight deck, where she took the controls off their automatic setting.

"How do you know about Valentine?" asked Tom.

"Oh, everyone has heard about Thaddeus Valentine," she laughed. "I know that he is London's greatest Historian, and I also know that that is just a cover for his *real* work: as Crome's secret agent."

"That's not true!" Tom started to say, still instinctively defending his ex-hero. But there had always been rumors that Valentine's expeditions involved something darker than mere archaeology, and now that he had seen the great man's ruthless handiwork, he believed them. He blushed, ashamed for Valentine, and ashamed of himself for having loved him.

Miss Fang watched him with a faint, sympathetic smile. "Hester told me a great deal more last night, while I was tending to her wound," she said gently. "You are both very lucky to be alive."

"I know," agreed Tom, but he could not help feeling uneasy that Hester had shared their story with this stranger.

He sat down in the copilot's seat and studied the controls: a baffling array of knobs and switches and levers labeled in mixtures of Airsperanto, Anglish, and Chinese. Above them a little lacquered shrine had been fixed to the bulkhead, decorated with red ribbons and pictures of Miss Fang's ancestors. That smiling Manchu air-merchant must be her father, he supposed. And had that red-haired lady from the Ice Wastes been her mum?

"So tell me, Tom," asked Miss Fang, setting the ship on a new course, "where is London going?"

The question was unexpected. "I don't know!" Tom said.

"Oh, surely you must know *something!*" she laughed. "Your city has left its hidey-hole in the west, come back across the land-bridge, and now it is whizzing off into the central Hunting Ground 'like a bat out of Hull,' as the saying goes. You must have heard at least a rumor. No?"

Her long eyes slid toward Tom, who licked his lips nervously, wondering what to say. He had never paid any attention to the stupid tales the other apprentices swapped about where London was heading; he really had no idea. And even if he had, he knew it would be wrong to go revealing his city's plans to mysterious foreign aviatrices. What if Miss Fang flew off and told some larger city where to lie in wait for London, in exchange for a finder's fee? And yet, if he didn't tell her *something*, she might kick him off her airship — perhaps without even bothering to land it first!

"Prey!" he blurted out. "The Guild of Navigators say there are lots and lots of prey in the central Hunting Ground."

The red smile grew even broader. "Really?"

"I heard it from the Head Navigator himself," said Tom, growing bolder.

Miss Fang nodded, beaming. Then she hauled on a long brass lever. Gas valves grumbled up inside the envelope and Tom's ears popped as the *Jenny Haniver* started to descend, plunging into a thick, white layer of cloud. "Let me show you the central Hunting Ground," she chuckled, checking the charts that were fastened to the bulkhead beside her shrine.

Down, and down, and then the cloud thinned and parted and Tom saw the vast Out-Country spread below him like a crumpled sheet of gray-brown paper, slashed with long, blue shapes that were the flooded track-marks of countless towns. For the first time since the airship lifted away from Stayns he felt afraid, but Miss Fang murmured, "Nothing to fear, Tom."

He calmed himself and gazed out at the amazing view. Far to the north he could see the cold glitter of the Ice Wastes and the dark cones of the Tannhäuser fire-mountains. He looked for London, and eventually thought he saw it, a tiny, gray speck that raised a cloud of dust behind it as it trundled along, much farther off than he had hoped. There were other towns and cities too, dotted here and there across the plain, or lurking in the shadows of half-eaten mountain ranges, but not nearly as many as he had expected. To the southeast there were none at all, just a dingy layer of mist above a tract of marshland, and beyond that the silvery shimmer of water.

"That is the great inland Sea of Khazak," said the aviatrix, when he pointed to it. "I'm sure you've heard the old land-shanty," and in a lilting, high-pitched voice she sang, "*Beware, beware of the Sea of Khazak, for the town that goes near it will never come back. . . .*"

But Tom wasn't listening. He had noticed something much more terrible than any inland sea.

Directly below, with the tiny shadow of the *Jenny Haniver*

flickering across its skeletal girders, lay a dead city. It stood on ground scarred by the tracks of hundreds of smaller towns, tilting over at a strange angle, and as the *Jenny Haniver* swept down for a closer look Tom realized that its tracks and gut were gone, and that its deckplates were being stripped out by a swarm of small towns that seethed in the shadows of its lower levels, tearing off huge rusting sections in their jaws and landing salvage parties whose blowtorches glittered and sparked in the shadows between the tiers like fairy lights on a Quirkemas tree.

There was a puff of smoke from one of the towns and a rocket came winding up toward the airship and exploded a few hundred feet below. Miss Fang's hands moved swiftly over the controls and Tom felt the ship lift again. "Half the scavengers of the Hunting Ground are working on the wreck of Motoropolis," she said, "and they are a jealous lot. Shoot at anybody who comes near, and when nobody does, they shoot at each other."

"But how did it get like that?" asked Tom, staring back at the huge skeleton as the *Jenny Haniver* carried him up and away.

"It starved," said the aviatrix. "It ran out of fuel, and as it stood motionless there a pack of smaller towns came and started tearing it apart. The feeding frenzy has been going on for months, and I expect another city will come along soon and finish off the job. You see, Tom, there isn't enough prey to go around in the central Hunting Ground — so it can't be that that has brought London out of hiding."

Tom twisted around to watch as the dead city fell behind. A pack of tiny predator-suburbs were harrying the scavenger towns on the northwestern side, singling out the weakest and slowest and charging after it, but before they caught it the *Jenny Haniver* rose up again into the pure, clean world above the clouds, and the carcass of Motoropolis was hidden from view.

When Miss Fang looked at him again she was still smiling, but there was an odd gleam in her eyes. "So if it isn't prey that Magnus Crome is after," she said, "what can it be?"

Tom shook his head. "I'm only an Apprentice Historian," he confessed. "Third Class. I don't *really* know the Head Navigator."

"Hester mentioned something," the aviatrix went on. "The thing Mr. Valentine took from her poor parents. MEDUSA. A strange name. Have you heard of it? Do you know what it means?"

Tom shook his head and she watched him closely, watched his eyes until he felt as if she were looking right into his soul. Then she laughed. "Well, no matter. I must get you to Airhaven, and we'll find a ship to take you home."

❊

Airhaven! It was one of the most famous towns of the whole Traction Era, and when the warble of its homing beacon came over the radio that evening Tom went racing forward to the flight deck. He met Hester in the companionway outside the sick bay, tousled and sleepy and limping. Anna Fang had done her best with the wounded leg, but she hadn't improved the girl's manners; she hid her face when she saw Tom and only glared and grunted when he asked her how she felt.

On the flight deck the aviatrix turned to greet them with a radiant smile. "Look, my dears!" she said, pointing ahead through the big windows. "Airhaven!"

They went and stood behind her seat and looked, and far away across the sea of clouds they saw the westering sun glint on a single tier of lightweight alloy and a nimbus of brightly colored gasbags.

Long ago, the town of Airhaven had decided to escape the hungry cities by taking to the sky. It was a trading post and meeting place for aviators now, drifting above the Hunting Ground all summer, then flying south to winter in warmer skies. Tom remembered how it had once anchored over London for a whole week; how the sightseeing balloons had gone up and down from Kensington Gardens and Circle Park, and how jealous he had been of people like Melliphant who were rich enough to take a trip in one and come back full of stories about the floating town. Now he was going there himself, and not just as a sight-seer, either! What a story he would be able to tell the other apprentices when he got home!

Slowly the airship rose toward the town, and as the sun dipped behind the cloud banks in the west Miss Fang cut her engines and let her drift in toward a docking strut, while harbor officers in sky-blue livery waved multicolored flags to guide her safely to her berth. Behind them the dock was crowded with sightseers and aviators, and even a little gaggle of airship-spotters who duti-fully jotted down the *Jenny Haniver's* number in their notebooks as the mooring clamps engaged.

A few moments later Tom was stepping out into the twilight and the chill, thin air, gazing at the airships coming and going; elegant high-liners and rusty scows, trim little air-cutters with see-through envelopes and tiger-striped spice-freighters from the

Hundred Islands. "Look!" he said, pointing up at the rooftops. "There's the Floating Exchange, and that church is St. Michael's-in-the-Sky, there's a picture of it in the London Museum!" But Miss Fang had seen it many, many times before, and Hester just scowled at the crowds on the quayside and hid her face.

The aviatrix locked the *Jenny*'s hatches with a key that hung on a lanyard around her neck, but when a barefoot boy ran up and tugged at her coat saying, "Watch yer airship for yer, Missus?" she laughed and dropped three square bronze coins into his palm. "I won't let nobody sneak aboard!" he promised, taking up his post beside the gangplank. Uniformed dockhands appeared, grinning at Miss Fang but staring suspiciously at her new groundling friends. They checked that the newcomers had no metal toe-caps on their boots or lighted cigarettes about their persons, then led them back to the harbor-office where huge, crudely-lettered notices insisted NO SMOKING, TURN OFF ALL ELECTRICS, and MAKE NO SPARKS. Sparks were the terror of the air-trade, because of the danger that they might ignite the gas in the airships' envelopes. In Airhaven even over-vigorous hair-brushing was a serious crime, and all new arrivals had to sign strict safety agreements and convince the harbormaster that they were not likely to burst into flames.

At last they were allowed up a metal stairway to the High Street. Airhaven's single thoroughfare was a hoop of lightweight alloy deckplates lined with shops and stalls, chandleries, cafés, and airshipmen's hotels. Tom turned around and around, trying to take everything in and make sure he would remember it forever. He saw turbines whirling on every rooftop, and mechanics crawling like spiders over the huge engine-pods. The air was thick with the exotic smells of foreign food, and everywhere he looked there were aviators, striding along with the careless confidence of people who had lived their whole lives in the sky, their long coats fluttering behind them like leathery wings.

Miss Fang pointed along the curve of the High Street to a building with a sign in the shape of an airship. "That's the Gasbag and Gondola," she told her companions. "I'll buy you dinner, and then we'll find a friendly captain to take you back to London."

They strode toward it, the aviatrix in the lead, Hester hiding from the world behind her upraised hand, Tom still looking about in wonder and thinking it a pity that his adventures would soon be over. He didn't notice a Goshawk 90 circling among a shoal of larger vessels, waiting for a berth. Even if he had, he would not have been able to read its registration numbers at this distance, or see that the insignia on its envelope was the red wheel of the Guild of Engineers.

12

THE GASBAG AND GONDOLA

The inn was big and dark and busy. The walls were decorated with airships in bottles and the propellers of famous old sky-clippers with their names carefully painted on the blades: *Nadhezna* and *Aerymouse* and *Invisible Worm*. Aviators clustered around the metal tables, talking of cargoes and the price of gas. There were Jains and Tibetans and Xhosa, Inuit and Air-Tuareg and fur-clad giants from the Ice Wastes. An Uighur girl played "Slipstream Serenade" on her forty-string guitar, and now and then a loudspeaker would announce, "Arrival on Strut Three: the *Idiot Wind* fresh from the Nuevo-Mayan Palatinates with a cargo of chocolate and vanilla," or, "Now boarding at Strut Seven: *My Shirona* outbound for Arkangel. . . ."

Anna Fang stopped at a little shrine just inside the door and said her thanks to the gods of the sky for a safe journey. The God of Aviators was a friendly-looking fellow — the fat red statue on the shrine reminded Tom of Chudleigh Pomeroy — but his wife, the Lady of the High Heavens, was cruel and tricky; if offended she might brew up hurricanes or burst a gas-cell. Anna made her an offering of rice cakes and lucky money, and Tom and Hester nodded their thank-yous just in case.

When they looked up the aviatrix was already hurrying away from them toward a group of aviators at a corner table. "Khora!" she shouted, and by the time they caught up with her she was being whirled around and around in the arms of a handsome young African and talking quickly in Airsperanto. Tom was almost sure he heard her mention "MEDUSA" as she glanced back at him and Hester, but by the time they drew near the talk had switched into Anglish and the African was saying, "We rode high-level winds all the way from Zagwa!" and shaking red Sahara sand out of his flying helmet to prove it.

He was Captain Khora of the gunship *Mokele Mbembe* and he came from a static enclave in the Mountains of the Moon, an ally of the Anti-Traction League. Now he was bound for Shan Guo, to begin a tour of duty in the League's great fortress at Batmunkh Gompa. Tom was shocked at first to be sharing a table with a soldier of the League, but Khora seemed a good man, as kind and welcoming as Miss Fang herself. While she ordered food he introduced his friends: the tall gloomy one was Nils Lindstrom of the *Garden Aeroplane Trap*, and the beautiful Arab lady with the laugh was Yasmina Rashid of the Palmyrene privateer *Zainab*. Soon the aviators were all laughing together, reminding each other of battles above the Hundred Islands and drunken parties in the airmen's quarter on Panzerstadt-Linz, and between stories Anna Fang pushed dishes across the table to her guests. "More battered dormouse, Tom? Hester, try some of this delicious deviled bat!"

While Tom poked the strange foreign food around his plate with the pair of wooden sticks he had been given instead of a knife and fork, Khora leaned close and said softly, "So are you and your girlfriend crewing aboard the *Jenny* now?"

"No, no!" Tom assured him quickly. "I mean, no, she's not my girlfriend, and no, we are just passengers. . . ." He fumbled with some mashed locust and asked, "Do you know Miss Fang well?"

"Oh, yes!" laughed Khora. "The whole air-trade knows Anna. And the whole of the League, too, of course. In Shan Guo they call her 'Feng Hua,' the Wind-Flower."

Tom wondered why Miss Fang would have a special name in Shan Guo, but before he could ask, Khora went on. "Do you know she built the *Jenny Haniver* herself? When she was just a girl she and her parents had the bad luck to be aboard a town that was eaten by Arkangel. They were put to work as slaves in the airship-yards there, and over the years she managed to sneak an engine here, a steering vane there, until she built herself the *Jenny* and escaped."

Tom was impressed. "She didn't *say*," he murmured, looking at the aviatrix in a new light.

"She doesn't talk about it," said Khora. "You see, her parents did not live to escape with her; she watched them die in the slave-pits."

Tom felt a rush of sympathy for poor Miss Fang, his fellow orphan. Was that why she smiled all the time, to hide her sorrow? And was that why she had rescued Hester and himself, to save them from her parents' fate? He smiled at her as kindly as he could, and she caught his eye and smiled back and passed him a plate of crooked black legs. "Here, Tom, try a sautéed tarantula. . . ."

"Arrival on Strut Fourteen!" blared the loudspeaker overhead. "London airship GE47 carrying passengers only."

Tom jumped up and his chair fell backward with a crash. He could remember the little fast-moving scout ships that the Engineers used to survey London's tracks and superstructure, and he remembered how they didn't have names, just registration codes, and how all the codes started with GE. "They've sent someone after us!" he gasped.

Miss Fang was rising to her feet as well. "It might just be coincidence," she said. "There must be lots of airships from London. . . . And even if Valentine has sent someone after you, you are among friends. We are more than a match for your horrible Beefburgers."

"Beefeaters," Tom corrected her automatically, although he knew that she had made the mistake deliberately, just to break the tension. He saw Hester smile and felt glad that she was there, and fiercely determined to protect her.

Then all the lights went out.

There were shouts, boos, a crash of falling crockery from the kitchens. The windows were dim twilight-colored shapes cut out of the dark. "The electrics are off all over Airhaven!" said Lindstrom's gloomy voice. "The power plant must have failed!"

"No," said Hester quickly. "I know this trick. It's meant to create chaos and stop us leaving. Someone's here, coming for us. . . ." There was an edge of panic in her voice that Tom hadn't heard before, not even in the chase at Stayns. Suddenly he felt very frightened.

From the far end of the room, where crowds of people were spilling out onto the moonlit High Street, a sudden scream arose.

Then came another, and a long crash of breaking glass, shrieks, curses, the clatter of chairs and tables falling. Two green lamps bobbed above the crowd like corpse-lanterns.

"That's no Beefeater!" said Hester.

Tom couldn't tell if she was frightened or relieved.

"HESTER SHAW!" screeched a voice like a saw cutting metal. Over by the doorway a sudden cloud of vapor bloomed, and out of it stepped a Stalker.

It was seven feet tall, and beneath its coat shone metal armor. The flesh of its long face was pale, glistening with a sluglike film of mucus, and here and there a blue-white jag of bone showed through the skin. Its mouth was a slot full of metal teeth. Its nose and the top of its head were covered by a long metal skull-piece with tubes and flexes trailing down like dreadlocks, their ends plugged into ports on its chest. Its round glass eyes gave it a startled look, as if it had never gotten over the horrible surprise of what had happened to it.

Because that was the worst thing about the Stalkers: They had been human once, and somewhere beneath that iron cowl a human brain was trapped.

"It's impossible!" Tom whimpered. "There *aren't* any Stalkers! They were all destroyed centuries ago!" But the Stalker stood there still, horribly real. Tom tried to back away, but he couldn't move. Something was trickling down his legs, as hot as spilled tea, and he realized that he had wet himself.

The Stalker came forward slowly, shoving aside the empty chairs and tables. Fallen glasses burst under its feet. From the shadows behind, an aviator swung at it with a sword, but the blade rebounded from its armor and it smashed the man aside with a sweeping blow of one huge fist, not even bothering to glance back.

"HESTER SHAW," it said. "THOMAS NATSWORTHY."

It knows my name! he thought.

"I . . ." began Miss Fang, but even she seemed lost for words. She pulled Tom backward while Khora and the others drew their swords and stepped between the creature and its prey. But Hester pushed past them. "It's all right," she said in a strange, thin voice. "I know him. Let me talk to him."

The Stalker swung its dead-white face from Tom to Hester, lenses whirring inside mechanical eyes. "HESTER SHAW," it said, caressing her name with its gas-leak hiss of a voice.

"Hello, Shrike," said Hester.

The great head tilted to stare down at her. A metal hand rose, hesitated, then touched her face, leaving streaks of oil.

"I'm sorry I never got the chance to say good-bye. . . ."

"I WORK FOR THE LORD MAYOR OF LONDON NOW," said Shrike. "HE HAS SENT ME TO KILL YOU."

Tom whimpered again. Hester gave a brittle little laugh. "But . . . you won't do it, will you, Shrike? You wouldn't kill me?"

"YES," said Shrike flatly, still staring down at her.

"No, Shrike!" whispered Hester, and Miss Fang seized her chance. She drew a little fan-shaped sliver of metal from a pocket in the sleeve of her coat and sent it whirling toward the Stalker's throat. It made an eerie moaning sound as it flew, unfolding into a shimmering, razor-edged disc.

"A Nuevo-Mayan Battle Frisbee!" gasped Tom, who had seen

91

such weapons safe in glass cases in the Weapons & Warfare section at the Museum. He knew that they could sever a man's neck at sixty paces, and he tensed, waiting for the Stalker's skull to drop from its shoulders — but the Frisbee just hit Shrike's armored throat with a clang and lodged there, quivering.

The slit of a mouth lengthened into a long smile and the Stalker darted forward, quick as a lizard. Miss Fang sidestepped, jumped past it and swung a high kick, but it was far too fast for her. "Run!" she shouted at Hester and Tom. "Get back to the *Jenny*! I'll follow!"

What else could they do? They ran. The thing snatched at them as they ducked past, but Khora was there to grab its arm and Nils Lindstrom swung his sword at its face. The Stalker flung Khora off and raised its hand; there were sparks and a shriek of metal on metal, and Lindstrom dropped the broken sword and howled and clutched his arm. It threw him aside and lifted Anna off her feet as she came at it again, swinging her hard against Khora and Yasmina when they rushed to her aid.

"Miss Fang!" shouted Tom. For a moment he thought of going back, but he knew enough about Stalkers to know that there was nothing he could do. He ran after Hester, over a heap of bodies in the doorway, and out into shadows and twilight and the frightened, milling crowds. A siren was keening mournfully. There was acrid smoke on the breeze and over by the power plant he thought he saw the flicker of the thing all aviators feared the most: fire!

"I don't understand," gasped Hester, talking to herself, not Tom. "He wouldn't kill *me*, he *wouldn't*!" But she kept running, and together they dashed out onto Strut Seven, where the *Jenny Haniver* was waiting for them.

But Shrike had already made certain that the little airship would not be going anywhere that night. The envelope had been slashed; the cowling of the starboard engine-pod had been wrenched open like an old tin can and a spaghetti of torn wiring spilled out onto the quay. Among it lay the broken body of the boy Miss Fang had paid to guard her ship.

Tom stood staring at the wreckage. Behind him, faintly, growing closer, footsteps trod the metal deck: *pung, pung, pung, pung.*

He looked around for Hester, and found her gone; limping away along the docking ring — running *downhill*, he realized, for the damaged air-town was developing a worrying tilt. He shouted her name and sprinted after her, following her out onto a neighboring strut. A tattered-looking balloon had just arrived there, spilling out a family of startled sightseers who weren't sure if the darkness and the shouting meant an emergency or some sort of carnival. Hester shouldered her way through them and grabbed the balloonist by his goggles, heaving him out of his basket. It sagged away from the quay as she leaped in. "Stop! Thieves! Hijackers! Help!" the balloonist was shouting, but all Tom could hear was that faint, appalling *pung-pung-pung* approaching fast along the High Street.

"Tom! Come on!"

He summoned all his courage and leaped after Hester. She was fumbling at the mooring ropes as he landed in the bottom of the basket. "Throw everything overboard," she shouted at him.

He did as he was told and the balloon lurched upward, level

with the first-floor windows, with the rooftops, with the spire of St. Michael's. Soon Airhaven was a doughnut of darkness falling away behind them and below, and Shrike was just a speck, his green eyes glowing as he stalked out along the strut to watch them go.

13

The Resurrected Man

In the dark ages before the dawn of the Traction Era, nomad empires had battled one another across the volcano-maze of Europe. It was they who had built the Stalkers, dragging dead warriors off the battlefields and bringing them back to a sort of life by wiring weird old-tech machines into their nervous systems.

The empires were long forgotten, but the terrible Resurrected Men were not. Tom could remember playing at being one when he was a child in the Guild Orphanage, stomping about with his arms held out straight in front of him, shouting, "I-AM-A-STAL-KER! EX-TER-MIN-ATE!" until Miss Plym came and told him to keep the noise down.

But he had never expected to *meet* one.

As the stolen balloon scudded eastward on the night wind, he sat shuddering in the swaying basket, twisted sideways so that Hester wouldn't see the wet stain on his breeches, and said, "I thought they all died hundreds of years ago! I thought they were all destroyed in battles, or went mad and tore themselves apart. . . ."

"Not Shrike," said Hester.

"And he *knew* you!"

"Of course he did," she said. "We're old friends, Shrike and me."

❋

She had met him the morning after her parents died, the morning when she woke up on the shores of the Hunting Ground in the whispering rain. She had no idea how she came to be there, and the pain in her head was so bad that she could barely move or think.

Drawn up nearby was the smallest, filthiest town that she had ever seen. People with big wicker baskets on their backs were coming down out of it on ladders and gangplanks and sifting through the flotsam on the tide-line before returning with their baskets full of scrap and driftwood. A few were carrying her father's rowboat away, and it wasn't long before some of them discovered Hester. Two men came and looked down at her. One was a typical scavenger, small and filthy, with bits of an old bug piled in his basket. After he had peered at her for a while he stepped back and said to his companion, "Sorry, Mr. Shrike — I thought she might be one for your collection, but she's flesh and blood all right. . . ."

He turned and stumped away across the steaming garbage, losing all interest in Hester. He only wanted stuff he could sell, and there was no value in a half-dead child. Old bug tires, now — *those* were worth something. . . .

The other man stayed where he was, looking down at Hester. It was only when he reached down and touched her face and she felt the cold, hard iron beneath his gloves that she realized he was not really a man at all. When he spoke, his voice sounded like a wire brush being scraped across a blackboard. "YOU CAN'T STAY HERE, CHILD," he said, and picked her up and slung her over his shoulder and took her aboard the town.

It was called Strole, and it was home to fifty tough, dust-hardened scavengers who robbed old-tech sites when they could find them and scrounged salvage from the leavings of larger towns when they could not. Shrike lived with them, but he was no scavenger. When criminals from one of the great Traction Cities escaped into the Out-Country, Shrike would track them and cut off their heads, which he carefully preserved. When he crossed that city's path again he would take the head to the authorities, and collect his reward.

Why he bothered to rescue her Hester never did discover. It could not have been out of pity, for he had none. The only sign of tenderness she ever saw in him was when he busied himself with his collection. He was fascinated by old automata and mechanical toys, and he would buy any that passing scavengers brought to him. His ramshackle quarters in Strole were full of them: animals, knights in armor, clockwork soldiers with keys in their backs, even a life-size Angel of Death pulled from some elaborate clock. But his favorites were all women or children: beautiful ladies in moth-eaten gowns and pretty girls and boys with porcelain faces. All night long Shrike would patiently dis-mantle and repair them, exploring the intricate escapements of their hearts as if searching for some clue to the workings of his own.

Sometimes it seemed to Hester that she, too, was part of his col-lection. Did she remind him of the wounds that he had suffered on the battlefields of forgotten wars, when he had still been human?

She shared his home for five long years, while her face healed badly into a permanent ruined scowl and her memories came slowly back to her. Some were startlingly clear: the waves on the shores of Oak Island, her mum's voice, the moor-wind with its smells of wet grass and the dung of animals. Others were murky and hard to understand; they flashed into her mind just as she was falling asleep, or caught her unawares while she wandered amongst the silent mechanical figures in Shrike's house. *Blood on the star-charts. A metallic noise. A man's long, handsome face with sea-gray eyes.* They were broken shards of memory, and they had to be carefully collected and pieced together, just like the bits of machinery the scavengers dug up.

It was not until she overheard some men telling stories about the great Thaddeus Valentine that she started to make sense of it all. She found that she recognized that name: It was the name of the man who had killed her mum and dad and turned her into a monster. She knew what she had to do without even having to think about it. She went to Shrike and told him she wanted to go after Valentine.

"YOU MUST NOT," was all the Stalker said. "YOU'LL BE KILLED."

"Then come with me!" she had pleaded, but he would not. He had heard about London and about Magnus Crome's love of technology. He thought that if he went there the Guild of Engineers would overpower him and cut him into pieces to study in their secret laboratories. "YOU MUST NOT GO," was all that he would say.

So she went anyway, waiting till he was busy with his automata, then slipping out of a window and out of Strole, and setting off across the wintry Out-Country with a stolen knife in her belt, in search of London and revenge.

❄

"I've never seen him since that," she told Tom, shivering in the basket of the stolen balloon. "Strole was down on the shores of the Anglish Sea when I left, but here Shrike is, working for Magnus Crome, and wanting to kill me. It doesn't make sense!"

"Maybe you hurt his feelings when you ran away?" suggested Tom.

"Shrike doesn't have feelings," said Hester. "They cleaned all his memories and feelings away when they made a Stalker of him."

She sounds as if she envies him, thought Tom. But at least the sound of her voice had helped to calm him, and he had stopped shaking. He sat and listened to the wind sigh through the balloon's rigging. There was a black stain on the western clouds that he thought must be the smoke from Airhaven. Had the aviators managed to get the fires under control, or had their town been destroyed? And what about Anna Fang? He realized that Shrike had probably murdered her, along with all her friends. That kind, laughing aviatrix was dead, as dead as his own parents. It was as if there was a curse on him that destroyed everybody who was kind to him. If only he had never met Valentine! If only he had stayed safely in the Museum where he belonged!

"She might be all right," said Hester suddenly, as if she had guessed what he was thinking about. "I think Shrike was just playing with her; he didn't have his claws out or anything."

"He's got *claws?!*"

"As long as she didn't annoy him too much he probably wouldn't waste time killing her."

"What about Airhaven?"

"I suppose if it's really badly damaged it'll put down somewhere for repairs."

Tom nodded. Then a happy thought occurred to him. "Do you think Miss Fang'll come after us?"

"I don't know," said Hester. "But Shrike will."

Tom looked over his shoulder again, horrified.

"Still," she said, "at least we're heading in the right direction for London."

He peered gingerly over the edge of the basket. The clouds lay below them like a white eiderdown drawn across the land, hiding anything that might give a clue as to where they were or where they were going. "How can you tell?" he asked.

"From the stars, of course," said Hester. "Mum showed me. She was an aviator, too, remember? She'd been all over the place. She even went to America once. You have to use the stars to find your way in places like that where they don't have charts or landmarks. Look, that's the Pole Star, and that constellation is what the Ancients used to call the Great Bear, but most people nowadays call it the City. And if we keep *that* one to starboard we'll know we're heading northeast. . . ."

"There are so many!" he said, trying to follow her pointing finger. Here above the clouds, without veils of city-smoke and Out-Country dust to hide it, the night sky sparkled with a million cold points of light. "I never knew there were so many stars before!"

"They're all suns, burning away far out in space, thousands and thousands of miles away," said Hester, and Tom had the feeling that she felt proud to show him how much she knew. "Except for the ones that aren't really stars at all. Some of the really bright ones are mechanical moons that the Ancients put up into orbit thousands of years ago, still circling and circling the poor old Earth."

Tom stared up at the glittering dark. "And what's that one?" he asked, pointing to a bright star low in the west.

Hester looked at it, and her smile faded away. He saw her hands clench into fists. "That one?" she said. "That's an airship, and it's coming after us."

"Perhaps Miss Fang has come to rescue us?" said Tom hopefully.

But the distant airship was gaining quickly, and in another few minutes they could see that it was a small, London-built scoutship, a Spudbury Sunbeam or a Goshawk 90. They could almost feel Shrike's green eyes watching them across the deserts of the sky.

Hester started fumbling with the rusty wheels and levers that controlled the gas pressure in the balloon. After a few seconds she found the one she wanted and a fierce hiss came from some where overhead.

"What are you doing?" squeaked Tom. "You'll let the gas out! We'll crash!"

"I'm hiding us from Shrike," said the girl, and she opened the valve still farther. Looking up, Tom saw the gasbag start to sag. He glanced back at the pursuing airship. It was gaining, but it was still a few miles away. Hopefully from that distance it would look as if some accident had struck the balloon. Hopefully Shrike would not guess Hester's plan. Hopefully his little ship was not armed with rocket projectors. . . .

And then they sank down into the clouds and could see nothing but swirling dark billows and sometimes a quick glimpse of the moon scudding dimly above them. The basket creaked and the envelope flapped and the gas valve hissed like a tetchy snake.

"When we touch down, get out of the basket as quick as you can," said Hester.

"Yes," he said, and then, "but . . . you mean we're going to leave the balloon?"

"We don't stand a chance against Shrike in the air," she explained. "Hopefully on the ground I can outwit him."

"On the ground?" cried Tom. "Oh, not the Out-Country again!"

The balloon was sinking fast. They saw the black landscape looming up below, dark blots of vegetation and a few thin glimmers of moonlight. Overhead, thick clouds were racing into the east. There was no sign of Shrike's airship. Tom braced himself. The ground was a hundred feet below, then fifty, then ten. Branches came rattling and scraping along the keel and the basket bucked and plunged, crashing against muddy earth and leaping up into the sky and down again and up.

"Jump!" screamed Hester, the next time it touched down. He jumped, falling through scratchy branches into a soft mattress of mud. The balloon shot upward again and for a moment he was afraid that Hester had abandoned him to perish on the bare earth. "Hester!" he shouted, so loud it hurt his throat.

"Hester!" And then there was a rustling in the scrub away to his left and she was limping toward him. "Oh, thank Quirke!" he whispered.

He expected her to stop and sit down with him to rest awhile and thank the gods for dropping them onto soft, wet earth instead of hard stone. Instead, she walked straight past him, limping away toward the northeast.

"Stop!" shouted Tom, still too winded and shivery to even stand. "Wait! Where are you going?"

She looked back at him as if he were mad. "London," she said.

Tom rolled onto his back and groaned, gathering his strength for another weary trek.

Above him, freed of their weight, the balloon was returning to the sky, a dark teardrop that was quickly swallowed into the belly of the clouds. A few moments later he heard the purr of engines as Shrike's airship went hurrying after it. Then there were only the night and the cold wind, and rags of moonlight prowling the broken hills.

14

THE GUILDHALL

Katherine decided to start at the top. The day after her father left London she sent a message up the pneumatic tube system to the Lord Mayor's office from the terminal in her father's room, and half an hour later a reply came back from Crome's secretary: The Lord Mayor would see Miss Valentine at noon.

Katherine went to her dressing room and put on her most businesslike clothes — her narrow black trousers and her gray coat with the shoulder-fins. She tied back her hair with a clip made from the taillights of an Ancient car and fetched out a stylish hat with trailing ear-flaps that she had bought six weeks before but hadn't got around to wearing yet. She put color on her lips and soft oblongs of rouge high on her cheekbones and painted a little blue triangle between her eyebrows, a mock Guild-mark like the fashionable ladies wore. She found a notebook and a pencil and slipped them both into one of Father's important-looking black briefcases along with the pass he had given her on her fifteenth birthday, the gold pass that allowed her access to almost every part of London. Then she studied her appearance in the mirror, imagining herself a few weeks from now going to meet the returning expedition. She would be able to tell Father, "*It's all right now, I understand everything; you needn't be afraid anymore. . . .*"

At a quarter to twelve she walked with Dog to the elevator station in Quirke Circus, enjoying the looks that people gave her as she passed. "*There goes Miss Katherine Valentine,*" she imagined them saying. "*Off to see the Lord Mayor . . .*" The elevator staff all knew her face, and they smiled and said, "Good morning, Miss Katherine," and patted Dog and didn't bother looking at her pass as she boarded the 11:52 for Top Tier.

The elevator hummed upward. She walked briskly across Paternoster Square, where Dog stared thoughtfully at the wheeling pigeons and pricked up his ears at the sounds of the repair work going on inside St. Paul's. Soon she was climbing the steps of the Guildhall and being ushered into a tiny internal elevator, and at one minute to twelve she was shown through the circular bronze door of the Lord Mayor's private office.

"Ah, Miss Valentine. You are one minute early." Crome glanced up at her from the far side of his huge desk and went back to the report that he had been reading. Behind his head was a round window with a view of St. Paul's, looking wavery and unreal through the thick glass, like a sunken temple seen through clear water. Sunlight shone dimly on the tarnished bronze panels of the office walls. There were no pictures, no hangings or decorations of any sort, and the floor was bare metal. Katherine shivered, feeling the cold rise up through the soles of her shoes.

The Lord Mayor kept her waiting for fifty-nine silent seconds that seemed to stretch on forever. She was feeling thoroughly uncomfortable by the time he set down the report. He smiled faintly, like somebody who had never seen a smile but had read a book on how to do it.

"You will be glad to hear that I have just received a coded radio signal sent from your father's expedition shortly before he flew out of range," he said. "All is well aboard the 13*th Floor Elevator*."

"Good!" said Katherine, knowing that it would be the last she would hear of Father until he was on his way home; even the Engineers had never been able to send radio signals more than a few hundred miles.

"Was there anything else?" asked Crome.

"Yes . . ." said Katherine, and hesitated, afraid that she was going to sound foolish. Faced with Crome's cold office and still colder smile, she found herself wishing she had not put on so much makeup or worn these stiff, formal clothes. But this was what she had come here for, after all. She blurted out, "I want to know about that girl, and why she tried to kill my father."

The Lord Mayor's smile vanished. "Your father has never seen fit to tell me who she is. I have no idea why she is so keen to murder him."

"Do you think it is something to do with MEDUSA?"

Crome's gaze grew a few degrees colder. "That matter does not concern you!" he snapped. "What has Valentine told you?"

"Nothing!" said Katherine, getting flustered. "But I can see he's scared, and I need to know why, because . . ."

"Listen to me, child," said Crome, standing up and coming around the desk at her. Thin hands gripped her shoulders. "If Valentine has secrets from you it is for good reason. There are aspects of his work that you could not begin to understand. Remember, he started out with nothing; he was a mere Out-Country scavenger before I took an interest in him. Do you want to see him reduced to that again? Or worse?"

Katherine felt as if he had slapped her. Her face burned red with anger, but she controlled herself.

"Go home and wait for his return," ordered Crome. "And leave grown-up matters to those who understand them. Don't speak to anyone about the girl, or MEDUSA."

Grown-up matters? thought Katherine angrily. *How old does he think I am?* But she bowed her head and said meekly, "Yes, Lord Mayor," and "Come along, Dog."

"And do not bring that animal to Top Tier again," called Crome, his voice following her into the outer office, where the secretaries turned to stare at her furious, tearful face.

Riding the elevator back to Quirke Circus, she whispered in her wolf's ear, "We'll show him, Dog!"

Instead of going straight home she called in at the Temple of Clio on the edge of Circle Park. There in the scented darkness she calmed herself and tried to work out what to do next.

Ever since Nikolas Quirke had been declared a god, most Londoners had stopped giving much thought to the older gods and goddesses, and so Katherine had the temple to herself. She liked Clio, who had been her mother's goddess back in Puerto Angeles, and whose statue looked a bit like Mama, too, with its kind dark eyes and patient smile. She remembered what Mama had taught her, about how the poor goddess was being blown constantly backward into the future by the storm of progress, but how she could reach back sometimes and inspire people to change the whole course of history. Looking up now at the statue's gentle face she said, "What must I do, Clio? How can I help Father if the Lord Mayor won't tell me anything?"

She hadn't really expected an answer, and none came, so she said a quick prayer for Father and another for poor Tom Natsworthy, and made her offerings and left.

It wasn't until she was halfway back to Clio House that the idea struck her, a thought so unexpected that it could have been sent to her by the goddess herself. She remembered how, as she ran toward the waste chutes on the night Tom fell, she had passed someone heading in the other direction: a young Apprentice Engineer, looking so white and shocked that she was *sure* he must have witnessed what happened.

She hurried homeward through the sunlit park. That young Engineer would have the answer! She would go back to the Gut and find him! She would find out what was going on without any help from wicked old Magnus Crome!

15

THE RUSTWATER MARSHES

Tom and Hester had walked all night, and when the pale, flat sun rose behind drifts of morning fog they kept walking, stopping only now and then to catch their breaths. This landscape was quite different from the mud-plains they had crossed a few days ago. Here they had to keep making detours around bogs and pools of brackish water, and although they sometimes stumbled into the deep, weed-choked scars of old town-tracks it was clear that no town had been this way for many years. "See how the scrub has grown up," said Hester, pointing out ruts filled with brambles and hillsides green with young trees. "Even a little semi-static would have felled those saplings for fuel."

"Perhaps the earth here is just too soft," suggested Tom, sinking to his waist for the twentieth time in the thick mud. He was recalling the huge map of the Hunting Ground that hung in the lobby of the London Museum, and the great sweep of marsh-country that stretched all the way from the central mountains to the shores of the Sea of Khazak, mile after mile of reedbeds and thin blue creeks and all of it marked, *Unsuitable for Town or City.*

He said, "I think this must be the edge of the Rustwater Marshes. They call it that because the water is supposed to be stained red with the rust of towns that have strayed into it and sunk. Only the most foolhardy mayor would bring his town here."

"Then Wreyland and Anna Fang brought us much farther south than I thought," whispered Hester to herself. "London must be almost a thousand miles away by now. It'll take months to catch it up again, and Shrike will be on my tail the whole way."

"But you fooled him!" Tom reminded her. "We escaped!"

"He won't stay fooled for long," she said. "He'll soon pick up our tracks again. Why do you think he's called a Stalker?"

✢

On and on she led him, dragging him over hills and through mires and down valleys where the air was speckly with swarms of whining, stinging flies. They both grew weary and peevish. Once, Tom suggested they sit down and rest a while, and Hester snapped back, "Do what you like. What do I care?" After that he trudged on in silence, angry at her. What a horrible, ugly, vicious, self-pitying girl she was! After all they had come through, and the way he had helped her in the Out-Country, she was still ready to abandon him. He wished Shrike had gotten her and it was Miss Fang or Khora whom he had escaped with. They would have let him rest his aching feet. . . .

But he was glad enough of Hester when the darkness fell, when thick clots of fog rose out of the marshes like the ghosts of mammoths and every rustle in the undergrowth sounded like a Stalker's footfall. She found a place for them to spend the night, in the shelter of some stunted trees, and later, when the sudden shriek of a hunting owl brought him leaping out of his uneasy sleep he found her sitting guard beside him like a friendly gargoyle. "It's all right," she told him. And after a moment, in one of those sudden flashes of softness that he had noticed before, she said, "I miss them, Tom. My mum and dad."

"I know," he said. "I miss mine, too."

"You've got no family at all in London?"

"No."

"No friends?"

He thought about it. "Not really."

"Who was that girl?" she asked, after a little while.

"What? Where?"

"In the Gut that night, with you and Valentine."

"That was Katherine," he said. "She's . . . Well, she's Valentine's daughter."

Hester nodded. "She's pretty," she said.

After that he slept easier, dreaming that Katherine was coming down to rescue them in an airship, carrying them back into the crystal light above the clouds. When he next opened his eyes it was dawn and Hester was shaking him.

"Listen!"

He listened, and heard a sound that was not the sound of woods or water.

"Is it a town?" he asked hopefully.

"No . . ." Hester tilted her head to one side, tasting the sound. "It's a Rotwang aero-engine. . . ."

It grew louder, throbbing down out of the sky. Above the swirling mist a London scoutship flickered by.

They froze, hoping that the wet black cage of branches

overhead would hide them. The growl of the airship faded and then rose again, circling. "Shrike can see us," whispered Hester, staring up at the blind, white fog. "I can feel him watching us. . . ."

"No, no," Tom insisted. "If we can't see the airship, how can he see us? It stands to reason. . . ."

❀

But high overhead, the Resurrected Man tunes his eyes to ultra-red and switches on his heat sensors and sees two glowing human shapes amid the soft gray static of the trees. "TAKE ME CLOSER," he orders.

"If you can see them so clearly now," the airship's pilot grumbles, "it's a pity you couldn't tell that bloomin' balloon was empty before we went chasing it across half the Hunting Ground."

Shrike says nothing. Why should he explain himself to this whining Once-born? He had seen that the balloon was empty as soon as it popped back up above the clouds, but he had decided to keep it to himself. He was pleased at Hester Shaw's quick thinking, and he decided to let her live a few more hours as a reward, while this slow-witted Engineer Aviator pursued her empty balloon.

He flicks his eyes back to their normal setting. He will hunt Hester the hard way, with scent and sound and ordinary vision. He calls up a memory of her face and sets it turning in his mind as the airship sweeps down through the fog.

❀

"Run!" said Hester. The airship loomed out of the whiteness a few yards away, settling toward the ground with its rotors beating the fog like egg whisks. She hauled Tom out of their useless hiding place and away across sodden ground, knuckled with tree roots. White scuts of water spurted at every step, and black slime gurgled into their boots. They ran blindly, until Hester came to such an abrupt stop that Tom crashed into her from behind and they both went sprawling.

They had come in a circle. The airship hung just ahead of them, and a giant shape barred their path. Two beams of pale green light stabbed toward them, filled with dancing water droplets. "HESTER," grated a metal voice.

Hester groped for something she could use as a weapon and came up with a gnarled old length of wood. "Don't come any closer, Shrike!" she warned. "I'll smash those pretty green eyes of yours! I'll bash your brains out!"

"Come on!" squeaked Tom, plucking at her coat and trying to drag her away.

"Where to?" asked Hester, risking a quick glance back at him. She shifted her grip on the makeshift club and stood her ground as Shrike stalked closer.

"YOU HAVE DONE WELL, HESTER, BUT THE HUNT IS ENDED." The Stalker was moving carefully over the wet ground. Each time he set down his metal foot a wreath of steam hissed up. He raised his hands and clawlike blades slid out.

"What made you change your mind about London, Shrike?" shouted Hester angrily. "How do you come to be Crome's odd-job man?"

"YOU LED ME TO LONDON, HESTER." Shrike paused, and his dead face widened in a steely smile. "I KNEW YOU WOULD GO THERE. I SOLD MY COLLECTION AND CHARTERED AN AIRSHIP SO THAT I COULD GET THERE BEFORE YOU."

"You sold your clockwork people?" Hester sounded astonished. "Shrike, if you wanted me back that badly, why didn't you just track me down?"

"I DECIDED TO LET YOU CROSS THE HUNTING GROUND ALONE," said Shrike. "IT WAS A TEST."

"Did I pass?"

Shrike ignored her. "WHEN I REACHED LONDON I WAS TAKEN STRAIGHT TO THE ENGINEERIUM, AS I EXPECTED. I SPENT EIGHTEEN MONTHS THERE WAITING FOR YOU TO ARRIVE. THE ENGINEERS TOOK ME APART AND PUT ME TOGETHER AGAIN A DOZEN TIMES. BUT IT WAS WORTH IT. I MADE A DEAL WITH MAGNUS CROME. HE HAS PROMISED ME MY HEART'S DESIRE."

"Oh, good," said Hester weakly, wondering what on earth he was talking about.

"BUT FIRST YOU MUST DIE."

"But, Shrike, why?"

The reply was drowned out by a thick, warbling hum that made Tom wonder if the Stalker's airship was about to lift off without him. He glanced up at it. It was still holding the same position as before, but the steady chirrup of the propellers had been masked by the new noise, a rumbling, slithering roar that grew louder every second. Even Shrike seemed disturbed: His eyes flickered and he tilted his head to one side, listening. Underfoot, the ground began to tremble.

Out of the fog behind the Stalker burst a wall of mud and water, curling over at the top, capped with white foam. Behind it came a town, a very small, old-fashioned town, racing along on eight fat wheels. Hester scrambled backward, and Shrike saw the look on her face and turned to see what caused it. Tom dived sideways, grabbing the girl by the scruff of her neck and hurling her to safety. The airship tried to veer away but the wheels of the speeding town caught it and blew it apart and plowed the blazing debris down into the mud. An instant later they heard the Stalker bellow "HESTER!" as the huge front wheel came crashing down on him.

They clung together, rolling over and over as the town howled past, a flicker of spokes and pistons, firelight on metal, tiny figures staring down from observation decks, the long-drawn-out moan of a Klaxon echoing through the fog. Then, just as suddenly as it had appeared, it was gone. The air stank of smoke and hot metal.

They sat up. Bits of airship were drifting down, blazing merrily. Where the Stalker had been standing a deep wheel-mark was quickly filling with black, glistening mud. Something that might have been an iron hand jutted from the ooze and a pale cloud of steam rose into the air above it and slowly faded.

"Is it . . . *dead?*" asked Tom, his voice all quivery with fright.

"A town just ran over him," said Hester. "I shouldn't think he's very well. . . ."

Tom wondered dimly what Shrike had meant about his "heart's desire." Why would he have sold his precious collection to come after Hester if all he wanted to do was kill her? There was no way of knowing now. "And the poor men on that airship . . ." he whispered.

"They were sent to help him kill us, Natsworthy," said the girl. "Don't waste your pity on them."

They were quiet for a moment, staring at the mist. Then Tom said, "I wonder what it was running from?"

"What do you mean?"

"That town," said Tom. "It was moving so fast. . . . Something must be chasing it. . . ."

Hester looked at him and slowly realized what he meant.

"Oh, *knackers!*" she said.

The second town was upon them almost at once. It was bigger than the first, with vast, barrel-shaped wheels. On its gaping jaws some wag had drawn a toothy grin and the words HAPPY EETER.

There was no time to run out of its way. Hester grabbed Tom this time and he saw her shouting something, but the shrieking thunder of the engines meant that it took him a moment to work out what it was.

"*We can jump it! Do as I do!*"

The town rolled over them, its wheels passing on either side so that they were lifted up like two ants in the path of a plow, lifted on a wave of mud that almost smashed them against the lumbering metal belly overhead. Hester crouched on the crest of the wave like a surfer and Tom wobbled beside her, expecting at any moment to be swatted out of his life by a passing derrick or hurled under the wheels. Hester was shouting at him again, and pointing. An exhaust duct was rushing past them like a monstrous snake, and by the flare of furnace-light from vents on the town's underside he made out the handrail of a maintenance platform. Hester grabbed at it and swung herself up, and Tom flung himself after her. For a moment his hands clutched wildly at nothing, then there was rusty iron under his fingers, almost jerking his arms from their sockets, and Hester reached down and took a firm grip on his belt and hauled him to safety.

It was a long time before they stopped shaking and clambered to their feet. They both looked as if they had been modeled crudely from the Out-Country mud; it covered their clothes and clagged in their hair and plastered their faces. Tom was laughing helplessly at the closeness of their escape and at the sheer surprise of finding himself still alive, and Hester laughed with him. He had never heard her laugh before, and he had never felt as close to anyone as he felt to her at that moment.

"We'll be all right!" she said. "We'll be all right now! Let's go up and find out whom we've hitched a lift with!"

※

Whatever the town was, it was small, only a suburb, really. Tom amused himself by trying to work out what it might be while Hester picked the lock on a hatchway and led him up a long stairwell with rusty walls that steamed in the heat from the engines. He thought it looked a bit like Crawley, or Purley Spokes, the suburbs that London had built back in the great old days when there was so much prey that cities could afford to build little satellite towns. If so, it might have its own merchant airships, licensed to trade with London.

But something still nagged at the back of his mind. *Only the most foolhardy mayor would bring his town here. . . .*

Why on earth would Crawley or Purley Spokes be chasing a townlet into the dreaded Rustwater Marshes?

They climbed on up the stairwell until they reached a second hatch. It wasn't locked, and swung open to let them out onto the upper deck. A cold wind blew fog between the metal buildings, and the deckplates shook and lurched as the suburb raced onward. The streets seemed deserted, but Tom knew that small towns often had only a few hundred inhabitants. Perhaps they were all busy in the engine rooms, or waiting safe indoors until the chase was over.

117

But there was something about this place he didn't like; it certainly wasn't the trim little suburb he had been hoping for. The deckplates were rusty and pitted and the shabby houses were dwarfed by huge auxiliary engines that had been ripped out of other towns and bolted haphazardly to this one, linked to the main engines on the deck below by a cat's cradle of gigantic ducts that wrapped around the buildings and burrowed down through holes cut in the deck-plate. Beyond them, where Tom would have expected parks and observation platforms, a mess of gun emplacements and wooden palisades ringed the edge of the suburb.

Hester motioned for him to keep quiet and led him toward the foggy stern, where he could see a tall building that must be the Town Hall. As they drew nearer they made out a sign above the entrance that read:

Welcome to
TUNBRIDGE WHEELS
Population: ~~500~~ ~~467~~ 212
and still rising!

Above it flapped a black and white flag, a grinning skull and two crossed bones.

"Great Quirke!" Tom gasped. "This is a pirate suburb!"

And suddenly, from foggy side streets all around them, came men and women as shabby as the town, lean and hard and fierce-eyed, and carrying the biggest guns that he had ever seen.

As the pirate suburb speeds on its way, silence returns to the Rustwater, broken only by the sounds of small creatures moving in the reedbeds. Then

the ooze in one of the deep wheel-ruts burbles and heaves and vomits up the jerking wreck of Shrike.

He has been driven far down into the mud like a screaming tent peg, ground and crushed and twisted. His left arm hangs by a few frayed wires; his right leg will not move. One of his eyes is dark and blind and the view from the other is cloudy, so that he has to keep twitching his head to clear it. Bits of his memory have vanished, but others come up unbidden. As he wades out of the suburb's wheel-marks he remembers the ancient wars that he was built for. At Hill 20 the Tesla Guns crackled like iced lightning, wrapping him in fire until his flesh began to fry on his iron bones. But he survived. He is the last of the Lazarus Brigade, and he always survives. It will take a lot more than being run over by a couple of towns to finish Shrike.

Slowly, slowly, he claws his way to firmer ground, and sniffs and scouts and scans until he is sure that Hester escaped alive. He feels very proud of her. His heart's desire! Soon he will find her again, and the loneliness of his everlasting life will be over.

The suburb has left deep grooves across the landscape. It will be easy to track, even with his leg dragging uselessly, even with an eye gone and his mind misfiring. The Stalker throws back his head and bellows his hunting cry at the empty marshes.

16

The Turd Tanks

London kept on moving, day after day, grinding its way across the continent formerly known as Europe as if there were some fantastic prize ahead — but all that the lookouts had sighted since the city ate Salthook were a few tiny scavenger towns, and Magnus Crome would not even alter course to catch them. People started to grow restless, asking each other in whispers what the Lord Mayor thought he was playing at. London had never been meant to go so far, so fast. There was talk of food shortages, and the heat from the engines spread up through the deckplates until it was said you could fry an egg on the pavements of Tier Six.

Down in the Gut the heat was appalling, and when Katherine stepped off the elevator at Tartarus Row she felt as if she had just walked into an oven. She had never been so deep into the Gut before, and for a while she stood blinking on the steps of the elevator terminus, dazed by the noise and darkness. Up on Tier One she had left the sun shining down on Circle Park and a cool wind stirring the rosebushes; down here gangs of men were running about, Klaxons were honking, and huge hoppers of fuel were grinding past her on their way to the furnaces.

For a moment she felt like going home, but she knew that she had do what she had come here for, for Father's sake. She took a deep breath and went out into the street.

It was nothing like High London. Nobody knew her face down here; passersby were surly when she asked them for directions, and off-duty laborers lounging on the pavements whistled as she went by and shouted, "Hello, darling!" and "Where'd you get that hat?" A burly foreman shoved her aside to lead a gang of shackled convicts past. From shrines under the fuel ducts leered statues of Sooty Pete, the hunchbacked god of engine rooms and smokestacks. Katherine lifted her chin and kept a tight grip on Dog's leash, glad that he was there to protect her.

But she knew that this was the only place where she could hope to find the truth. With Father away and Tom lost or dead, and Magnus Crome unwilling to talk, there was only one person left in London who might know the secret of the scarred girl.

It had been hard work finding him, but luckily the staff in the records office at the Guild of Salvagemen, Stokers, Wheel-Tappers, and Associated Gut Operatives were happy enough to oblige Thaddeus Valentine's daughter. If there was an Apprentice Engineer near the waste chutes that night, they said, he must have been supervising convict laborers, and if he was supervising convict laborers he must have come from the Engineers' experimental prison in the Deep Gut. A few more questions and a bribe to a Gut foreman and she had a name: Apprentice Engineer Pod.

Now, nearly a week after her meeting with the Lord Mayor, she was on her way to talk to him.

✳

The Deep Gut Prison was a complex of buildings the size of a small town that clustered around the base of a giant support pillar. Katherine followed signposts to the administration block, a spherical metal building jacked up on rust-streaked gantries and slowly revolving so that the supervisors could look down from its windows and watch their cellblocks and exercise yards and algae-mat farms spin endlessly around them. In the entrance hall, neon light glimmered on acres of white metal. An Engineer came gliding up to Katherine as she stepped inside. "No dogs allowed," he said.

"He's not a dog, he's a wolf," replied Katherine, with her sweetest smile, and the man jumped back as Dog sniffed at his rubber coat. He was prim-looking, with a thin, pursed mouth and patches of eczema on his bald head. The badge on his coat said *Gut Supervisor Nimmo*. Katherine smiled at him, and before he could raise any more objections she showed her gold pass and said "I'm here on an errand for my father, the Head Historian. I have to see one of your apprentices, a boy called Pod."

Supervisor Nimmo blinked at her and said, "But . . . But . . ."

"I've come straight from Magnus Crome's office," Katherine lied. "Call his secretary if you want to check. . . ."

"No, I'm sure it's all right . . ." mumbled Nimmo. Nobody from outside the Guild had ever wanted to interview an apprentice before, and he didn't like it. There was probably a rule against it. But he didn't want to argue with someone who knew the Lord Mayor. He asked Katherine to wait and he scurried away, vanishing into a glass-walled office on the far side of the hall.

Katherine waited, stroking Dog's head and smiling politely at bald, white-coated passersby. Soon Nimmo was back. "I have located Apprentice Pod," he announced. "He has been transferred to Section 60."

"Oh, well done, Mr. Nimmo!" Katherine beamed. "Can you send him up?"

"Certainly not," retorted the Engineer, who wasn't sure he liked being ordered about by a mere Historian's daughter. But if she wanted to see Section 60, he would take her there. "Follow me," he said, leading the way to a small elevator. "Section 60 is on the underdecks."

The underdecks were where London kept its plumbing. Katherine had read about them in her schoolbooks, so she was prepared for the long descent, but nothing could have prepared her for the smell. It hit her as soon as the elevator reached the bottom and the door slid open. It was like walking into a wall of wet sewage.

"This is Section 60, one of our most interesting experimental labor units," said Nimmo, who didn't seem to notice the smell. "The convicts assigned to this sector are helping to develop some very exciting new ways of recycling the city's waste products."

Katherine stepped out, clamping her handkerchief over her nose. She found herself standing in a huge, dimly lit space. Ahead of her were three tanks, each larger than Clio House and all its gardens. Stinking yellow-brown filth was dribbling into the tanks from a maze of pipes that clung to the low ceiling, and people in drab gray prison coveralls were wading chest-deep in it, skimming the surface with long-handled rakes.

"What are they doing?" asked Katherine. "What is that stuff?"

"Detritus, Miss Valentine," said Nimmo, sounding proud. "Effluent. Ejecta. Human nutritional by-products."

"You mean . . . poo?" said Katherine, appalled.

"Thank you, Miss Valentine; perhaps that is the word for which I was groping." Nimmo glared at her. "There is nothing disgusting about it, I assure you. We all . . . ah . . . use the toilet from time to time. Well, now you know where your . . . um . . . *poo* ends up. 'Waste not, want not' is the Engineers' motto, Miss. Properly processed human ordure makes very useful fuel for our city's engines. And we are experimenting with ways of turning it into a tasty and nutritious snack. We feed our prisoners on nothing else. Unfortunately they keep dying. But that is just a temporary setback, I'm sure."

Katherine walked to the edge of the nearest tank. *I have come down to the Sunless Country!* she thought. *Oh, Clio! This is the land of the dead!*

But even the Sunless Country could not be as terrible as this place. The slurry swilled and shifted, slapping at the edges of the tanks as London trundled over a range of rugged hills. Flies buzzed in thick clouds beneath the vaulted roof and settled on the faces and bodies of the laborers. Their shaven heads gleamed in the dim half-light, faces set in blank stares as they skimmed the thick crust from the surface and transferred it into hoppers that other convicts wheeled on rails along the sides of the tank. Grim-faced Apprentice Engineers looked on, swinging long, black truncheons. Only Dog seemed happy; he was straining at his leash, his tail wagging, and every now and then he would look up eagerly at Katherine as if to thank her for bringing him somewhere with such interesting smells.

She fought down her rising lunch and turned to Nimmo. "These poor people! Who are they?"

"Oh, don't worry about *them*," said the supervisor. "They're convicts. Criminals. They deserve it."

"What did they do?"

"Oh, this and that. Petty theft. Tax-dodging. Criticizing our Lord Mayor. They're very well-treated, considering. Now, let's see if we can find Apprentice Pod. . . ."

While he spoke, Katherine had been watching the nearest tank. One of the men working it had stopped moving and let go of his rake, holding his head as if overcome by dizziness. Now a girl apprentice had also noticed him, and stepping up to the edge of the tank she jabbed at the man with her truncheon. Blue sparks flickered where it touched him, and he thrashed and howled and floundered, finally vanishing under the heaving surface. Other prisoners stared toward the place where he had sunk, too scared to go and help.

"Do something!" gasped Katherine, turning to Nimmo, who seemed not to have noticed.

Another apprentice came running along the edge of the tank, shouting at the prisoners below him to help their comrade. Two or three of them dredged him up, and the new apprentice leaned down into the tank and hauled him out, splattering himself with slurry in the process. He was wearing a little gauze mask, like many of the warders, but Katherine was sure she recognized him, and at her side she heard Nimmo growl, "*Pod!*"

They hurried toward him. Apprentice Pod had dragged the half-drowned convict onto the metal walkway between the tanks and was trying to wash the slurry from his face with water from a standpipe nearby. The other apprentice, the one who had jabbed the poor man in the first place, looked on with an expression of disgust. "You're wasting water again, Pod!" she said as Katherine and Nimmo ran up.

"What is going on here, Apprentices?" asked Nimmo crossly.

"This man was slacking," the girl said. "I was just trying to get him to work a bit faster."

"He's feverish!" said Apprentice Pod, looking up plaintively, covered in stinking muck. "It's no wonder he couldn't work."

Katherine knelt beside him and he noticed her for the first time, his eyes widening in surprise. He had succeeded in washing most of the slurry from the man's face, and she reached out and laid her hand on the damp brow. Even by the standards of the Deep Gut it felt hot. "He's really sick," she said, looking up at Nimmo. "He's burning up. He should be in the hospital. . . ."

"Hospital?" replied Nimmo. "We have no hospital down here. These are prisoners, Miss Valentine. Criminals. They don't require medical care."

"He'll be another case for K Division soon," observed the girl apprentice.

"Be quiet!" hissed Nimmo.

"What does she mean, K Division?" asked Katherine.

Nimmo wouldn't answer. Apprentice Pod was staring at her, and she thought she saw tears trickling down his face, although it might have been perspiration. She looked down at the convict, who seemed to have slid into a sort of half sleep. The metal decking looked terribly hard, and on a sudden impulse she pulled off her hat and folded it and slipped it under his head as a pillow. "He shouldn't be here!" she said angrily. "He's far too weak to work in your horrible tanks!"

"It's appalling," agreed Nimmo. "The sort of prisoners we are being sent these days are just too feeble. If the Guild of Merchants made more of an effort to solve the food shortage they might be a bit healthier, or if the Navigators pulled their fingers out and tracked down some decent prey for once. . . . But I think you have seen enough, Miss Valentine. Kindly ask Apprentice Pod whatever it is your father wishes to know, and I shall take you back to the elevators."

Katherine looked at Pod. He had pulled down his mask, and he was unexpectedly handsome, with big dark eyes and a small, perfect mouth. She stared at him for a moment, feeling stupid. Here he was, being brave, trying to help this poor man, and she was bothering him with something that suddenly seemed quite trivial.

"It's Miss Valentine, Miss, isn't it?" he said nervously as Dog pushed past him to sniff at the sick man's fingers.

Katherine nodded. "I saw you in the Gut that night when we ate Salthook," she said. "Down by the waste chutes. I think you saw the girl who tried to kill my father. Could you tell me everything you remember?"

The boy stared at her, fascinated by the long dark strands of hair that were falling down across her face now that her hat was off. Then his eyes flicked away to look at Nimmo. "I didn't see anything, Miss," he said. "I mean, I heard shouting and I ran to help, but with all the smoke and stuff . . . I didn't see anybody."

"Are you sure?" pleaded Katherine. "It could be terribly important."

Apprentice Pod shook his head, and wouldn't meet her eye. "I'm sorry. . . ."

The man on the deck suddenly stirred and gave a great sigh, and they all looked down at him. It took Katherine a moment to understand that he was dead.

"See?" said the girl apprentice smugly. "Told you he was for K Division."

Nimmo was prodding the body with the toe of his boot. "Take him away, Apprentice."

Katherine was shaking. She wanted to cry, but she couldn't. If only she could do something to help these poor people! "I'm going to tell my father all about this when he gets home," she promised. "And when he finds out what's going on in this dreadful place . . ." She wished she had never come here. Beside her she heard Pod say again, "Sorry, Miss Valentine," and wasn't sure if he was sorry because he couldn't help her or sorry for her because she had learned the truth of what life was like under London.

Nimmo was growing edgy. "Miss Valentine, I insist that you leave now. You shouldn't be here. Your father should have sent an official member of his Guild if he had business with this apprentice. What did he hope to learn from the boy, anyway?"

"I'm coming," said Katherine, and did the only thing she could for the dead convict: She reached out and gently shut his eyes.

"I'm sorry," whispered Apprentice Pod as they led her away.

17

THE PIRATE SUBURB

Late that night, and deep in the Rustwater Marshes, Tunbridge Wheels finally caught up with its prey. The exhausted townlet had blundered into a sinkhole and the suburb hit it side-on without bothering to slow its thunderous speed. The impact tore the townlet to pieces and splinters came raining down into the suburb's streets as it turned and sped back to swallow the wreckage. "Meals on wheels!" the pirates howled.

From their cage in the suburb's gut, Tom and Hester watched in horror as the dismantling-engines went to work, ripping the townlet into heaps of scrap without even bothering to let the survivors off. The few who did come stumbling out were grabbed by the waiting pirates. If they were young and fit they were dragged off to other tiny cages like the one in which Hester and Tom had been imprisoned. If not, they were killed, and their bodies were added to the rubbish heap at the edge of the Digestion Yard.

"Oh, great Quirke!" Tom whispered. "This is horrible! They're breaking every rule of Municipal Darwinism. . . ."

"It's a pirate suburb, Natsworthy," said Hester. "What did you expect? They strip their prey as quickly as they can and make the captives slaves in their engine rooms. They don't waste food and space on people who·are too weak to work. It's not really so different from what your precious London gets up to. At least this lot have the honesty to call themselves pirates."

The flash of a crimson robe out in the Digestion Yards caught Tom's eye. The mayor of the pirate suburb had come down to take a look at his latest catch, and he was strutting along the walkway outside the cells, surrounded by his bodyguards. He was a tiny little man, stooping and hunch-shouldered, a bald head and scrawny neck jutting from the cat-fur collar of his gown. He didn't look friendly. "He looks more like a moth-eaten vulture than a mayor!" whispered Tom, tugging at Hester's sleeve and pointing. "What do you think he'll do with us?"

She shrugged, glancing up at the approaching party. "We'll be slung into the engine rooms, I suppose. . . ." Then she stopped short, staring at the mayor as if he was the most amazing thing she had ever seen. Shouldering Tom aside, she thrust her face against the bars of the cage and started to shout. "Peavey!" she hollered, straining to make herself heard over the thunder of the gut. "Peavey! Over here!"

"Do you know him?" asked Tom, confused. "Is he a friend? Is he all right?"

"I don't have friends," snapped Hester, "and he's not all right; he's a ruthless, murdering animal and I've seen him kill people for just looking at him in a funny way. So let's hope the catch has put him in a good mood. Peavey! Over here! It's me! It's Hester Shaw!"

The ruthless, murdering animal turned toward their cage and scowled.

"His name's Chrysler Peavey," Hester explained hoarsely. "He stopped to trade in Strole a couple of times when I lived there with Shrike. He was mayor of another little scavenger town. The gods alone know how he got himself a flash suburb like this. . . . Now hush, and let me do the talking!"

Tom studied Chrysler Peavey as he came stalking over to peer at the captives, henchmen clustering behind. He wasn't much to look at. His lumpy scalp reflected the glare of furnaces and the sweat draining off it made pale stripes in the grime on his face. As if to make up for his bald head he had hair almost everywhere else: grubby white bristles pushing out of his chin, thick gray tufts sprouting from his ears and nostrils, and a pair of enormous, bushy, wriggling eyebrows. A tarnished chain of office hung around his neck, and on one shoulder perched a scrawny monkey.

"Who're they?" he said.

"Couple of hitchhikers, boss — I mean, Your Worship . . ." said one of his guards, a woman whose hair had been plaited and lacquered into two long, curving horns.

"Come aboard in the middle of the chase, Your Worship," added another, the man who had overseen the newcomers' capture. He showed Peavey the coat he was wearing: the fleece-lined aviator's coat he had taken from Tom. "I got this off one of 'em. . . ."

Peavey grunted. He seemed about to turn away, but Hester kept grinning her crooked grin at him and saying, "Peavey! It's me!" until she lit a spark of recognition in his greedy black eyes.

"Bloody Hull!" he growled. "It's the tin man's kid!"

"You're looking good, Peavey," said Hester, and Tom noticed that she didn't try to hide her face from the pirates, as if she knew that she mustn't let them see any sign of weakness.

"Blimey!" said Peavey, looking her up and down. "Blimey! It really is you! The Stalker's little helper, all growed up and uglier than ever! Where's old Shrikey then?"

"Dead," said Hester.

"Dead? What was it, metal fatigue?" He gave a great guffaw and the bodyguards all joined in obediently, until even the monkey on his shoulder started shrieking and rattling its chain. "Metal fatigue! Get it?"

"So how come you're running Tunbridge Wheels?" asked Hester, while he was still wiping the tears from his eyes and chuckling. "The last I heard of this place it was a respectable suburb. It used to hunt up north, on the edges of the ice."

Peavey chuckled, leaning against the bars. "Flashy, innit?" he said. "This place ate my old town a couple of years back. Come racing up one day and scoffed it straight down. They was soft, though: They hadn't reckoned with me and my boys. We busted out of the Gut and took over the whole place — set the mayor and the council to work stoking their own boilers, settled ourselves down in their comfy houses and their posh Town Hall. No more scavenging for me! I'm a proper mayor now. His Worship Chrysler Peavey at your service!"

Tom shuddered, imagining the dreadful things that must have happened here when Peavey's roughs took over — but Hester just nodded as if she was impressed. "Congratulations," she said. "It's a good town. Fast, I mean. Well built. You're taking a risk, though. If your prey hadn't stopped when it did, you'd've plunged straight into the heart of the Rustwater and sunk like a stone."

Peavey waved the warning away. "Not Tunbridge Wheels, sweethcart. This suburb's specialized. Mires and marshes don't bother us. There're fat towns hiding in these swamps, and fatter prey still where I'm planning to go next."

Hester nodded. "So how about letting us out then?" she asked casually. "With all this prey to catch you could probably use a couple of good tough helpers up top."

"Ha ha!" chortled Peavey. "Nice try, Hettie, but you're out of luck. Prey's been short these last couple of years. I need all the loot and grub I can find just to keep the lads happy, and they won't be happy if I start bringing new faces aboard. 'Specially not faces as 'orrible as yours." He bellowed with laughter again, looking around at his bodyguards to make sure they were joining in. The monkey ran up onto the top of his head and squatted there, chattering.

"But you need me, Peavey!" Hester told him, forgetting all about Tom in her desperation. "I'm not soft. I'm probably tougher than half of your best lads. I'll fight for a place up top, if that's what it takes. . . ."

"Oh, I can use you, all right," agreed Peavey. "But not up top. It's in the engine rooms where I need help. Sorry, Hettie!" He turned away, and beckoned to the woman with the horns. "Chain 'em up, Maggs, and take 'em to the slave-pits."

Hester slumped down on the floor of the cage, despairing. Tom touched her shoulder, but she shrugged him irritably away. He looked past her, at Peavey stalking away across his bloodstained

Yards and the pirates advancing on the cage with guns and manacles. To his surprise, he felt more angry than afraid. After all that they had been through, they were going to become slaves after all! It wasn't *fair*! Before he knew what he was doing he was on his feet and pounding at the greasy bars, and, in a strange, thin-sounding voice, he heard himself shouting, "NO!"

Peavey turned around. His eyebrows climbed his craggy forehead like mountaineering caterpillars.

"NO!" shouted Tom again. "You know her, and she asked you for help, and you ought to help her! You're just a coward, eating up little towns that can't escape, and murdering people, and sticking people in the slave-pit because you're too scared of your own men to help them!"

Maggs and the other guards all raised their guns and looked at Peavey expectantly, waiting for him to give the order to blow the impertinent prisoner to pieces. But he just stood and stared, and then came walking slowly back toward the cage.

"What did you say?" he asked.

Tom took a step backward. When he tried to speak again, no words came out.

"You're from London, ain't yer?" asked Peavey. "I'd recognize that accent anywhere! And you're not from the Nether Boroughs, neither. What Tier d'you come from?"

"T-two," stammered Tom.

"Tier Two?" Peavey looked around at his companions. "You 'ear that? That's almost High London, that is! This bloke's a High London gentleman. What did you want to go slinging a gentleman like this in the lockups for, Maggs?"

"But you said . . ." Maggs protested.

"Never mind what I SAID," screamed Peavey. "Get him OUT!"

The horned woman fumbled at the lock until the door slid open, and the other pirates grabbed Tom and dragged him out of the cage. Peavey pushed them aside and started dusting him down with a sort of rough gentleness, muttering, "That's no way to treat a gentleman! Spanner, give him back his coat!"

"What?" cried the pirate wearing Tom's coat. "No way!"

Peavey pulled out a gun and shot him dead. "I said, give the gentleman back his COAT!" he shouted at the startled-looking corpse, and the others hurried to pull the coat off and put it back on Tom. Peavey patted at the smoldering bullet hole on the breast. "Sorry about the blood," he said earnestly. "These blokes, they've got no manners. Please allow me to apologize most 'umbly for the misunderstanding, and welcome you aboard my 'umble town. It's an honor to 'ave a real gentleman aboard at last, sir. I do hope you'll join me for afternoon tea in the Town Hall. . . ."

Tom gaped at him. He had only just realized that he wasn't going to be killed. Afternoon tea was the last thing he was expecting. But as the pirate mayor started to lead him away he remembered Hester, still cowering in the cage. "I can't leave her down here!" he said.

"What, Hettie?" Peavey looked bewildered.

"We're traveling together," explained Tom. "She's my friend. . . ."

"There's plenty of other girls in Tunbridge Wheels," said Peavey. "Much better ones, with noses and everyfink. Why, my own lovely daughter would be very pleased to make your acquainternce. . . ."

"I can't leave Hester behind," said Tom, as firmly as he dared, and the mayor simply bowed and gestured to his men to open the cage again.

※

At first Tom thought that Peavey was interested in the same thing as Miss Fang — information about where London was headed, and what had brought it out into the central Hunting Ground. But although the pirate mayor was full of questions about Tom's life in the city, he didn't seem to have much interest in its movements; he was just pleased to have what he called "a High London gent" aboard his town.

He gave Tom and Hester a guided tour of the Town Hall, and introduced them to his "councillors," a rough-looking gang with names to match: Janny Maggs and Thick Mungo and Stadtsfesser Zeb, Pogo Nadgers and Zip Risky and the Traktiongrad Kid. Then it was time for afternoon tea in his private quarters, a room full of looted treasures high in the Town Hall where his rabble of whining, snot-nosed children kept getting under everybody's feet. His eldest daughter, Cortina, brought tea in delicate porcelain cups, and cucumber sandwiches on a blast-glass tray. She was a dim, terrified girl with watery blue eyes, and when her father saw that she hadn't cut the crusts off the sandwiches he knocked her backward over the pouffe. "Thomas 'ere is from LONDON!" he shouted, hurling the sandwiches at her. "He expects fings POSH! And you should 'ave done 'em in little TRIANGLES!

"What can you do?" he said plaintively, turning to Tom. "I've tried to brung her up lady-like, but she won't learn. She's a good girl, though. I look at her sometimes and almost wish I hadn't shot her mum. . . ." He sniffed and dabbed at his eyes with a huge skull-and-crossbones hanky, and Cortina came trembling back with fresh sandwiches.

"The fing is," Peavey explained, through a mouthful of bread and cucumber, "the fing is, Tom, I don't want to be a pirate all me life."

"Um, no?" said Tom.

"No," said Peavey. "You see, Tommy boy, I didn't have the advantages what you've got when I was a kid. I didn't get no education or nuffink, and I've always been ugly as sin. . . ."

"Oh, I wouldn't say that," Tom mumbled politely.

"I had to look out for meself, in the dust heaps and the ditches. But I always knew one day I'd make it big. I saw London once, see. From a distance, like. Off on its travels somewhere. I fought it was the most beautiful place I'd ever seen, all them tiers, and the white villas up top all shining in the sun. And then I 'eard about them rich people what live up there, and I decided that's how I want to live, all them posh outfits and garden parties and trips to the theatre and that. So I become a scavenger, and then I got a little town of me own, and now I got a bigger one. But what I really want . . ." (he leaned close to Tom) "what I really want is to be *respectable*."

"Yes, yes, of course," agreed Tom, glancing at Hester.

"You see, what I'm finking is this," Peavey went on. "If this hunting trip works out like I hope, Tunbridge Wheels is goin' ter be rich soon. Really rich. I love this suburb, Tom. I wanna see it grow. I wanna 'ave a proper upper level wiv parks and posh mansions and no oiks allowed, and elevators goin' up and down. I want Tunbridge Wheels to turn into a city, a proper big city wiv me as Lord Mayor, sumfink I can 'and down to me sprogs. And

137

you, Tommy, I want you to tell me how a city ought to be, and teach me manners. Ettyket, like. So I can hobnob wiv other Lord Mayors and not 'ave them laugh at me behind my back. And all my lads as well; they live like pigs at the moment. So what do you say? Will you turn us into gentlemen?"

Tom blinked at him, remembering the hard faces of Peavey's gang and wondering what they would do if he started telling them to open doors for one another and not to chew with their mouths open. He didn't know what to say, but in the end Hester said it for him.

"It was a lucky day for you when Tom came aboard," she told the mayor. "He's an expert on etiquette. He's the politest person I know. He'll tell you anything you want, Peavey."

"But . . ." said Tom, and winced as she kicked his ankle.

"Lovely-jubbley!" cackled Peavey, spraying them both with half-eaten sandwich. "You stick with old Chrysler, Tommy boy, and you won't go far wrong. As soon as we've scoffed our big catch you can start work. It's waiting for us on the far side of these marshes. We should reach it by the end of the week. . . ."

Tom sipped at his tea. In his mind's eye he saw again the great map of the Hunting Ground; the broad sweep of the Rustwater, and beyond it . . . "Beyond the marshes?" he said. "But beyond the marshes there's nothing but the Sea of Khazak!"

"Relax, Tommy boy!" chuckled Chrysler Peavey. "Didn't I tell you? Tunbridge Wheels is *specialized*! Just you wait and see. Wait and *sea*, get it? Wait and *sea*, ha ha ha ha!" And he slapped Tom on the back and swigged his tea, his little finger delicately raised.

18

BEVIS

A few days later London sighted prey again: a scattering of small Slavic-speaking tractionvilles that had been trying to hide among the crags of some old limestone hills. To and fro the city went, snapping them up, while half of London crowded onto the forward observation platforms to watch and cheer. The dismal plains of the western Hunting Ground were behind them now, and the discontent of yesterday was forgotten. Who cared if people were dying of heat stroke down in the Nether Boroughs? Good old London! Good old Crome! This was the best run of catches for years!

The city chased down and ate the faster towns and then turned back for the slower ones. It was nearly a week before the last of them was caught, a big, once proud place that was limping along with its tracks ripped off after an attack by predator suburbs. On the night it was finally eaten there were catch-parties in all the London parks, and the celebrations grew still more frantic when a cluster of lights was sighted far away to the north. A rumor started to circulate that the lights belonged to a huge but crippled city; that it was what Valentine had been sent to find, and radio signals from the 13th *Floor Elevator* would lead London north to its greatest meal ever. Fireworks banged and racketed until two in the morning, and Chudleigh Pomeroy, the acting Head Historian, reduced Herbert Melliphant to Apprentice Third Class after he let off a firecracker in the Museum's Main Hall.

But at dawn the happiness and the rumors died away. The lights in the north belonged to a huge city all right, but it was not crippled; it was heading south at top speed, and it had a hungry look. The Guild of Navigators soon identified it as Panzerstadt-Bayreuth, a conurbation formed by the coupling together of four huge *Traktionstadts*, but nobody else cared very much what it was called; they just wanted to get away from it.

London fired up its engines and raced on into the east until the conurbation sank below the horizon. But next morning, there it was again, upperworks glinting in the sunrise, even closer than before.

❁

Katherine Valentine had not joined in with the parties and the merrymaking, nor did she join in the panic that now gripped her city.

Since her return from the Deep Gut she had kept to her room, washing and washing herself to get rid of the awful slurry-pit stink of Section 60. She hardly ate anything, and she made the servants fling all the clothes she had been wearing that day into the recycling bins. She stopped going to school. How could she face her friends, with all their silly talk of clothes and boys, knowing what she knew? Outside, sunlight dappled the lawns and the flowers were blooming and the trees were all unfurling fresh green leaves, but how could she enjoy the beauty of High

London ever again? All she could think of were the thousands of Londoners who were toiling and dying in misery so that a few lucky, wealthy people like herself could live in comfort.

She wrote a letter to the Goggle-screen people about it, and another to the police, but she tore them both up. What was the point of sending them, when everyone knew that Magnus Crome controlled the police and the Goggle-screens? Even the High Priest of Clio had been appointed by Crome. She would have to wait for her father's return before anything could be done about the Deep Gut — providing that London hadn't gotten itself eaten by the time he came home.

As for her search for the truth about the scarred girl, it had ground to a halt. Apprentice Pod had known nothing — or pretended as much — and she could think of nowhere else to turn.

Then, at breakfast time on the third day of London's flight from Panzerstadt-Bayreuth, a letter came for her. She had no idea who would have written to her, and she turned the envelope over in her hands a couple of times, staring at the Tier Six postmark and feeling oddly afraid.

When she finally tore it open a sliver of paper dropped into her algae-flakes: ordinary London notepaper, recycled so many times that it was as soft and hairy as felt, with a watermark that said "Waste not — want not."

Dear Miss Vallentine,
    Please help me there is something I must tell you. I will be at Pete's Eats in Belsize Park, Tier Five today at 11 am.
    Signed yours truly,
    A Friend.

141

A few weeks earlier Katherine would have been excited, but she was in no mood for mysteries anymore. It was probably somebody's idea of a joke, she thought. She was in no mood for jokes, either. How could she be, with London fleeing for its life and the lower tiers full of suffering and misery? She flung the note into the recycling bin and pushed her breakfast away uneaten, then went off to wash again.

But she was curious, in spite of herself. When nine o'clock came she said, "I will not go."

At nine-thirty she told Dog, "It would be pointless; there won't be anybody there."

At ten she muttered, "Pete's Eats — what sort of name is that? They probably made it up."

Half an hour later she was waiting at the Central Shaft terminus for a down elevator.

She got off at Low Holborn and walked to the tier's edge through streets of shabby metal flats. She had put on her oldest clothes and walked fast with her head down and Dog close against her. She didn't feel proud anymore when people stared. She imagined them saying, *"That's Katherine Valentine, a stuck-up little miss from Tier One. They don't know they're born, those High Londoners."*

Belsize Park was almost deserted, the air thick with grainy smog from London's engines. The lawns and flower beds had all been given over to agriculture years and years before and the only people she could see were some laborers from Parks & Gardens who were moving along the rows of cabbages, spraying them with something to kill greenfly. Nearby stood a tattered conical building with a sign on its roof that read PETE'S EATS

142

and, in smaller letters underneath, "Café". There were metal tables under awnings on the pavement outside the door and more tables inside. People sat talking and smoking in the thin flicker of a half-power argon globe. A boy sitting alone at a table near the door stood up and waved. Dog wagged his tail. It took Katherine a moment to recognize Apprentice Pod.

"I'm Bevis," he said, smiling nervously as Katherine sat down opposite him. "Bevis Pod."

"I remember."

"I'm glad you came, Miss. I've been wanting to talk to you ever since you come down to Section 60, but I didn't want the Guild to know I'd been in touch with you. They don't like us talking to outsiders. But I've got the day off 'cos they're preparing for a big meeting, so I came up here. You don't see many Engineers eating in here."

"I'm not surprised," said Katherine to herself, looking at the menu. There was a big color picture of something called a "Happy Meal," a wedge of impossibly pink meat sandwiched between two rounds of algae-bread. She ordered mint tea. It came in a glastic tumbler and tasted of chemicals. "Are all Tier Five restaurants like this?"

"Oh no," said Bevis Pod. "This one's much nicer than the rest." He could not stop staring at her hair. He had spent his whole life in the Engineer warrens of the Gut and he had never seen anyone before with hair like hers, so long and shining and full of life. The Engineers said hair was unnecessary, a vestige of the ground-dwelling past, but when he saw Katherine's, it made him wonder. . . .

"You said you needed my help. . . ." Katherine prompted.

"Yes," said Bevis. He glanced over his shoulder as if to check that nobody was watching them. "It's about what you asked. I couldn't tell you down at the Turd Tanks. Not with Nimmo watching. I was in enough trouble already, for trying to help that poor man. . . ."

His dark eyes were full of tears again, and Katherine thought it strange that an Engineer could cry so easily. "Bevis, it's not your fault," she said. "Now what about the girl? Did you see her?"

Bevis nodded, thinking back to the night London ate Salthook. "I saw her run past, with that Apprentice Historian chasing after her. He shouted for help, so I ran after him. I saw the girl turn when she got to the waste chutes. There was something wrong with her face. . . ."

Katherine nodded. "Go on."

"I heard her shouting at him. I couldn't catch it all, over the engines and the noise of the Dismantling Yards. But she said something about your father, Miss. And then she pointed at herself and said, 'something something something Hester Shaw.' And then she jumped."

"And dragged poor Tom with her."

"No, Miss. He was left there, looking a bit stupid. Then the smoke came down and I couldn't see nothing, and next thing I knew there were policemen everywhere, so I made myself scarce. I wasn't supposed to leave my post, you see, so I couldn't tell anyone what I'd seen."

"But you're telling me," said Katherine.

"Yes, Miss." The apprentice blushed.

"Hester Shaw?" Katherine turned the name over in her mind, but it meant nothing to her. Nor did she understand his description of events, which didn't seem to tally with Father's. Bevis must have made a mistake, she decided.

He glanced around nervously again, then lowered his voice to a whisper. "Did you mean what you said, Miss, about your dad? Could he really do something to help the prisoners?"

"He will when I tell him what's happening," vowed Katherine. "I'm sure he doesn't know. But there's no need to call me Miss; I'm Katherine. Kate."

"Right," said Bevis solemnly. "Kate." He smiled again, but he still looked troubled. "I'm loyal to the Guild," he explained. "I never wanted to be anything but an Engineer. But I never expected to get assigned to the experimental prison. Keeping people in cages and making them work in the Gut, and wade about in those turd tanks — that's not Engineering. That's just wicked. I do what I can to help them, but I can't do much, and the supervisors just want to work them to death and then send them up to K Division in plastic bags, so even when they're dead they won't get no rest."

"What is this K Division?" asked Katherine, remembering how Nimmo had hushed the other apprentice when she mentioned it. "Is it part of the prison?"

"Oh, no. It's up top. In the Engineerium. It's some sort of experimental department, run by Dr. Twix."

"What does she use dead bodies for?" asked Katherine nervously, not at all sure that she wanted to know.

Bevis Pod went a little paler. "It's just a rumor, Miss, but some people in the Guild say she's building Stalkers. Resurrected Men."

"Great Clio!" Katherine thought of what she had been taught about the Stalkers. She knew that her father had dug up some rusty skeletons for the Engineers to study, but he had told her they were only interested in the electrical brains. Could they really be trying to make new ones?

"Why?" she asked. "I mean, they were soldiers, weren't they? Sort of human tanks, built for some old war . . ."

"Perfect workers, Miss," said Bevis, wide-eyed. "They don't need feeding or clothing or housing, and when there's no work to be done you can just switch 'em off and stack 'em in a warehouse, so they're much easier to store. The Guild says that in the future everybody who dies on the lower tiers will be resurrected, and we won't need living people at all, except as supervisors."

"But that's horrible!" protested Katherine. "London would be a city of the dead!"

Bevis Pod shrugged. "Down in the Deep Gut it feels like that already. I'm just telling you what I've heard. Crome wants Stalkers built, and that's what Dr. Twix does with the bodies from our section."

"I'm sure if people knew about this awful plan . . ." Katherine started to say. Then an idea occurred to her. "Does it have a code name? Do they call it MEDUSA?"

"Blimey! How do you know about MEDUSA?" Bevis's face had turned paler than ever. "Nobody's supposed to know about that!"

"Why?" asked Katherine. "What is it? If it's not to do with these new Stalkers . . ."

"It's a big Guild secret," whispered Bevis. "Apprentices aren't supposed to even know the name. But you hear the Supervisors talking about it. Whenever something goes wrong, or the city is in trouble, they talk about how everything will be all right once we awaken MEDUSA. Like this week, with this conurbation chasing us. Everybody's running around in a panic thinking it's the end of London, but the top Guildsmen just tell each other, 'MEDUSA will sort things out.' That's why they're having this big meeting at the Engineerium tonight. Magnus Crome is making an announcement about it."

Katherine shivered, thinking about the Engineerium and the mysterious things that went on behind its black windows. That was where she would find the clue to her father's troubles. MEDUSA. It all had something to do with MEDUSA.

She leaned closer to the boy and whispered, "Bevis, listen; are you going to this meeting? Can you tell me what Crome says?"

"Oh, no, Miss . . . I mean Kate. No! It's strictly Guildsmen only. No apprentices . . ."

"Couldn't you pose as a Guildsman or something?" Katherine urged him. "I have a feeling that there is something bad going on, and I think this MEDUSA thing is at the bottom of it."

"I'm sorry, Miss," said Bevis, shaking his head. "I wouldn't dare. I don't want to get killed and carted off to Top Tier and turned into a Stalker."

"Then help *me* go!" said Katherine eagerly. She reached across the table to take his hand, and he flinched at her touch and pulled back, staring at his fingers in amazement, as if it had never occurred to him that anybody would want to touch them. Katherine persisted, gently taking both his trembling hands in hers and looking deep into his eyes.

"I have to find out what Crome is really up to," she explained, "for Father's sake. Please, Bevis. I have to get inside the Engineerium!"

19

THE SEA OF KHAZAK

A few hours later, as the evening mists came curling from the Rustwater Marshes, Tunbridge Wheels rolled down to the edge of the sea. It paused there awhile, gazing out toward a cluster of islands that rose dark and rugged from the silver water. Birds were streaming in off the sea in long skeins and as the suburb cut its engines the beat of their wings came echoing over the mudflats. Small waves beat steadily against the shore and a wind from the east blew hissing through the thin, gray marram grass. There was no other sound, no other movement, no light or smoke trail of a wandering town anywhere on the marshes or the sea.

"Natswurvy!" shouted Chrysler Peavey, standing with a telescope to his eye at the window of his observation bridge, high in the Town Hall. "Where is the lad? Pass the word for Natswurvy!" When a couple of his pirates ushered Tom and Hester in he turned with a broad grin and held out the telescope, saying, "Take a look, Tommy boy! I told you I'd get you here, didn't I? I told you I'd get you through these marshes safe? Now, have a look at where we're going!"

Tom took the telescope and put it to his eye, blinking at the trembling, blurred circle of view until it came clear. There were dozens of little islands speckling the sea ahead, and a larger one that loomed in the east like the back of an enormous prehistoric monster breaking the water.

He lowered the telescope and shuddered. "But there's nothing there . . ." he said.

❋

It had taken more than a week for Tunbridge Wheels to pick its slow way through the quagmire, and although Chrysler Peavey had taken quite a shine to Tom he had still not explained what he hoped to find on the far side. His men had not been told, either, but they were happy enough snapping up the tiny townships that had taken shelter in the mazes of the Rustwater, semi-static places with moss-covered wheels and delicate, beautiful carvings on their wooden upperworks. They were so small that they were barely worth eating, but Tunbridge Wheels ate them anyway, and murdered or enslaved their people and fed the lovely carvings to its furnaces.

It was a horrible, confusing time for Tom. He had been brought up to believe that Municipal Darwinism was a noble, beautiful system, but he could see nothing noble or beautiful about Tunbridge Wheels.

He was still an honored guest in the Town Hall, and so was Hester, although Peavey clearly didn't understand his attachment to the scarred, sullen, silent girl. "Why don'cha ask my Cortina out?" he wheedled one night, sitting next to Tom in the old council chamber that was now his dining hall. "Or why not one of them girls we took off the last catch? Lovely lookers they was, an' not a word of Anglish, so they can't give you any lip. . . ."

"Hester isn't my girlfriend!" Tom started to say, but he didn't want to have to go out with the mayor's daughter and he knew Peavey would never understand the truth — that he was in love with the image of Katherine Valentine, whose face had hung in his mind like a lantern through all the miles of his adventures. So he said, "Hester and I have been through a lot together, Mr. Peavey. I promised I'd help her catch up with London."

"But that was before," the mayor reasoned. "You're a Tunbridge-Wheelsian now. You're going to stay here with me, like the son I never had, and I'm just thinking that maybe the lads would accept you a bit more easily if you had a better-looking girl; you know, more lady-like."

Tom looked across the clutter of tables and saw the other pirates glaring at him, fingering their knives. He knew that they would never accept him. They hated him for being a soft city dweller, and for being Peavey's favorite, and he couldn't really blame them.

Later, in the little room he shared with Hester, he said, "We have to get off this town. The pirates don't like us, and they're starting to get tired of Peavey going on at them about manners and stuff. I don't even like to think about what will happen to us if they mutiny."

"Let's wait and see," muttered the girl, curled up in a far corner. "Peavey's tough, and he'll be able to keep his lads in line as long as he finds them this big catch he's been promising. But Quirke alone knows what it is."

"We'll find out tomorrow," said Tom, drifting into an uneasy sleep. "This time tomorrow these horrible bogs will be behind us. . . ."

❋

This time tomorrow, and the horrible bogs *were* behind them. As Peavey's navigator spread out his maps in the observation bridge, a strange hissing sound echoed up the stairwells of the Town Hall. Tom glanced up at the faces of Peavey's henchmen as they clustered around the chart table, but apart from Hester no one seemed to have heard it. She looked nervously at him and shrugged.

The navigator was a thin, bespectacled man named Mr. Ames. He had been the suburb's schoolteacher until Peavey took over. Now he was settling happily into his new life as a pirate: It was a lot more fun, and the hours were better, and Peavey's ruffians were better behaved than most of his old pupils. Smoothing his maps with his long, thin hands he said, "It used to be the hunting ground for hundreds of little aquatic towns, but they all ate each other, and now Anti-Tractionist squatters have started coming down out of the mountains and setting up home on islands like this one. . . ."

Tom craned closer. The great inland Sea of Khazak was speckled with dozens of islands, but the one Ames was pointing to was the biggest, a tattered diamond shape some twenty miles long. He couldn't imagine what was so interesting about it, and most of the other pirates looked baffled, too, but Peavey was chuckling and rubbing his hands together in glee.

"The Black Island," he said. "Not much to look at, is it? But it's goin' ter make us rich, boys, rich. After tonight, ol' Tunbridge Wheels'll be able to set up as a proper city."

"How?" demanded Mungo, the pirate who trusted Chrysler Peavey least, and most resented Tom. "There's nothing there, Peavey. Just a few old trees and some worthless Mossies."

"What are 'Mossies'?" Tom whispered to Hester.

"He means people who live in static settlements," she hissed back. "You know, like in that old saying, 'A rolling town gathers no moss. . . .'"

"The fact is, ladies and gentlemen," announced Peavey, "that there is something on the Black Island. A few days ago — just before you come aboard, Tom — we shot down an airship that was footling about over the marshes. Its crew told me something very interesting before we killed 'em. It seems there's been a big battle up in Airhaven: fires, engine damage, gas spills, the whole place knocked about so bad they couldn't stay up in the sky but had to come down for repairs. And where d'you fink they've landed?"

"The Black Island?" suggested Tom, guessing as much from Peavey's greedy grin.

"That's my boy, Tommy! There's an air-caravanserai there, where sky-convoys refuel on their way up from the League's lands south of the mountains. That's where Airhaven's put down. They think they're safe, with sea all round them and their Mossie friends to help 'em. But they ain't safe from Tunbridge Wheels!"

A ripple of excitement ran through the assembled pirates. Tom turned to Hester, but she was staring out across the sea toward the distant island. Half of him was appalled by the thought that the lovely flying town was lying crippled there, waiting to be eaten — the other half was busy wondering how on earth Peavey planned to reach it.

152

"To yer stations, me hearties!" the pirate mayor yelled. "Fire up the engines! Prime the guns! By dawn tomorrow, we'll all be rich!"

The pirates scrambled to obey his orders, and Tom ran to the window. It was almost dark outside now, with a last ominous glow of sunset bruising the sky above the marshes. But the streets of Tunbridge Wheels were full of light, and all around the edge of the suburb huge orange shapes were unfolding, growing like fungus in a speeded-up film. Now the hissing from the lower deck made sense; while Peavey talked, his town had been busily pumping air into flotation chambers and these inflatable rubber skirts.

"Let's go swimmin'!" shouted the pirate mayor, sitting back in his swivel chair and signaling the engine rooms. The huge motors rumbled into life, a plume of exhaust gases drifted aft, and Tunbridge Wheels surged forward across the beach and into the sea.

❋

At first all went well; nothing stirred on the darkening waters as Tunbridge Wheels went chugging eastward, and up ahead the Black Island grew steadily larger. Tom opened a small side window on the bridge and stood there feeling the salt night air spill over him, feeling strangely excited. He could see pirates gathering in the old market square at the suburb's forward end, readying grappling hooks and boarding-ladders, because Airhaven would be far too large to fit into the Jaws — they would have to take it by force and tear it apart at their leisure. He didn't like the idea, especially when he remembered that his aviator friends might still be on Airhaven, but it was a town eat town world, after all — and there *was* something exciting about the cutthroat recklessness of Peavey's plan.

And then suddenly something fell out of the sky and exploded in the market square, and there was a black gash in the deck and the men he had been watching weren't there anymore. Others came running with buckets and fire extinguishers. "Airship! Airship! Airship!" someone was shouting, and then there were more rushing things and buildings were exploding all over the suburb, with people flung tumbling high up into the air like mad acrobats.

"For Sooty Pete's sake!" shouted Peavey, running to the shattered observation window and staring down into the smoke-filled streets. His monkey jumped up and down on his shoulders, jabbering. "These Mossies are better organized than we gave 'em credit for," he said. "Searchlights, quick!"

Two wavering fingers of light rose above the town, feeling their way across the smoke-dappled sky. Where they met, Tom saw a fat rising shape shine briefly red. The suburb's guns swung upward and fired a rippling broadside, and pulses of flame stalked the drifting clouds.

"Missed!" hissed Peavey, squinting through his telescope. "Curse it, I should have known Airhaven would send up spotter ships. And if I'm not mistaken it was that witch Fang's old rustbucket!"

"The *Jenny Haniver!*" gasped Tom.

"No need to sound so pleased about it," snarled Peavey. "She's a menace. Ain't you heard of the Wind-Flower?"

Tom hadn't told the pirate mayor of his adventures aboard

154

Airhaven. He tried to hide his happiness at the thought that Miss Fang was still alive and said, "I've *heard* of her. She's an air-trader. . . ."

"Oh, yeah?" Peavey spat on the deck. "You think a trader carries that sort of firepower? She's one of the Anti-Traction League's top agents. She'll stop at nothing to hurt us poor traction towns. It was her who planted the bomb that sank Marseilles, and her what strangled the poor Sultana of Palau Pinang. She's got the blood of a thousand murdered townsfolk on her hands! Still, we'll show her, won't we, Tommy boy? I'll have her guts for goulash! I'll hang her carcass out for the buzzards! Mungo! Pogo! Maggs! An extra cut of the spoils to whoever shoots down that red airship!"

No one did shoot down that red airship; it was long out of range, buzzing back toward the Black Island to warn Airhaven of the approaching danger. But Tom could not have been more filled with grief and anger if he had seen it falling in flames. So that was why Miss Fang had rescued him, and been so kind! All she had wanted was information for the League — and her friend Captain Khora had been in on it, spinning that tale about her just to win Tom's sympathy. Thank Quirke he had not been able to tell her anything!

Tunbridge Wheels was battered and burning, but the *Jenny Haniver*'s rockets had been too small to do any serious damage, and now that the element of surprise was lost Miss Fang did not risk another attack. The suburb chugged on into the east, pushing a thick bore of flame-lit water ahead of it. Tom could see lights on the Black Island now, lanterns flickering along the shore.

Closer, between the island and the suburb, shone another cluster of lights. "Boats!" shouted Mungo, peering through the sights of his gun.

Peavey went and stood at the window, robes flapping on the rising breeze. "Fishing fleet!" he grunted, sounding satisfied. "First meal of the night; we'll eat 'em up by way of an aperitif. That's 'starters' to you lot."

The fishing boats started scattering as Tunbridge Wheels bore down, running goose-winged for the shelter of the shore, but one, bigger and slower than the rest, sagged away to windward. "We'll have him," growled Peavey, and Maggs relayed his order into the intercom. The suburb changed course slightly, engines grumbling. The steep crags of the Black Island filled the sky ahead, blotting out the eastern stars. *What if there are guns on the heights?* thought Tom — but if there were any, they stayed silent. He could see the white wake of the boat ahead, and beyond it a faint pale line of breakers on the shore. . . .

And then there were other, closer breakers, dead ahead, and Hester was shouting, "Peavey! It's a trap!"

They all saw it then, but it was much too late. The fishing boat with its shallow keel ran clear through the reef, but the great lumbering bulk of Tunbridge Wheels struck at full speed and the sharp rocks clawed its belly open. The suburb lurched and settled, throwing Tom off his feet and rolling him hard against the legs of the chart table. The engines failed, and in the terrible silence that followed a Klaxon began lowing like a frightened bull.

Tom crawled back to the window. Down below he saw the streets going dark as a great rush of water came bursting through

156

the palisades. White geysers of foam sprayed up through gratings from the flooded underdeck, and mingled with the whiteness he saw black flecks of debris and tiny, struggling figures. The boat was far away, tacking to admire her handiwork. A hundred yards of sea separated the doomed suburb from the steep shores of the island.

A hand grabbed his shoulder, heaving him toward the exits. "You're coming wiv me, Tommy boy," snarled Chrysler Peavey, snatching a huge gun from a rack on the wall and swinging it onto his shoulder. "You, too, Amesy, Mungo, Maggs, you're wiv me. . . ."

They were with him, the pirates forming a tight protective knot around their mayor as he hurried Tom down the stairs. Hester came limping behind. There were screams below, and frightened faces staring up at them from a third-floor landing already knee-deep in water. "Abandon town!" hollered Peavey. "Women and mayors first!"

They crashed into his private quarters, where his daughter stood clutching her frightened sisters. Peavey ignored her and waded to a chest in the corner, scowling with concentration as he twirled the combination lock this way and that. The chest sprang open, he dragged out a little orange bundle, and then they were on the move again, out onto the balcony where the sea was already spilling through the railings. Tom turned back into the room, meaning to help Cortina and the children, but Peavey had forgotten all about them. He flung the bundle down into the waves and it unfolded with a complicated hiss, flowering into a small, circular life raft. "Get aboard," he snapped, taking hold of Tom and thrusting him toward it.

"But . . ."

"Get aboard!" A boot in the seat of his breeches sent him tumbling over the balcony rail and down onto the yielding rubber floor of the raft. Mungo was next, then the others piled in so fast that the raft wallowed deep and water spilled over the gunwales. "Oh! Oh! Oh!" wailed Cortina Peavey somewhere away to the left, but by the time Tom had scrambled out from under Mr. Ames the suburb was already far away, its stern submerged and its bows tilted high into the night sky. He looked for Hester and found her crouching beside him. Peavey's monkey jabbered with fear, bouncing up and down on his head. "Oh! Oh! Oh!" came the distant cries, and there were white splashes, dozens of splashes as people leaped from palisades and the useless tatters of the airbags. Hands clutched at the sides of the raft and Mungo and Peavey beat them away. Frantic figures came splashing through the swell toward them, and Janny Maggs stood up and fired her machine gun, churning up red water all around the raft. The suburb was tilting steeper, steeper; there was a rush of steam as the sea poured into its boilers and then with sudden, shocking speed it slid under. The water boiled and heaved. For a while there were screams, faint cries for help, a brief rattle of gunfire as a drifting fragment of debris changed hands, a longer one as a few lucky pirates battled their way onto a beach.

Then there was silence, and the raft turning slow circles as the current drew it in toward the shore.

THE BLACK ISLAND

At dawn Shrike comes to the edge of the sea. The tide is turning and the deep wheel-marks that lead down into the surf are already starting to blur. Eastward, smoke rises from settlements on the shores of the Black Island. The Stalker wrenches his dead face into a smile, feeling very pleased with Hester Shaw and the trail of destruction that she has left behind her.

The thought of Hester is all that dragged him through the marshes. On and on it has drawn him, through mud that sucked at his damaged leg and sloughs whose bitter waters sometimes closed over his head. But at least the tracks the suburb left were easy to follow. He follows them again now, stalking down the beach and into the waves like a swimmer bent on a morning dip. Saltwater slaps at the lenses of his eyes and seeps stinging through the gashes in his armor. The sounds of the gulls and the wind fade, replaced by the dim hiss of the underneath of the sea. Air or water, it makes no difference to the Resurrected Men. Fish goggle at him and dart away into forests of kelp. Crabs sidle out of his path, rearing up and waving their pincers at him, as if they are worshipping a crab-god, armored, invincible. He plows on, following the water-scent of oil and axle grease that will lead him to Tunbridge Wheels.

A few miles from the inlet where they had come ashore, Chrysler Peavey paused at the top of a steep rise and waited for the others to catch up. They came slowly, first Tom and Hester, then Ames with his map, finally Maggs and Mungo, bent under the weight of their guns. Looking back they could see the steep rocky flanks of the island falling to the sea and a cluster of boats gathered above the wreck of Tunbridge Wheels, where a raft with a crane on it had already been anchored. The islanders were wasting no time in looting the drowned suburb.

"Mossie scum," growled Peavey.

Tom had barely spoken to the mayor since they first came struggling ashore. Now he was surprised to see tears gleaming in the little man's eyes. He said, "I'm so sorry about your family, Mr. Peavey. I tried to reach them, but . . ."

"Little twerps!" snorted Peavey. "I wasn't sniffling over *them*. It's my lovely suburb! Look at it! Damn Mossies . . ."

Just then, from somewhere to the south, they heard the faint clatter of gunfire.

Peavey's face brightened. He turned to the others. "Hear that! Some of the lads must have got ashore! They'll be more'n a match for them Mossies! We'll link up with 'em! We'll capture Airhaven yet, keep a few of its people alive to repair it, kill the rest, and fly back to the mainland rich. Drop out of the sky on a few fat towns before word gets around that Airhaven's gone pirate! Catch ourselves a city, maybe!"

He set off again, hauling himself up from boulder to boulder with the monkey riding on his hunched shoulders. The others followed behind. Maggs and Mungo seemed dazed by the loss of

160

Tunbridge Wheels and not convinced by Peavey's latest plan. They kept exchanging glances and muttering together when their mayor was out of earshot — but they were in strange country, and Tom didn't think they had the nerve to move against Peavey, not yet. As for Mr. Ames, he had never set foot on the bare earth before. "It's horrible!" he grumbled. "So difficult to walk on . . . All this grass! There may be wild animals, or snakes. . . . I can quite see why our ancestors decided to stop living on the ground!"

Tom knew exactly how he felt. To north and south of them the steep side of the Black Island stretched away, and above them the slope climbed almost vertically to dark crags that moaned with ghostly voices as the wind blew around them. Some of the higher pinnacles of rock had been sculpted into such wild shapes that from the beach they had looked like fortresses, and Peavey had led his party on a long detour to avoid them before he realized they were only stones.

"It's lovely," sighed Hester, limping along at Tom's side. She was smiling to herself, which he had never seen her do, and whistling a little tune through her teeth.

"What are you so happy about?" he asked.

"We're going to Airhaven, aren't we?" she replied in a whisper. "It's laired up ahead somewhere, and Peavey's little gang will never take it, not with Mossies and the Airhaven people ranged against them. They'll be killed, and we'll find a ship to take us north to London. Anna Fang's there, remember. She might help us again."

"Oh, her!" said Tom angrily. "Didn't you hear what Peavey said? She's a League spy."

"I thought so," admitted Hester. "I mean, all those questions she kept asking us about London, and Valentine."

"You should have told me!" he protested. "I might have revealed an important secret!"

"Why would I care?" asked Hester. "And since when have Apprentice Historians known any important secrets? Anyway, I thought you realized she was a spy."

"She didn't look like one."

"Well, spies don't, generally. You can't expect them to wear a big sandwich board with SPY on it, or a special spying hat." She was in a strange, jokey mood, and Tom wondered if it was because these dismal steeps reminded her of her girlhood on that other island. Suddenly she touched his arm and said, "Poor Tom. You're learning what Valentine taught me all those years ago: You can't trust anybody."

"Huh," said Tom.

"Oh, I don't mean *you*," she added hurriedly. "I think I trust you, almost. And what you did for me back in Tunbridge Wheels — making Peavey let me out of the lockups like that . . . a lot of people wouldn't have bothered. Not for somebody like me."

Tom looked at her, and saw more clearly than ever before the kind, shy Hester peeping from behind the grim mask. He smiled at her with such warmth that she blushed (at least, her strange face turned red in patches and her scar went purple) and Peavey looked back at them and hollered, "Come on, you two lovebirds! Stop whispering sweet nothings and *march!*"

✾

Afternoon, the cloud clearing eastward and sunlight dazzling down through the wave-tops, flickering on the upperworks of Tunbridge Wheels. Shrike moves through the suburb's streets with his head swinging slowly from side to side. Bodies drift in the flooded rooms like cold tea bags left too long in the pot. Small fish dart in and out of a pirate's mouth. A girl's hair coils on the current. Dark keels of salvage boats move overhead. He waits hidden in the shadows while three naked boys come diving down, flying past him with urgent motions of their arms and legs and leaving trails of silver bubbles. They kick back to the surface carrying guns, bottles, a leather belt.

Hester is not here. Shrike turns away from the sunken suburb, following the shadows of drifting oil slicks over the silt. Wreckage is strewn along the sea floor, and floating bodies beckon him toward the roots of the Black Island.

It is evening by the time he walks out of the surf, trailing flags of sea-weed, water draining from inside his battered armor. He shakes his head to clear his vision and stares around him at a beach of black sand beneath dark cliffs. It takes him most of another hour to find the life raft, hidden in a tumble of house-size boulders. He unsheathes his metal claws and tears the bottom out of it, cutting off her escape. Hester is his again now. When she is dead he will carry her gently through the drowned sunlight and the forests of kelp, back through the marshes and the long leagues of the Hunting Ground to Crome. He will take her into London in his arms like a father carrying his sleeping child.

He drops on all fours in the sand and starts sniffing for her scent.

✸

Toward sundown, they finally reached the top of the slope, and found themselves looking down into the center of the Black Island.

Tom hadn't realized until now that it was an extinct volcano, but from here it was obvious; the steep, black crags ringed an almost circular bowl of land, green and patched with fields. Almost directly below the place where the pirates crouched, a small static settlement stood beside a blue lake. There were airship hangars and mooring masts beside the stone buildings, and on the flat ground behind them, dwarfing the whole place, Airhaven perched on a hundred skinny landing legs, looking as helpless as a grounded bird.

"The air-caravanserai!" chuckled Peavey. He pulled out his telescope and put it to his eye. "Look at 'em work! They're pumping their gasbags back up, desperate to get back into the sky. . . ." He swung the glass quickly across the surrounding hillsides. "No sign of any of our boys. Oh, if only we had a cannon left! But we'll manage, eh, lads? A bunch of airy-fairies is no match for us! Come on, let's get closer. . . ."

There was a strange edge to the mayor's voice. *He's frightened*, Tom realized. But *he can't admit it, in case Mungo and Maggs and Ames lose faith in him*. He had never thought he would feel sorry for the pirate mayor, but he did. Peavey had been kind to him, in his way, and it hurt to see him reduced to this, scrambling across the wet ground with his people muttering and cursing him behind his back.

They still followed him, though, down between the screes into the crater of the old fire-mountain. Once, they saw riders silhouetted on a distant crag; a patrol of islanders hunting for survivors from the sunken pirate town. Once, an airship flew low overhead, and Peavey hissed at everybody to lie flat and stay still, wrapping his monkey under his robes to muffle its shrill complaints. The airship circled, but by that time the sun had gone down, and the pilot did not see the figures who cowered in the twilight below him like mice hiding from an owl. He flew back down to land at the caravanserai as a fat moon heaved itself over the eastern crags.

Tom gave a sharp sob of relief and scrambled up. Around him the others were also starting to move, grunting, dislodging small stones that went clattering away down the hillside. He could see people hurrying about with lanterns and torches in the streets of the air-caravanserai, and lamp-lit windows that made him think how wonderful it would be to be warm and safe indoors. Airhaven was bright with electric lights, and the wind brought the distant sounds of shouted orders, music, cheering.

"For Pete's sake!" hissed Mungo. "We're too late! It's leaving!"

"Never," scoffed Peavey.

But they could all see that Airhaven's gasbags were almost full. A few minutes later the growl of its engines came rumbling up the slope, rising and falling as the wind gusted. The flying town was straining upward, its crablike legs folding back into place underneath it. "No!" shouted Peavey.

Then he was running downhill, scrambling and tumbling down clattering spills of scree toward the flat, boggy land in the crater floor, and as he ran they heard him screaming, "Come back! You're my *catch*! I sank my town for you!"

Mungo and Maggs and Ames set off after him, with Hester and Tom behind. At the foot of the slope the ground grew soft and squashy underfoot and pools of water reflected the moon and the lights of the rising town.

"Come back!" they could hear Peavey shouting, somewhere ahead of them. "Come back!" and then, "Ah! Oh! Help!"

165

They hurried toward the sound of his voice and the harsh screams of the monkey, and all came to a halt together at the edge of a deep patch of bog. Peavey was already up to his waist in it. The monkey perched on top of his head like a sailor on a foundering ship, grinning with fear. "Give me a hand, boys!" the mayor pleaded. "Help me! We can still get it! It's only testing its liftin' engines! It'll come down again!"

The pirates watched him silently. They knew they had no chance of taking the flying town, and that his shouts had probably warned the islanders of their presence.

"We've got to help him!" whispered Tom, starting forward, but Hester held him back.

"Too late," she said.

Peavey was sinking deeper, the weight of his chain of office pulling him down. He spluttered as the black mud swilled into his mouth. "Come on, lads! Maggs? Mungo? I'm your mayor! I done all this for you!" He searched for Tom with wild, terrified eyes. "Tell 'em, Tommy boy!" he whimpered. "Tell 'em I wanted to make Tunbridge Wheels great! I wanted to be respectable! Tell 'em —"

Mungo's first shot blew the monkey off the top of Peavey's head in a cloud of singed fur. The second and third went through his chest. He bowed his head, and the mud gulped him down with soft farting noises.

The pirates turned to look at Tom.

"We prob'ly wouldn't be 'ere if it weren't for you," muttered Mungo.

"If you hadn't of gone filling the Chief's head up with all them ideas about manners and cities and stuff," agreed Maggs.

"Different forks for every course, and no talking with your mouth full!" sneered Ames.

Tom started to back away. To his surprise, Hester stepped quickly between him and the pirates. "It's not Tom's fault!" she said.

"An' you're no use to us, neither," Mungo growled. "Neither of you is. We're pirates. We don't need no lessons in etiquette an' we don't need no lame scarface girl to hold us up." He raised his gun, and Maggs followed suit. Even Mr. Ames pulled out a little revolver.

And a voice out of the darkness said, "THEY'RE MINE."

21

IN THE ENGINEERIUM

London was climbing toward a high plateau where the town-torn earth was dusted with thin layers of snow. Far behind it — but not nearly far enough — rolled Panzerstadt-Bayreuth, not just a threatening blur on the horizon anymore but a huge dark mass of tracks and tiers, the gold filigree-work of its ornate top deck clearly visible above the smoke of factories and engines. Londoners crowded onto the aft observation platforms and watched in silence as the gap between the two cities slowly narrowed. That afternoon the Lord Mayor announced that there was no need for panic and that the Guild of Engineers would bring the city safely through this crisis — but there had already been riots and looting on the lower tiers, and squads of Beefeaters had been sent down to keep order in the Gut.

"Old Crome doesn't know what he's talking about," muttered one of the men on duty at the Quirke Circus Elevator Station that evening. "I never thought I'd hear myself say it, but he's a fool. Bringing poor old London way out east like this, day after day of traveling, week after week, just to get scoffed by some big old conurbation. I wish Valentine was here. He'd know what to do. . . ."

"Quiet, Bert," hissed his companion, "here comes some more of 'em."

Both men bowed politely as two Engineers strode up to the turnstiles, a young man and a girl, dressed identically in green glastic goggles and white rubber hoods and coats. The girl flashed a gold pass. When she and her companion had gone up into the waiting elevator Bert turned to his friend and whispered, "It must be important, this do at the Engineerium. They've been swarming up out of their nests in the Deep Gut like a load of old white maggots. Imagine having a Guild meeting at a time like this!"

✸

Inside the elevator Katherine sat down next to Bevis Pod, already feeling hot and self-conscious inside the coat that he had lent her. She glanced at him, and then checked her reflection in the window, making sure that the red wheels they had drawn so carefully on each other's foreheads had not gotten smudged. She thought they both looked ridiculous in these hoods and goggles, but Bevis had assured her that a lot of Engineers wore them these days, and the other occupant of the elevator, a fat Navigator, didn't so much as look at them while the car lurched toward Top Tier.

Katherine had spent the whole day restlessly waiting for Bevis to arrive with her disguise. To while away the time she had looked up the name HESTER SHAW in the indices of all her father's books, but couldn't find it. A *Complete Catalogue of the London Museum* contained one brief reference to a *Pandora* Shaw, but it just said she was an Out-Country scavenger who had supplied a few minor fossils and pieces of old-tech to the Historians' Guild, and gave the date of her death, seven years ago. After that she tried looking up MEDUSA, only to learn that it was some sort of monster in an old story. She didn't think Magnus Crome and his Engineers believed in monsters.

Nobody gave a second glance as she and Bevis strode across Top Tier toward the main entrance of the Engineerium. Scores of Engineers were already hurrying up the steps. Katherine joined them, clutching her gold pass and keeping close to the apprentice, terrified that she might lose him in this crowd of identical white coats. *This will never work!* she kept thinking, but the Guildsman on duty at the door wasn't bothering to look at passes. She took a last look at the fading sunset behind the dome of St. Paul's, then stepped inside.

It was bigger than she expected, and brighter, lit by hundreds of argon globes that hung in the great open shaft at the center of the building like planets hanging in space. She looked around for the staircase, but Bevis tugged at her arm and said, "We go up by monorail. Look. . . ."

The Engineers were clambering into little monorail cars. Katherine and Bevis joined the line, listening to their muttered conversations and the squeaky rustle of their coats rubbing together. Bevis's eyes were wide and frightened behind his goggles. Katherine had hoped that they would be able to get a monorail car to themselves so that they could talk, but more Engineers were arriving all the time and she ended up sitting on the far side of a packed car from him, wedged tightly in with a group from the Mag-Lev Research Division.

"Where are you from, Guildsperson?" asked the man sitting beside her.

"Um . . ." Katherine looked frantically at Bevis, but he was too far away to whisper an answer. She blurted out the first thing that came to mind. "K Division."

"Old Twixie, eh?" said the man. "I hear she's having amazing results with her new models!"

"Oh, yes, very," she replied. Then the car moved off with a lurch and her neighbor turned to the window, fascinated by the passing view.

Katherine had expected the monorail to feel like an elevator, but the speed and the spiraling movement made it quite different and for a moment she had to concentrate hard on not being sick. The other Engineers seemed not to notice. "What do you think the Lord Mayor's speech will be about?" one of them asked.

"It must be MEDUSA," said another. "I heard they are preparing for a test."

"Let's hope it works," said a woman sitting just in front of Katherine. "It was Valentine who found the machine, after all, and he's only a Historian, you know. You can't trust them."

"Oh, Valentine is the Lord Mayor's man," said another. "Don't let that Historians' Guild-mark fool you. He's as loyal as a dog, so long as we give him plenty of money and he gets to pretend that foreign daughter of his is a High London lady."

Around and around they went, and up past offices and workshops full of busy Engineers, like an enormous hive of insects. The car stopped on level five and Katherine climbed out, still flushed with anger at what the others had said. She linked up with Bevis again and they all trotted together along chilly, white corridors and through hanging curtains of transparent plastic. She could hear the babble of voices ahead, and after a few twists and turns they emerged into an immense auditorium. Bevis led the way to a seat near one of the exits. She looked around to see if she could spot Supervisor Nimmo, but it was impossible to make him out. The auditorium was a sea of white coats and bald or hooded heads, and more were pouring through the entrances all the time.

"Look!" hissed Bevis, nudging her. "That's Dr. Twix, the one I told you about!" He pointed to a squat little barrel-shaped woman who was taking a seat in the front row, chattering animatedly with her neighbors. "All the top Guildspersons are here! Twix, Chubb, Garstang . . . and there's Dr. Vambrace, the head of security!"

Katherine began to feel frightened. If she had been unmasked at the door she might have been able to pass it off as a silly prank, but now she was deep in the Engineers' inner sanctum, and she could tell that something important was about to happen. She reminded herself that even if they discovered her, the Engineers would never dare harm Thaddeus Valentine's daughter. She tried not to think about what they might do to Bevis.

At last the doors were closed and the lights dimmed. An expectant hush filled the auditorium, broken only by the slithery whisper of five hundred Engineers rising to their feet.

Katherine and Bevis jumped up with them, peering at the stage over the shoulders of the people in front. Magnus Crome was standing at a metal lectern, his cold eyes sweeping the audience. For a moment he seemed to stare straight at Katherine, and she had to remind herself that he couldn't possibly recognize her, not with her hood and her goggles and the tall collar of her coat turned up.

"You may be seated," said Crome, and waited until they had settled themselves before going on. "This is a glorious day for our Guild, my friends."

A ripple of excitement ran through the auditorium, and through Katherine, too. Crome motioned for quiet.

Up in the ceiling of the auditorium a slide projector whirred into life, and a picture appeared on a screen behind his head. It was a diagram of an enormous, complicated machine.

"MEDUSA," announced Crome, and there was a sort of echo as all the Engineers sighed, "MEDUSA!"

"As some of you already know," he went on, "MEDUSA is an experimental energy weapon from the Sixty Minute War. We have known about it for some time — in fact, ever since Valentine found these documents on his trip to America, twenty years ago."

The projector screen was flickering with faded diagrams and spidery writing. *Father never told me that!* Katherine thought.

"Of course, these fragmentary plans were not enough to let us reconstruct MEDUSA," Crome was saying. "But seven years ago, thanks again to Valentine, we acquired a remarkable piece of old-tech, taken from a long-lost military site in the American desert. It is perhaps the best-preserved Ancient computer-core ever discovered, and it is more than that; it is the brain of MEDUSA, the artificial intelligence that once powered this remarkable machine. Thanks to the hard work of Dr. Splay and his comrades in B Division, we have at last been able to restore it to working order. Guildspersons, the days when London had to run and hide from other hungry cities are at an end! With MEDUSA at our command we will be able to reduce any one of them to ashes in the blink of an eye!"

The Engineers applauded wildly, and Bevis Pod nudged at Katherine to join in, but her hands seemed to have become frozen to the metal armrests of her seat. She felt giddy with shock. She remembered everything she had heard about the Sixty Minute War and how the Ancients' terrible thunder-weapons had blasted their static cities and poisoned the earth and sky. Father would never have helped the Engineers to re-create such a terrible thing!

"Nor will we have to go chasing after scraps like Salthook," Crome continued. "In another week London will be within range of Batmunkh Gompa, the Shield-Wall. For a thousand years the Anti-Traction League has cowered behind it, holding out against the tide of history. MEDUSA will destroy it at a single stroke. The lands beyond it, with all their huge static cities, their crops and forests, their untapped mineral wealth, will become London's new hunting ground!"

You could hardly hear him now; the cheers of the Engineers rolled like breakers against the wall behind him, and it slid slowly open, revealing a long window that looked out toward St. Paul's Cathedral and the turrets of the Guildhall.

"But first," he shouted, "we have more pressing business to attend to. Although I had hoped we might keep MEDUSA hidden until we reached the Shield-Wall, it has become necessary to give a demonstration of its power. Even as I speak, Dr. Splay's team is preparing a test firing of the new weapon."

Even if Katherine had wanted to hear more it would soon have become impossible, for Crome's audience were all talking excitedly among themselves. A few Engineers, presumably those connected with the MEDUSA project, were hurrying to the exits. Standing up, Katherine started pushing her way to the door. A moment later she was out in the antiseptic corridor, wondering what to do next.

"Kate?" Bevis Pod appeared behind her. "Where are you going? People noticed you leave! I saw some Guild security people watching us!"

"We've got to get out of here," whispered Katherine. "Where's the way out?"

"I don't know," admitted the boy. "I've never been to this level before. I suppose we'll have to find our way back to the monorail. . . ." He shook Katherine away as she tried to take his hand. "No! Somebody will see. Engineers aren't supposed to touch each other."

They hurried along the tubular corridors, and Katherine said, "Crome was lying! My father didn't go to America seven years ago. He just went on a little trip to the islands of the Western Ocean. And he never told me he'd found anything important. He'd have told me, if he'd really found MEDUSA. He wouldn't want anything to do with old-world weapons, anyway."

"But why would the Lord Mayor lie?" asked Bevis, who was secretly rather pleased that his Guild had stumbled upon the keys to yet another Ancient secret. "Anyway, he didn't say your dad went to America for this thing, he just said he acquired it. Maybe he bought it from a scavenger or something. I wonder what Crome meant about a demonstration. . . ."

He stopped. They had come to the end of the corridor, and there were no monorails in sight. Three doorways faced them.

Two were locked; the third led only onto a narrow balcony that jutted out from the Engineerium's flank, high above Paternoster Square.

"What now?" asked Katherine, hearing her own voice high and thin with fright, and Bevis, just as nervously, replied, "I don't know."

She stepped out onto the balcony to catch her breath. The moon was up, but veiled by thin clouds, and a cool drizzle was falling. She pulled off her goggles and let the rain spill down her face, glad to be free of the heat and the chemical stench. She thought about Father. Had he really found MEDUSA? Bevis was right; Crome had no reason to lie. Poor Father! He would be in the air now, somewhere above the snow-peaks of Shan Guo. If only she had some way to warn him what they were planning to do with his discovery!

A low, mechanical rumble came drifting across the moonlit square. She looked down at the wet deckplates, but could not see what was making the noise. Then something made her glance up at St. Paul's. She gasped. "Bevis! Look!"

Slowly, like a huge bud blooming, the dome of the Ancient cathedral was splitting open.

22

SHRIKE

Had the Stalker only just arrived, or had he been standing watching them squabble, dark and still on the stone-strewn hillside like a stone himself? He took a step forward, and the damp grass smoldered where he set his foot. "THEY ARE MINE."

The pirates swung around, Maggs's machine gun spraying streams of tracer at the iron man while Mungo's hand-cannon punched black holes in his armor and Ames blazed away with his revolver. Caught in the web of gunfire, Shrike stood swaying for a moment. Then, slowly, like a man walking into a strong wind, he started forward. Bullets sparked off his armor and his coat tore away in rags and tatters. The holes the cannon made spewed something that might have been blood, might have been oil. He stretched out his arms, and an iron claw was ripped away, and another. Then he reached Maggs and she made a choking sound and went backward into the bracken and down. Ames flung down his gun and turned to run, but Shrike was suddenly behind him and he stopped short, gawping at a handful of red spikes that sprouted from his chest.

Mungo's gun was empty. He threw it aside and pulled his sword out, but before he could swing it Shrike had grabbed him by the hair and wrenched his head back and severed his neck with one scything blow.

"Tom," said Hester. "Run!"

Shrike flung the head aside and stalked forward, and Tom ran. He didn't want to; he knew there was no point, and he knew he should stand by Hester, but his legs had other ideas; his whole body wanted only to be away from the terrible, dead thing that was coming toward him down the hill. Then the ground gave way under him; he plunged into cold mud and fell, rolled over, and came to a rest against an outcrop of stone on the edge of the same mire that had swallowed Chrysler Peavey.

He looked back. The Stalker stood among the sprawling bodies. Airhaven was overhead, testing its engines one by one, and its lights kindled cold reflections on his moon-silvered skull.

Hester stood facing him, bravely holding her ground. Tom thought, *She's trying to save me! She's buying time so that I can get away! But I can't just let him kill her, I can't!*

Ignoring the countless voices of his body that were still screaming at him to run, he started to crawl back up the hill.

"HESTER SHAW," he heard Shrike say, and the voice slurred and caught like a faulty recording. Steam hissed from holes in the Stalker's chest and black ichor dripped from him and bubbled at the corners of his mouth.

"Are you going to kill me?" the girl asked.

Shrike nodded his great head, just once. "FOR A LITTLE WHILE."

"What do you mean?"

The long mouth dragged sideways, smiling. "WE ARE TWO OF A

178

KIND, YOU AND I. I KNEW IT AS SOON AS I FOUND YOU THAT DAY ON THE SHORE. AFTER YOU LEFT ME, THE LONELINESS . . ."

"I had to go, Shrike," she whispered. "I wasn't part of your collection."

"YOU WERE VERY DEAR TO ME."

Something's wrong with him, thought Tom, inching up the hill. Stalkers weren't meant to have *feelings.* He remembered what he had been taught about the Resurrected Men all going mad. Was that seaweed hanging from the ducts on Shrike's head? Had his brains gone rusty? Sparks were flickering inside his chest, behind the bullet holes. . . .

"HESTER," Shrike grated, falling heavily to his knees so that his face was at the same level as hers. "CROME HAS MADE ME A PROMISE. HIS SERVANTS HAVE LEARNED THE SECRET OF MY CONSTRUCTION."

Fear prickled the back of Tom's neck.

"I WILL TAKE YOUR BODY TO LONDON," Shrike told the girl. "CROME WILL RESURRECT YOU AS AN IRON WOMAN. YOUR FLESH WILL BE REPLACED WITH STEEL, YOUR NERVES WITH WIRE, YOUR THOUGHTS WITH ELECTRICITY. YOU WILL BE BEAUTIFUL! YOU WILL BE MY COMPANION, FOR ALL TIME."

"Shrike," Hester snorted. "Crome won't want *me* Resurrected. . . ."

"WHY NOT? NO ONE WILL RECOGNIZE YOU IN YOUR NEW BODY; YOU WILL HAVE NO MEMORIES, NO FEELINGS, YOU WILL BE NO THREAT TO HIM. BUT I WILL REMEMBER FOR YOU, MY DAUGHTER. WE WILL HUNT DOWN VALENTINE TOGETHER."

Hester laughed, a strange, mad, terrible sound that set Tom's teeth on edge as he reached the place where Mungo's body lay. The heavy sword was still clamped in the pirate's fist, and Tom reached out and started prying it free. Glancing up, he saw that

Hester had taken a step closer to the Stalker. She tilted her head back, baring her throat, readying herself for his claws. "All right," she said. "But let Tom go."

"HE MUST DIE," insisted Shrike. "IT IS PART OF MY BARGAIN WITH CROME. YOU WILL NOT REMEMBER HIM WHEN YOU WAKE IN YOUR NEW BODY."

"Oh please, Shrike, no," begged Hester. "Tell Crome he escaped or drowned or something, died somewhere in the Out-Country and you couldn't bring him back. Please."

Tom clung to the sword, its hilt still clammy with Mungo's sweat. Now that the moment had come he was so scared that he could barely breathe, let alone stand up and confront the Stalker. *I can't do this!* he thought. *I'm a Historian, not a warrior!* But he couldn't desert Hester, not while she was bargaining away her life for his. He was close enough to see the fear in her eye, and the sharp glitter of Shrike's claws as he reached for her.

"VERY WELL," the Stalker said. Gently, he stroked Hester's face with the tips of the blades. "THE BOY CAN LIVE." The hand drew back to strike. Hester shut her eye.

"Shrike!" howled Tom, hurling himself up and forward with the sword held out stiffly in front of him, feeling the green light spill across his face as Shrike spun hissing to meet him. An iron arm lashed out, hurling him backward. He felt a searing pain in his chest and for a moment he was sure that he had been torn in two, but it was the Stalker's forearm that struck him, not the bladed hand, and he landed in one piece and rolled over, gasping at the pain, expecting to see Shrike lunge at him and then nothing, ever again.

But Shrike was on the ground, and Hester was bending over

him, and as Tom watched the Stalker's eye flickered and some-thing exploded inside him with a flash and a crack and a coil of smoke leaking upward. The hilt of the sword jutted from one of the gashes in his chest, crackling with blue sparks.

"Oh, Shrike!" whispered Hester.

Shrike carefully sheathed his claws so that she could take his hand. Unexpected memories fluttered through his disinte-grating mind, and he suddenly knew who he had been before they dragged him onto the Resurrection Slab to make a Stalker of him. He wanted to tell Hester, and he lifted his great iron head toward her, but before he could force the words out his death was upon him, and it was no easier this time than the last.

The great iron carcass settled into stillness, and smoke blew away on the wind. Down in the valley, horns were blowing, and Tom could see a party of riders starting up the hill from the cara-vanserai, alerted by the sound of gunfire. They carried spears and flaming torches, and he didn't think they would be friendly. He tried to push himself upright, but the pain in his chest almost made him faint.

Hester heard him groan and swung toward him. "What did you do that for?" she shouted.

Tom could not have been more surprised if she had slapped him. "He was going to kill you!" he protested.

"He was going to make me like *him!*" screamed Hester, hug-ging Shrike. "Didn't you hear what he said? He was going to make me everything I ever wanted: no memories, no feelings. Imagine Valentine's face when I came for him! Oh, *why* do you keep *interfering?*"

"He would have turned you into a monster!" Tom heard his own voice rising to a shout as all his pain and fear flared into anger.

"I'm already a monster!" she shrieked.

"No, you're not!" Tom managed to heave himself to his knees. "You're my friend!" he shouted.

"I hate you! I hate you!" Hester was yelling.

"Well, I care about you, whether you like it or not!" Tom screamed. "Do you think you're the only person who's lost their mum and dad? I feel just as angry and lonely as you, but you don't see me going around wanting to kill people and trying to get myself turned into a Stalker! You're just a rude, self-pitying —"

But the rest of what he had been planning to tell her died away in an astonished sob, because suddenly he could see the town below him and Airhaven and the approaching riders as clearly as if it were the middle of the day. He saw the stars fade; he saw Hester's face freeze in mid-shout with spittle trailing from the corners of her mouth; he saw his own wavering shadow dancing on the blood-soaked grass.

Above the crags, the night sky was filling with an unearthly light, as if a new sun had risen from the Out-Country, somewhere far away toward the north.

23

MEDUSA

Katherine watched, transfixed, as the dome of St. Paul's split along black seams and the sections folded outward like petals. Inside, something was rising slowly up a central tower and opening as it rose, an orchid of cold, white metal. The grumble of vast hydraulics echoed across the square and shivered through the fabric of the Engineerium.

"MEDUSA!" whispered Bevis Pod, standing behind her in the open doorway. "They haven't really been repairing the cathedral at all! They've built MEDUSA inside St. Paul's!"

"Guildspersons?"

They turned. An Engineer was standing behind them. "What are you doing?" he snapped. "This gantry is off-limits to everyone but L Division —"

He stopped, staring at Katherine, and she saw that Bevis was staring, too, his dark eyes wide and horrified. For a moment she couldn't imagine what was wrong with him. Then she understood. The rain! She had forgotten about the Guild-mark he had painted so carefully between her eyebrows, and now it was trickling down her face in thin red rills.

"What in Quirke's name?" the Engineer gasped.

"Kate, run!" shouted Bevis, pushing the Engineer aside, and Katherine ran, and heard the man's angry shout behind her as he fell. Then Bevis was with her, grabbing her by the hand, darting left and right down empty corridors until a stairway opened ahead. Down one flight and then another, and behind them they heard more shouts and the sudden jarring peal of an alarm bell. Then they were at the bottom, in a small lobby, somewhere at the rear of the Engineerium. There were big glass doors opening onto Top Tier, and two Guildsmen standing guard.

"There's an intruder!" panted Bevis, pointing back the way they had come. "On the third floor! I think he's armed!"

The Guildsmen were already startled by the sudden ringing of the alarm bell. They exchanged shocked glances, then one started up the stairs, dragging a gas-pistol from his belt.

Bevis and Katherine seized their chance and hurried on. "My colleague's been hurt," explained Bevis, pointing at Katherine's red-streaked face. "I'm taking her around to the infirmary!" The door swung open and spilled them out into the welcome dark.

They ran as fast as they could into the shadow of St. Paul's, then stopped and listened. Katherine could hear the heavy throbbing of machinery, and a closer, louder throb that was the beat of her own heart. A man's voice was shouting orders somewhere, and there was a crash of armored feet, coming closer. "Beefeaters!" she whimpered. "They'll want to see our papers! They'll take off my hood! Oh, Bevis, I should never have asked you to get me in there! Run! Leave me!"

Bevis looked at her and shook his head. He had defied his

Guild and risked everything to help her, and he wasn't about to abandon her now.

"Oh, Clio *help us!*" breathed Katherine, and something made her glance toward Paternoster Square. There was old Chudleigh Pomeroy standing on the Guildhall steps with his arms full of envelopes and folders, staring upward. She had never been so happy to see anyone in her whole life, and she ran to him, dragging Bevis Pod along with her and calling softly, "Mr. Pomeroy!"

He looked blankly at them, then gasped in surprise as Katherine pulled the stupid hood off and he saw her face and her sweat-draggled hair. "Miss Valentine! What in Quirke's name is happening? Look what those damned interfering Engineers have done to St. Paul's!"

She looked up. The metal orchid was open to its full extent now, casting a deep shadow on the square below. Only it was not an orchid. It was a cowled, flaring thing like the hood of some enormous cobra, and it was swinging around to point at Panzerstadt-Bayreuth.

"MEDUSA!" she said.

"Who?" asked Chudleigh Pomeroy.

A bug siren wailed. "Oh, please!" she cried, turning to the plump Historian. "They're after us! If they catch Bevis, I don't know what will happen to him. . . ."

Bless him — he did not say "Why?" or "What have you done wrong?" Just took Katherine by one arm and Bevis Pod by the other and hurried them toward the Guildhall garage where his bug was waiting. As the chauffeur helped them into it a squad of

185

Beefeaters came clattering past, but they paid no attention to Pomeroy and his companions. He hid Katherine's coat and hood behind his seat, and made Bevis Pod crouch down on the floor of the bug. Then he squeezed himself in beside Katherine on the backseat and said, "Let me do the talking," as the bug went purring out into Paternoster Square.

There was a throng of people outside the elevator station, gazing up in amazement at the thing that had sprouted from St. Paul's. Beefeaters stopped the bug while a young Engineer peered in. Pomeroy opened a vent in the glastic lid and asked, "Is there a problem, Guildsman?"

"A break-in at the Engineerium. Anti-Tractionist terrorists . . ."

"Well, don't look at us," laughed Pomeroy. "I've been working in my office at the Guildhall all evening, and Miss Valentine has been kindly helping me to sort out some papers."

"All the same, sir, I'll have to search your bug."

"Oh, really!" cried Pomeroy. "Do we look like terrorists? Haven't you got better things to do, on the last night of London, with a dirty great conurbation bearing down on us? I shall complain to the Council in the strongest possible terms! It's outrageous!"

The man looked uncertain, then nodded and stepped aside to let Pomeroy's chauffeur steer the bug into a waiting freight elevator. As the doors closed behind it Pomeroy let out a sigh of relief. "Those damned Engineers. No offense, Apprentice Pod."

"None taken," said Bevis's muffled voice from somewhere below.

"Thank you!" whispered Katherine. "Oh, thank you for helping us!"

"Don't mention it," chuckled Pomeroy. "I'm always happy to do anything that upsets Crome and his lackeys. Thousands of years old, that cathedral, and they go and turn it into a . . . into whatever they've turned it into, without so much as a by-your-leave. . . ." He looked nervously at Katherine and saw that she wasn't really listening. Gently he asked, "But whatever have you done to stir them up, Miss Valentine? You don't have to tell me if you don't want to, but if you and your friend are in trouble, and if there's anything an old coot like me can do . . ."

Katherine felt helpless tears prickling her eyes. "Please," she whispered, "could you just take us home?"

"Of course."

They sat in awkward silence as the bug drove through the streets of Tier One into the park. The darkness was full of people running and shouting, pointing up toward the cathedral. But there were other runners, too: Engineer security men leading squads of Beefeaters. When the bug stopped outside Clio House, Pomeroy climbed out to walk Katherine to the door. She whispered a heartfelt good-bye to Bevis and followed him. "Could you take Apprentice Pod to an elevator station?" she asked. "He needs to get back to the Gut."

Pomeroy looked worried. "I don't know, Miss Valentine," he sighed. "You've seen how het up the Engineers are. If I know them they'll have all their factories and dormitory blocks locked down tight by now, and security checks in progress. They may already have worked out that he's missing, along with two coats and hoods. . . ."

"You mean, he can't go back?" Katherine felt dizzy at the thought of what she had done to poor Pod. "Not ever?"

Pomeroy nodded.

"Then I'll keep him with me at Clio House!" Katherine decided.

"He's not a stray cat, my dear."

"But when Father gets home he'll be able to sort everything out, won't he? Explain to the Lord Mayor that it was nothing to do with Bevis. . . ."

"It's possible," agreed Pomeroy. "Your father is very close to the Guild of Engineers. A damned sight too close, some people say. But I don't think Clio House is the place to keep your friend. I'll take him down to the Museum. There's plenty of room for him there, and the Engineers won't be able to search for him without giving us warning first."

"Would you really do that?" asked Katherine, afraid that she was dragging yet another innocent person into the trouble she had created. But after all, it would only be for a few days, until Father came home. Then everything would be all right. "Oh, thank you!" she said happily, standing on tiptoe to kiss Pomeroy's cheek. "Thank you!"

Pomeroy blushed and beamed at her, and started to say something else — but although his mouth moved she could not hear the words. Her head was filled with a strange sound, a whining roar that grew louder and louder until she realized that it wasn't inside her at all, but pounding down from somewhere overhead.

"Look!" shouted the Historian, pointing upward.

Her fear had made her forget St. Paul's. Now, looking up at Top Tier, she saw the cobra-hood of MEDUSA start to crackle with violet lightning. The hair on her arms and the back of her neck prickled, and when she reached for Pomeroy's hand pale sparks jumped between the tips of her fingers and his robes. "Mr. Pomeroy!" she shouted. "What's happening?"

"Great Quirke!" the Historian cried. "What have those fools awoken now?"

Ghostly spheres of light detatched themselves from the glowing machine and drifted down over Circle Park like fire-balloons. Lightning danced around the spires of the Guildhall. The rushing, whining roar grew louder and louder, higher and higher, until even with her hands clapped over her ears Katherine felt she could not bear a moment more of it. Then, quite suddenly, a stream of incandescent energy burst from the cobra's hood and stretched northward, a snarling, spitting cat-o'-nine-tails lashing out to lick at the upperworks of Panzerstadt-Bayreuth. The night split apart and went rushing away to hide in the corners of the sky. For a second Katherine saw the tiers of the distant conurbation limned in fire, and then it was gone. A pulse of brightness lifted from the earth, blinding white, then red, a pillar of fire rushing up in silence into the sky, and across the flame-lit snow the sound wave came rolling, a low, long-drawn-out boom as if a great door had slammed shut somewhere in the depths of the earth.

The beam snapped off, plunging Circle Park into sudden darkness, and in the silence she heard Dog howling madly inside the house.

"Great Quirke!" Pomeroy whispered. "All those poor people . . . !"

"No!" Katherine heard herself say. "Oh, no, no, no!" She

started to run across the garden, staring toward the lightning-flecked cloud that wreathed the wreckage of the conurbation. From Circle Park and all the observation platforms came the sound of wordless voices, and she thought at first that they were crying out in horror, the way she wanted to — but no; they were cheering, cheering, cheering.

PART TWO

24

AN AGENT OF THE LEAGUE

The strange light in the north had died away and the long thunderclap had spent itself, echoing and re-echoing from the walls of the old volcano. Mastering their panicked horses, the men of the Black Island came on along the margins of the bog amid a drumroll of galloping hooves and the torn-silk sound of windblown torches.

Tom raised his hands and shouted, "We're friends! Not pirates! Travelers! From London!" But the horsemen were in no mood to listen, even the few who understood. They had been hunting survivors from the sunken suburb all day, they had seen what Peavey's pirates had done in the fishing villages along the western shore, and now they shouted to one another in their own language and galloped closer, raising their bows. A gray-feathered arrow thudded into the ground at Tom's feet, making him stumble backward. "We're friends!" he shouted again.

The leading man drew his sword, but another rider spurred in front of him, shouting something in the Island tongue, then in Anglish. "I want them alive!"

It was Anna Fang. She reined in her horse, swung herself

down from the saddle, and ran toward Tom and Hester, her coat flapping against the firelight like a red flag. She wore a sword in a long scabbard on her back, and on her breast Tom saw a bronze badge in the shape of a broken wheel — the symbol of the Anti-Traction League.

"Tom! Hester!" She hugged them one by one, smiling her sweetest smile. "I thought you were dead! I sent Lindstrom and Yasmina to look for you, the morning after the fight at Airhaven. They found your balloon wrecked in those horrible marshes, and said you must be dead, dead. I wanted to search for your poor bodies, but the *Jenny* had been damaged, and I was so busy helping guide the town down to the repair-yard here. . . . But we said prayers for you, and made funeral sacrifices to the gods of the sky. Do you think we could ask them for a refund?"

Tom kept quiet. His chest was hurting so that he could hardly breathe, let alone speak. Anyway, the badge on the aviatrix's coat told him that Peavey's stories had been true: She was an agent of the League. He wasn't charmed anymore by her kindness and her tinkling laugh.

She shouted something over her shoulder to the waiting riders, and a couple jumped down from their ponies and led them forward, staring in wonder at Shrike's corpse. "I have to leave you for a while," she explained. "I'm taking the *Jenny* north to see what devilry has lit up the sky. The islanders will look after you. Can you ride?"

Tom had never even seen a horse before, let alone sat on one, but he was so dazed with pain and shock that he could not protest as they heaved him up into the saddle of a shaggy little pony and started to lead it downhill. He looked back for Hester and saw her scowling at him, hunched in the saddle of a second pony. Then the knot of riders closed around her, and he lost sight of her in the narrow, crowded streets of the caravanserai, where whole families were standing outside their homes to stare at the northern sky, and dust and litter whirled between the buildings as Airhaven dipped overhead, trying out its rotors one by one.

There was a small stone house where someone found a seat for him, and a man in black robes and a big, white turban who examined his bruised chest. "Broken!" he said cheerfully. "I am Ibrahim Nazghul, physician. Four of your ribs are quite smashed up!"

Tom nodded, giddy with the pain and shock, but starting to feel lucky that he was still alive, and glad that these people weren't the Anti-Tractionist savages he had been expecting. Dr. Nazghul wound bandages around his chest, and his wife brought a steaming bowl of mutton stew and helped Tom eat, spooning it into his mouth. Lantern light lapped at the corners of the room, and in the doorway the doctor's children stood staring at Tom with huge dark eyes.

"You are a hero!" explained the doctor. "They say you fought with an iron djinn who would have killed us all."

Tom blinked sleepily at him. He had almost forgotten the squalid little battle at the edge of the bog: The details were fading quickly, like a dream. *I killed Shrike*, he thought. *All right, so he was dead already, technically, but he was still a person. He had hopes and plans and dreams, and I put a stop to them all.* He didn't feel like a hero, he felt like a murderer, and the feeling of guilt and shame stayed with him, staining his dreams as his head drooped over the bowl of stew and he slipped away into sleep.

Then he was in another room, in a soft bed, and there was a blustery blue-and-white sky beyond the window and a patch of sunlight coming and going on the lime-washed wall.

"How are you feeling, Stalker-killer?" a voice asked. Miss Fang stood over him, watching him with the gentle smile of an angel in an old picture.

Tom said, "Everything hurts."

"Well enough to travel? The *Jenny Haniver* is waiting, and I would like to be away before sundown. You can eat once we're airborne; I've made toad-in-the-hole, with real toad."

"Where's Hester?" Tom asked groggily.

"Oh, she's coming, too."

He sat up, wincing at the sharp pain in his chest and the memory of all that had happened. "I'm not going anywhere with *you*," he said.

The aviatrix laughed as if she thought he was joking, then realized he wasn't and sat down on the bed, looking concerned. "Tom? Have I done something to upset you?"

"You work for the League!" he said angrily. "You're a spy, no better than Valentine! You only helped us because you hoped we'd tell you things about London!"

Miss Fang's smile faded entirely. "Tom," she said gently, "I helped you because I like you. And if you had seen your family slave to death aboard a ruthless city, might you not have decided to help the League in its fight against Municipal Darwinism?"

She reached out to brush the tousled hair away from his forehead, and Tom remembered something he had forgotten, a time when he was little and very ill and his mother had sat with him like this. But the badge of the League was still on Miss Fang's breast, and the wound of Valentine's betrayal was still raw: He would not let himself be tricked by smiles and kindness again. "You kill people!" he said, pushing her hand away. "You sank Marseilles. . . ."

"If I had not, it would have attacked the Hundred Islands, killing or enslaving hundreds more people than I drowned with my little bomb."

"And you strangled the . . . the Raisin of Somewhere-or-Other!"

"The Sultana of Palau Pinang?" The smile came flickering back. "I didn't strangle her! What a horrible suggestion! I simply broke her neck. She let amphibious raft-cities refuel at her island, so she had be disposed of."

Tom didn't see that it was anything to smile about. He remembered Wreyland's men slumped in the shadows of the air-quay at Stayns, and Miss Fang telling him they were just unconscious.

"I may be no better than Valentine," she went on, "but there is a difference between us. Valentine tried to kill you, and I want to keep you alive. So, will you come with me?"

"Where to?" asked Tom suspiciously.

"To Shan Guo," she replied. "I'm willing to bet that what lit up the sky last night had something to do with the thing Valentine took from Hester's mother. And I have learned that London is heading straight for the Shield-Wall."

Tom was amazed. Could the Lord Mayor really have found a way to breach the League's borders? If so, it was the best news for years! As for going to Shan Guo, that was the heart of the

Anti-Traction League, the last place in the world a decent Londoner should go. "I won't do anything to help you harm London," he told her. "It's still my home."

"Of course," she replied. "But if the Wall is about to be attacked, don't you think the people who live behind it deserve a chance to get away? I am going to warn them of their danger, and I want Hester to come with me and tell her side of the story. And Hester will only go if you come, too."

Tom laughed, and found that it hurt. "I don't think so!" he said. "Hester hates me!"

"Nonsense," giggled Miss Fang. "She likes you very much. Did she not spend half the night telling me how kind you have been, and how wonderfully brave you were, killing that machine-man?"

"Did she?" Tom blushed, feeling suddenly proud. He didn't think he would ever get used to Hester Shaw and her seesawing moods. Nevertheless, she was the closest thing he had to a friend in this huge, confusing world, and he still remembered how she had pleaded with Shrike for his life. Wherever she was going, he had to go, too: even into the savage heartland of the League; even to Shan Guo.

"All right," he said. "I'll come."

25

THE HISTORIANS

It is raining on London, steady rain out of the low, bruised sky, raining hard enough to wash away the snow and churn the mud beneath the city's tracks into thick yellow slurry, but not to quench the fires of Panzerstadt-Bayreuth, which are still blazing like a titan's pyre away in the northwest.

Magnus Crome stands on the windswept roof of the Engineerium and watches the rising smoke. An apprentice holds an umbrella over him, and behind her wait six tall, motionless figures dressed in black versions of the Guild's rubber coats. The terrorists who breached the Engineerium last night have still not been caught, and security is being strengthened: From now on the Lord Mayor will go nowhere without his new bodyguard, the first batch of Dr. Twix's Stalkers.

A Guild spotter-ship swings overhead and touches down. Dr. Vambrace, the Engineers' security chief, steps out and comes hurrying to where the Lord Mayor waits, his rubber coat flapping thickly in the wind.

"Well, Doctor?" Crome asks eagerly. "What did you see? Were you able to land?"

Vambrace shakes his head. "Fires are still burning all over the wreck. But we circled as low as we dared and took photographs. The upper tiers have melted and collapsed onto the lower, and it looks as if all the boilers and fuel-stores exploded at the first touch of our energy beam."

Crome nods. "Were there any survivors?"

"A few signs of life, between the tiers, but otherwise . . ." The security man's eyes go wide behind his thick glasses, looking like a pair of jellyfish in an aquarium. His department is always keen to find new and inventive ways to kill people, and he is still excited at the thought of the dry, charred shapes he saw littering the streets and squares of Panzerstadt-Bayreuth, many of them still standing upright, flashed into clinker statues by the gaze of MEDUSA.

"Do you intend to turn back and devour the wreck, Lord Mayor?" he asks after a moment. "The fires will burn themselves out in a day or two."

"Absolutely not," snaps Crome. "We must press on toward the Shield-Wall."

"The people will not like that," Vambrace warns. "They have had their victory, now they want the spoils. The scrap metal and spare parts from that conurbation —"

"I have not brought London all this way for scrap metal and spare parts," Crome interrupts. He stands at the handrail on the roof's rim and stares east. He can already see the white summits of high mountains on the horizon, like a row of pearly teeth. "We must press on. A few more days will bring us within range of the Shield-Wall. I have announced a public holiday, and a reception at the Guildhall to mark the great event. Think of it, Vambrace! A whole new hunting ground!"

"But the League knows we are coming now," warns Vambrace. "They will try to stop us."

Crome's eyes are bright and cold, gazing at the future. He says, "Valentine has his orders. He will deal with the League."

❄

And so London kept moving, dragging itself eastward as the smoke of the dead conurbation towered up into the sky behind, and Katherine walked to the elevator stations through the wet wreckage of last night's celebrations. Broken Chinese lanterns blew across the shuddering deckplates, and men in the red livery of the Recycling Department wheeled bins around, gathering up abandoned party hats and soggy banners whose messages were still dimly to be read: We ♥ *Magnus Crome* and *Long Live London*. Dog played chase with a billowing paper chain, but Katherine called him sharply to heel. This was no time for games.

At least in the Museum there were no banners and no paper chains. The Historians' Guild had never been as quick as the rest of London to welcome new inventions from the Engineers, and they made no exception for MEDUSA. In the dusty shadows of the exhibition galleries there was a decent silence, as befitted the morning after the death of a whole city. The sounds of the streets outside seemed muffled, as if thick, soft curtains of time hung in the dim air between the display cabinets. The quietness helped Katherine to gather her thoughts, and by the time she reached Chudleigh Pomeroy's office she was quite clear about what she had to say.

She had not yet told Mr. Pomeroy what she had learned in the Engineerium, but he had seen how shaken she was when he left her at Clio House the night before. He did not seem surprised to find her and Dog at his door.

"Mr. Pomeroy," she whispered, "I have to talk to you. Is Bevis here? Is he all right?"

"Of course," he said at once. "Come in!"

Bevis Pod was waiting for her in the little teak-paneled office, dressed in borrowed Historian's robes, his pale skull looking as fragile as an eggshell in the dim yellow glow of the Museum lamps. She wanted to run to him and hold him and apologize for what she had led him into, but crammed in around him were about a dozen Historians, some perching on the arms of chairs and the corners of Pomeroy's desk. They all looked up guiltily at Katherine, and she looked back at them with a sudden, horrible fear that Pomeroy had betrayed her.

"Don't worry," said Pomeroy kindly. "If Pod's to be a guest of the Museum I thought my fellow Historians should be introduced to him. None of us are friends of the Lord Mayor. We have agreed that Apprentice Pod can stay as long as necessary."

The Historians made a space for her next to Bevis. "Are you all right?" she asked him, and was relieved when he managed a nervous smile.

"Not bad," he whispered. "It's strange here. All this wood everywhere, and old stuff. But the Historians are very kind. . . ."

Katherine looked around the room at them. She knew many of them by sight: Dr. Arkengarth, Dr. Karuna, Professor Pewtertide, young Miss Potts, Norman Nancarrow from Prints and Paintings, and Miss Plym, who was sniffling into her hankie.

"We've been talking about the destruction of Panzerstadt-Bayreuth," said Pomeroy, pressing a hot mug of cocoa into her hands. "This horrible MEDUSA device."

"Everybody else seems to think it's wonderful," said Katherine bitterly. "I could hear them laughing and shouting 'Good old Crome' half the night. I know they're relieved that we didn't get eaten, but . . . Well, I don't think blowing up another city is anything to be happy about."

"It's a disaster!" agreed old Dr. Arkengarth, wringing his bony hands. "The vibrations from that vile machine played havoc with my ceramics!"

"Oh, bother your ceramics, Arkengarth," snapped Pomeroy, who could see how upset Katherine was. "What about Panzerstadt-Bayreuth? Burned to a cinder!"

"That's what comes of the Engineers' obsession with old-tech!" said Professor Pewtertide. "Countless centuries of history to learn from, and all they are interested in is a few Ancient machines!"

"And what did the Ancients ever achieve with their devices, anyway?" whined Arkengarth. "They just made a horrible mess of their world and then blew themselves up!"

The others nodded dolefully.

"There was a great museum in Panzerstadt-Bayreuth," said Dr. Karuna.

"I believe they had some wonderful paintings," agreed Nancarrow.

"Unique examples of thirtieth-century c-c-cabinetmaking!" wailed Miss Plym, and collapsed in tears on Arkengarth's knobbly shoulder.

"You must excuse poor Moira, Katherine," whispered Pomeroy.

"She had terrible news this morning. Crome has ordered that our furniture collection be broken up to feed the furnaces. It's the fuel shortage, you see, a result of this mad journey east."

Katherine couldn't have cared less about furniture or ceramics at that moment, but she felt glad that she was not the only one in London appalled by what the Lord Mayor had unleashed. She took a deep breath, then quickly explained what she and Bevis had heard in the Engineerium about MEDUSA and the next step in Crome's great plan, the attack on the Shield-Wall.

"But that's terrible!" they whispered when she had finished.

"Shan Guo is a great and ancient culture, Anti-Traction League or no Anti-Traction League. Batmunkh Gompa can't be blown up . . . !"

"Think of all those temples!"

"Ceramics!"

"Prayer-wheels . . ."

"Silk paintings . . ."

"F-f-furniture!"

"Think of the *people!*" said Katherine angrily. "We must do something!"

"Yes! Yes!" they agreed, and then all looked sheepishly at her. After twenty years of Crome's rule they had no idea how to stand up to the Guild of Engineers.

"But what *can* we do?" asked Pomeroy at last.

"Tell people what is happening!" urged Katherine. "You're Acting Head Historian. Call a meeting of the Council! Make them see how wrong it is!"

Pomeroy shook his head. "They won't listen, Miss Valentine. You heard the cheering last night."

"But that was only because Panzerstadt-Bayreuth had been going to eat us! When they learn that Crome plans to turn his weapon on yet another city . . ."

"They'll just cheer all the louder," sighed Pomeroy.

"He has packed the other Guilds with his allies, anyway," observed Dr. Karuna. "All the great old Guildsmen are gone; dead or retired or arrested on his orders. Even our own apprentices are as besotted with old-tech as the Engineers, especially since Crome foisted his man Valentine on us as Head Historian. . . . Oh, I mean no offense, Miss Katherine. . . ."

"Father isn't Crome's man," said Katherine angrily. "I'm sure he's not! If he knew what Crome was planning he would never have helped him. That's probably why he was packed off on this reconnaissance mission, to get him out of the way. When he gets home and finds out he'll do something to stop it. You see, it was he who found MEDUSA in the first place. He would be horrified to think of it killing all those people. He will want to make amends, I'm sure he will!"

She spoke so passionately that some of the Historians believed her, even the ones like Dr. Karuna who had been passed over for promotion when Crome put Valentine in charge of their Guild. As for Bevis Pod, he watched her with shining eyes, filled with a feeling that he couldn't even name; something that they had never taught him about in the Learning Labs. It made him shiver all over.

Pomeroy was the first to speak. "I hope you're right, Miss Valentine," he said. "Because he is the only man who can hope to challenge the Lord Mayor. We must wait for his return."

"But . . ."

"In the meantime, we have agreed to keep Mr. Pod safe, here at the Museum. He can sleep up in the old Transport Gallery, and help Dr. Nancarrow catalogue the art collection, and if the Engineers come hunting for him we'll find a hiding place. It isn't much of a blow against Crome, I know. But please understand, Katherine: We are old, and frightened, and there really is nothing more that we can do."

26

BATMUNKH GOMPA

The world was changing. That was nothing new, of course; the first thing an Apprentice Historian learned was that the world was always changing, but now it was changing so fast that you could actually see it happening. Looking down from the flight deck of the *Jenny Haniver*, Tom saw the wide plains of the eastern Hunting Ground speckled with speeding towns, spurred into flight by whatever it was that had bruised the northern sky, heading away from it as fast as their tracks or wheels could carry them, too preoccupied to try and catch one another.

"MEDUSA," he heard Miss Fang whisper to herself, staring toward the far-off, flame-flecked smoke.

"What is a MEDUSA?" asked Hester. "You know something, don't you? About what my mum and dad were killed for?"

"I'm afraid not," the aviatrix replied. "I wish I did. But I heard the name once. Six years ago another League agent managed to get into London, posing as a crewman on a licensed airship. He had heard something that must have intrigued him, but we never learned what it was. The League had only one message from him, just two words: *Beware MEDUSA.* The Engineers caught him and killed him."

"How do you know?" asked Tom.

"Because they sent us back his head," said Miss Fang. "Cash on Delivery."

That evening she set the *Jenny Haniver* down on one of the fleeing towns, a respectable four-decker called Peripatetiapolis that was steering south to lair in the mountains beyond the Sea of Khazak. At the air-harbor there they heard more news of what had happened to Panzerstadt-Bayreuth.

"I saw it!" said an aviator. "I was a hundred miles away, but I still saw it. A tongue of fire, reaching out from London's Top Tier and bringing death to everything it touched!"

"London's dug up something from the Sixty Minute War," a freelance archaeologist told them. "The old American Empire was quite insane toward the end; I've heard stories about terrible weapons: quantum energy beams that drew their power from places outside the real universe. . . ."

"Who'll dare defy them now, when Magnus Crome has the power to burn any city that disobeys him?" asked a panic-stricken Peripatetiapolitan merchant. "'Come here and let us eat you,' London will tell us, and we will have to go. It's the end of civilization as we know it! Again!"

But one good thing had come out of it: The people of Peripatetiapolis were suddenly quite glad to accept Tom's London money. On an impulse he bought a red silk shawl to replace the scarf that Hester had lost on that long-ago night when he chased her through the Gut.

"For *me*?" she said incredulously when he gave it to her. She couldn't remember anyone ever giving her a gift before. She had not spoken to him much since they left the Black Island, ashamed of her outburst the night before, but now she said, "Thank you. And I suppose I should thank you for saving my life, too. Though I don't know why you keep bothering."

"I knew you didn't really want to end up as a Stalker," Tom told her.

"Oh, I did," she said. "It would make things so much easier. But you did the right thing." She looked away from him, embarrassed, staring down at the shawl in her hands. "I try to be nice," she said. "Nobody's ever made me feel they *like* me before, the way you do. So I try to be kind and smiley, like you want me to be, but then I catch sight of my reflection or I think of *him* and it all goes wrong and I can only think horrible things and scream at you and try and hurt you. I'm sorry."

"It's all right," said Tom awkwardly. "I know. It's OK." He picked up the shawl and tied it carefully around her neck, but as he had expected she pulled it up at once to hide her mouth and nose. He felt strangely sad: He had grown used to that face, and he would miss her lopsided smiles.

They flew on before dawn, crossing a range of steep hills like crumpled brown paper. All day the land rose up and up, and soon Tom realized that they were leaving the Hunting Ground altogether. By evening the *Jenny Haniver* was flying over landscapes too rugged for most towns to travel. He saw dense forests of pine and rhododendron, with now and then a little static village squatting in its cove of farmland, and once a white settlement perched on a mountaintop with roads reaching out from it like the spokes of a wheel, real roads with carts moving up and down and a bright flutter of prayer-flags at the intersections. He watched until they were out of sight. He had heard about roads in his history lessons, but he had never thought he'd *see* one.

Next day, Anna Fang handed out balls of reddish paste to her passengers. "Powdered betel-nut," she explained, "mixed with some dried leaves from Nuevo Maya. They help at these high altitudes. But don't make a habit of chewing them, or your teeth will turn as red as mine." The gritty paste made Tom's mouth tingle, but it cured the faint sense of nausea and light-headedness that had been growing in him as the airship flew higher and higher, and it also helped to numb the pain of his broken ribs.

By now the *Jenny*'s tiny shadow was flickering over high snow-clad summits, and ahead lay summits still higher, white spires that hung like a mirage above the clouds. Beyond them stretched an even higher range, and then another, higher yet. Tom strained his eyes, peering toward the south in the hope that he might catch a glimpse of old Chomolungma, Everest of the Ancients, but storms were brewing in the high Himalayas and it was wrapped in cloud.

On and on they flew, through a black-and-white world of snow and glaciers and the sheer dark rock of young mountains, where Tom or Hester sometimes had to mind the controls while Anna Fang took catnaps in the seat beside them, afraid to risk leaving her flight-deck. And still they climbed, until at last they were skimming over the lower buttresses of great Zhan Shan, tallest of the earth's new mountains, whose snowcapped crown jutted into the endless cold above the sky. After that the peaks were lower, white and lovely, with sometimes a green vale between, where huge herds of animals scattered and wheeled at the sound of the airship's engines. These were the Mountains of Heaven, and they swept away toward the north and east and sank down in the far distance to steppe and taiga and the glitter of impassable swamps.

"This is Shan Guo of the many horses," Anna Fang told Tom and Hester. "I had hoped to retire here, when my work for the League was done. Now I suppose it may all be eaten by London; our fortresses blasted by MEDUSA and our settlements devoured, the green hills split open and made to give up their minerals, the horses extinct, just like the rest of the world."

Tom didn't think it was such a bad idea, because it was only natural that Traction Cities should eventually spread right across the globe. But he couldn't help liking Miss Fang, even if she was a spy and an Anti-Tractionist, and to comfort her he said, "However powerful MEDUSA is, it will take years for London to gnaw its way through these great big mountains."

"It won't have to," she replied. "Look."

He looked where she pointed, and saw a break in the mountain chain ahead, a broad pass that a city could have crawled along — except that stretching across it, so vast that it seemed at first glance just another spur of the mountains, was the Shield-Wall.

It was like a wall of night, black, black, built from huge blocks of volcanic stone, armored with the rusting deckplates of cities that had dared to challenge it and been destroyed by the hundreds of rocket batteries on its western face. On its snow-clad summit, four thousand feet above the valley floor, the banner of the broken wheel snapped and raced in the wind and the sunlight gleamed on armored gun emplacements and the steel helmets of the League's soldiers.

"If only it were as strong as it looks," sighed the aviatrix, bringing the *Jenny Haniver* down toward it in a long sweeping curve. A small flying machine, little more than a motorized kite, came soaring to meet them, and she held a brief radio conversation with its pilot. It circled the *Jenny* once and then whirred ahead, guiding the newcomer over the top of the Shield-Wall. Tom looked down at broad battlements and the faces of soldiers gazing upward, yellow, brown, black, white, faces from every part of the world where barbarian statics still held out against Municipal Darwinism. Then they were gone; the *Jenny* was sinking down the sheltered eastern side of the Wall, and he saw that it was a city, a vertical city with hundreds of terraces and balconies and windows all carved into the black rock, tier upon tier of shops and barracks and houses with balloons and brightly colored kites drifting up and down between them like petals.

"Batmunkh Gompa," announced Miss Fang. "The City of Eternal Strength. Although the people who call it that have never heard of MEDUSA, of course."

It was beautiful. Tom, who had always been taught that static settlements were dingy, squalid, backward places, went to the window and stared, and Hester came and pressed her face to the glass beside him, safe behind her veil and almost girlish. "Oh! It's just like the cliffs on Oak Island where the seabirds nest!" she cried. "Look! Look!" Down at the base of the Wall a lake shone azure blue, flecked with the sails of pleasure boats. "Tom, we'll go swimming, I'll teach you how. . . ."

The *Jenny Haniver* landed among some other merchant ships at a mooring-terrace halfway down the Wall, and Miss Fang led Tom and Hester to a waiting balloon that took them up again past parks and tea shops to the governor's palace — the ancient monastery from which Batmunkh Gompa took its name, white-washed and many-windowed, carved out of the steep side of the mountain at the Wall's end. Other balloons were converging on the landing deck below the palace gardens, their envelopes bright in the mountain sunlight, and in one of the dangling baskets Tom saw Captain Khora waving.

They met on the landing deck, the young airman touching down just ahead of them and running across to embrace Miss Fang and help her friends out of the skittish gondola. He had flown here from Airhaven the morning after Shrike's attack, and he seemed amazed and happy to see Tom and Hester alive. Turning to the aviatrix he said, "The governor and his officers are eager for your report, Feng Hua. Terrible rumors have reached us about London. . . ."

It was good to meet a friendly face in this strange new city, and Tom fell into step beside Khora as he led the newcomers up the long stair to the palace entrance. He remembered seeing a trim Achebe 2100 berthed at one of the lower platforms and asked, "Was that your machine we saw at the mooring-place, the one with oxhide outriggers?"

Khora laughed delightedly. "That old air-scow? No, thank the gods! My *Mokele Mbembe* is a warship, Tom. Every ally of the League supplies a ship to the Northern Air-Fleet, and they are stabled together, up there." He stopped and pointed, and Tom saw the gleam of bronze doors far up near the summit of the Wall. "The High Eyries."

"We'll take you up there one day, Tom," promised Miss Fang, leading them past the warrior-monks who guarded the door and on into a maze of cool stone corridors. "The League's great Air Destroyers are one of the wonders of the skies! But first, Governor Khan must hear Hester's story."

✼

Governor Ermene Khan was a gentle old man with the long, mournful face of a kindly sheep. He welcomed them all into his private quarters and gave them tea and honey cakes in a room whose round windows looked down toward the lake of Batmunkh Nor, gleaming among patchwork farmlands, far below. For a thousand years his family had helped to man the Shield-Wall, and he seemed dazed by the news that all his guns and rockets were suddenly useless. "No city can pass Batmunkh Gompa," he kept saying as the room filled with officers eager to hear the aviatrix's advice. "My dear Feng Hua, if London dares to approach us, we will destroy it. As soon as it comes in range — boom!"

"But that is what I'm trying to tell you!" cried Miss Fang impatiently. "London doesn't need to come within range of your guns. Crome will park his city a hundred miles away and burn your precious Wall to ashes! You have heard Hester's story. I believe that the machine Valentine stole from her mother was a fragment of an Ancient weapon — and what happened to Panzerstadt-Bayreuth proves that the Guild of Engineers have managed to restore it to working order."

"Yes, yes," said an artillery officer, "so you say. But can we really believe that Crome has found a way to reactivate something that has been buried since the Sixty Minute War?

Perhaps Panzerstadt-Bayreuth was just destroyed by a freak accident."

"Yes!" Governor Khan clutched gratefully at the idea. "A meteorite, or some sort of gas leak . . ." He stroked his long beard, reminding Tom of one of the dithery old Historians back at the London Museum. "Perhaps Crome's city will not even come here. . . . Perhaps he has other prey in mind?"

But his other officers were more ready to believe the Wind-Flower's report. "He's coming here, all right," said one, an aviatrix from Kerala, not much older than Tom. "I took a scout-ship west the day before yesterday, Feng Hua," she explained, with an adoring look at Miss Fang. "The barbarian city was less than five hundred miles away, and approaching fast. By tomorrow night MEDUSA could be within range."

"And there have been sightings of a black airship in the mountains," put in Captain Khora. "The ships sent to intercept it never returned. My guess is that it was Valentine's 13th Floor Elevator, sent to spy out our cities so that London can devour them."

Valentine! Tom felt a strange mix of pride and fear at the thought of the Head Historian on the loose here in the very heart of Shan Guo. Beside him, Hester tensed at the mention of the explorer's name. He looked at her, but she was staring past him, out through the open windows toward the mountains as if she half expected to see the 13th Floor Elevator go flying past.

"No city can pass the Shield-Wall," said Governor Khan, loyal to his ancestors, but he did not sound convinced anymore.

"You must launch the Air-Fleet, Governor," Miss Fang insisted, leaning forward in her seat. "Bomb London before they can bring MEDUSA into range. It's the only way to be sure."

"No!" shouted Tom, springing up so that his chair fell backward with a clatter. He couldn't believe what she had said. "You said we were coming here to warn people! You can't attack London! People will get hurt! Innocent people!" He was thinking of Katherine, imagining League torpedoes crashing into Clio House and the Museum. "You promised!" he said weakly.

"Feng Hua does not make promises to savages," snapped the Keralan girl, but Miss Fang hushed her.

"We will just hit the Gut and tracks, Tom," she said. "Then the Top Tier, where MEDUSA is housed. We do not seek to harm the innocent, but what else are we to do, if a barbarian city chooses to threaten us?"

"London's not a barbarian city!" shouted Tom. "It's you who are the barbarians! Why shouldn't London eat Batmunkh Gompa if it needs to? If you don't like the idea, you should have put your cities on wheels long ago, like civilized people!"

A few of the League officers were shouting angrily at him to be quiet, and the Keralan girl had drawn her sword, but Miss Fang calmed them with a few words and turned her patient smile to Tom. "Perhaps you should leave us, Thomas," she said firmly. "I will come and find you later."

Tom's eyes stung with stupid tears. He was sorry for these people, of course he was. He could see that they weren't savages, and he didn't really believe anymore that they deserved to be eaten, but he couldn't just sit by and listen to them planning to attack his home.

He turned to Hester in the hope that she would take his side, but she was lost in her own thoughts, her fingers tracing and retracing the scars under her red veil. She felt guilty and stupid.

Guilty because she had been happy in the air with Tom, and it was wrong to be happy while Valentine was wandering about unpunished. Stupid because, when he gave her the shawl, she had started to hope that Tom really liked her, and thinking of Valentine made her remember that *nobody* could like her, not in that way, not ever. When she saw him looking at her she just said, "They can kill everybody in London for all I care, so long as they save Valentine for me."

Tom turned his back on her and stalked out of the high chamber, and as the door rolled shut behind him he heard the Keralan girl hiss, "Barbarian!"

Alone, he mooched down to the terrace where the taxi-balloons waited and sat on a stone bench there, feeling angry and betrayed and thinking of things that he should have said to Miss Fang, if only he had thought of them in time. Below him the rooftops and terraces of Batmunkh Gompa stretched away into the shadows below the white shoulders of the mountains, and he found himself trying to imagine what it must be like to live here and wake up every day of your life to the same view. Didn't the people of the Shield-Wall long for movement and a change of scene? How did they dream, without the grumbling vibrations of a city's engines to rock them to sleep? Did they *love* this place? And suddenly he felt terribly sad that the whole bustling, colorful, ancient city might soon be rubble under London's tracks.

He wanted to see more. Going over to the nearest taxi-balloon, he made the pilot understand that he was Miss Fang's guest and wanted to go down into the city. The man grinned and started weighting his gondola with stones from a pile that stood nearby, and soon Tom found himself traveling down past the many levels of the city again until he stepped out on a sort of central square, where dozens of other taxis were coming and going and stairways branched off across the face of the Shield-Wall, going up toward the High Eyries and down to the shops and markets of the lower levels.

News of MEDUSA was spreading fast through Batmunkh Gompa, and already a lot of the houses and shops were shuttered, their owners fled to cities farther south. The lower levels were still packed with people, though, and as the sun dipped behind the Wall, Tom wandered the crowded bazaars and steep ladderways. There were fortune-tellers' booths at the street corners, and shrines to the sky gods, dusty with the crumbly gray ash of incense sticks. Fierce-looking Uighur acrobats were performing in the central square, and everywhere he looked he saw soldiers and airmen of the League: blond giants from Spitzbergen and blue-black warriors from the Mountains of the Moon, the small dark people of the Andean statics and people the color of firelight from jungle strongholds in Laos and Annam.

He tried to forget that some of these young men and women might soon be dropping rockets on London, and started to enjoy the flow of faces and the incomprehensible mishmash of languages — and sometimes he heard someone say "Tom!" or "Thomasz!" or "Tao-mah!" as they pointed him out to their friends. The story of his battle with Shrike had spread through the mountains from trading post to trading post and had been waiting for him here in Batmunkh Gompa. He didn't mind. It felt like a different Thomas that they were talking about, someone brave and strong who understood what had to be done, and felt no doubts.

He was just wondering if he should go back to the governor's palace and find Hester, when he noticed a tall figure climbing a nearby stairway. The man wore a ragged red robe with the hood pulled down over his face, and carried a staff in one hand and a pack slung over his shoulder. Tom had already seen dozens of these wandering holy men in Batmunkh Gompa: monks in the service of the mountain gods who traveled from city to city through the high passes. (Up at the mooring platform Anna Fang had stooped to kiss the feet of one, and given six bronze coins for him to bless the *Jenny Haniver*.) But this man was different; something about him snagged Tom's gaze and would not let it go.

He started following the red robe. He followed it through the spice market with its thousand astonishing scents, and down the narrow Street of Weavers where hundreds of baskets swung from low poles outside the shops like hanging nests, brushing against the top of his head as he passed underneath. What was it about the way the man moved, and that long brown hand clutching the staff?

And then, under a lantern in the central square, the monk was stopped by a street girl asking for a blessing and Tom caught a glimpse of the bearded face inside the hood. He knew that hawklike nose and those mariner's eyes; he knew that the amulet hanging between the black brows hid the familiar Guild-mark of a London Historian.

It was Valentine!

27

DR. ARKENGARTH REMEMBERS

Katherine spent a lot of time in the Museum in those final days, as London went roaring toward the mountains. Safe in its dingy maze she could not hear the burr of the saws as they felled the trees in Circle Park to feed the engines, or the cheers of the noisy crowds who gathered each day in front of the public Goggle-screens where the details of Crome's great plan were being gradually revealed. She could even forget the Guild of Engineers' security people, who were everywhere now, not just the usual white-coated thugs, but a strange new breed in black coats and hoods, silent, stiff in their movements, with a faint greenish glow behind their tinted visors: Dr. Twix's Resurrected Men.

But if she was honest with herself, it wasn't only the peace and quiet that kept calling her down to the Museum. Bevis was there, his borrowed bedding spread out on the floor of the old Transport gallery, under the dusty hanging shapes of model gliders and flying machines. She needed his company more and more as the city hauled itself eastward. She liked the fact that he was her secret. She liked his soft voice, and the strange laugh that always sounded as if he were trying it on for size, as if he had never had much call for laughter down in the Deep Gut. She liked the way he looked at her, his dark eyes always lingering on her face and especially her hair. "I've never really known anybody with hair before," he told her one day. "In the Guild they use chemicals on us when we're first apprenticed, so it never grows back."

Katherine thought about his pale, smooth scalp. She liked that too. It sort of suited him. Was this what falling in love was like? Not something big and amazing that you knew about straight away, like in a story, but a slow thing that crept over you in waves until you woke up one day and found that you were head-over-heels with someone quite unexpected, like an Apprentice Engineer?

She wished that Father were here, so she could ask him.

In the afternoons Bevis would pull on a Historian's robe and hide his bald head under a cap and go down to help Dr. Nancarrow, who was busy recataloguing the Museum's huge store of paintings and drawings and taking photographs in case the Lord Mayor decided to feed those to the furnaces as well. Then Katherine would wander the Museum with Dog at her heels, hunting for the things that her father had dug up. Washing machines, pieces of computer, the rusty rib cage of a Stalker, all had labels that read, "Discovered by Mr. T. Valentine, Archaeologist." She could imagine him lifting them gently out of the soil that had guarded them, cleaning them, wrapping them in scrim for transport back to London. *He must have done the same thing with the MEDUSA fragment when he discovered it*, she thought. She·

whispered prayers to Clio, sure that the goddess must be present in these time-soaked halls. "*London needs him! I need him! Please send him safely home, and soon. . . .*"

But it was Dog, not Clio, who led her into the Natural History section that evening. He had glimpsed a display of stuffed animals from the far end of the corridor and gone prowling down to stare at them, a growl bubbling in the back of his throat. Old Dr. Arkengarth, who was passing through the gallery on his way home, backed away nervously, but Kate said, "It's all right, Doctor! He's quite safe!" and knelt down at Dog's side, looking up at the sharks and dolphins that swung above her and the great looming shape of the whale, which had been taken off its hawsers and propped against the far wall before the vibrations could bring it crashing down.

"Impressive, isn't it?" said Arkengarth, who was always ready to begin a lecture. "A blue whale. Hunted to extinction in the first half of the twenty-first century. Or possibly the twentieth: The records are unclear. We wouldn't even know what it looked like if Mrs. Shaw hadn't discovered those fossilized bones. . . ."

Katherine had been thinking about something else, but the name "Shaw" made her turn around. The display case Arkengarth was pointing at housed a rack of brownish bones, and propped against a vertebra was a label that said, "*Bones of a Blue Whale, Discovered by Mrs. P. Shaw, Freelance Archaeologist.*"

Pandora Shaw, thought Katherine, recalling the name she had seen in the Museum catalogue. *Not Hester. Of course not.* But just to get Dr. Arkengarth out of lecture-mode she said, "Did you know her? Pandora Shaw?"

"Mrs. Shaw, yes, yes," the old man nodded. "A lovely lady. She was an Out-Country archaeologist, a friend of your father's. Of course, her name was Rae in those days. . . ."

"Pandora Rae?" Katherine knew that name. "Then she was Father's assistant on the trip to America! I've seen her picture in his book!"

"That's right," said Arkengarth, frowning slightly at the interruption. "An archaeologist, as I said. She specialized in old-tech, of course, but she brought us other things when she found them — like these whale bones. Later she married this Shaw chappie and went to live on some grotty little island in the Western Ocean. Poor girl. A tragedy. Terrible. Terrible."

"She died, didn't she?" said Katherine.

"She was murdered!" Arkengarth waggled his eyebrows dramatically. "Six or seven years ago. We heard it from another archaeologist. Murdered in her own home, and her husband with her. Dreadful business. I say, my dear, are you all right? You look as if you've seen a ghost!"

But Katherine was not all right. In her mind, all the pieces of the puzzle were flying together. *Pandora Shaw was murdered, seven years ago, the same time that Father found the machine. . . . Pandora the aviatrix, the archaeologist, the woman who had been with him in America when he found the plans of MEDUSA. And now a girl called Shaw who wants to kill Father . . .*

She could hardly manage to force the words out, but at last she asked, "Did she have a child?"

"I think she did, I think she did," the old man mused. "Yes, I remember Mrs. Shaw showing me a picture once when she turned up with some ceramics for my department. Lovely pieces. A decorated vase from the Electric Empire Era, best of its kind in the collection . . ."

"Do you remember its name?"

"Ah, yes, let me see . . . EE27190, I believe."

"Not the vase! The baby!"

Katherine's impatient shout echoed through the gallery and out into the halls beyond, and Dr. Arkengarth looked first startled, then offended. "Well, really, Miss Valentine, there's no need to snap! How should I remember the child's name? It was fifteen, sixteen years ago and I have never liked babies — nasty creatures, leak at both ends and have no respect for ceramics. But I believe this particular one was called Hattie or Holly or . . ."

"Hester!" sobbed Katherine, and turned and ran, ran with Dog at her heels, ran and ran without knowing where or why, since there was no way that she could outrun the dreadful truth. She knew how Father had come by the key to MEDUSA, and why he had never spoken of it. At last she knew why poor Hester Shaw had wanted to kill him.

28

A STRANGER IN THE
MOUNTAINS OF HEAVEN

Valentine's hand drew subtle, complicated shapes in the air above the girl's bowed head, and her face was calm and smiling, little suspecting that she was being blessed by the League's worst enemy.

Tom watched from behind a shrine to the sky goddess. His eyes had known who the red-robed monk was all along, and now his brain caught up with them in a flurry of understandings. Captain Khora had said that the 13th *Floor Elevator* had been haunting the mountains. It must have dropped Valentine off in the crags near Batmunkh Gompa, and he had come the rest of the way on foot, creeping into the city like a thief. But why? What secret mission could have brought him here?

Tom didn't know what to feel. He was frightened, of course, to be so close to the man who had tried to murder him, but at the same time he was thrilled by Valentine's daring. What courage it must have taken, to sneak into the great stronghold of the League, under the very noses of London's enemies! It was the sort of adventure that Valentine had written about, in books that Tom had read again and again, huddled under the blankets in the Third Class Apprentices' dorm with a flashlight, long after lights-out.

Valentine finished his blessing and moved on. For a few moments Tom lost sight of him among the crowds in the square, but then he spotted the red robe climbing on up the broad central stairway. He followed at a safe distance, past beggars and guards and hot food vendors, none of whom guessed that the red-robed figure was anything more than one of those crazy holy men. Valentine had his head bowed now and he climbed quickly, so Tom did not feel in any danger as he hurried along, twenty or thirty paces behind. But he still didn't know what he should do. Hester deserved to know that her parents' murderer was here. Should he find her? Tell her? But Valentine must be on some important mission for London, maybe gathering information so that the Engineers would know exactly where to aim MEDUSA. If Hester killed him, Tom would have betrayed his whole city. . . .

He climbed upward, ignoring the pain of his broken ribs. Around him the terraces of Batmunkh Gompa were speckled with lamps and lanterns, and the envelopes of taxi-balloons glowed from within as they rose and fell, like strange sea creatures swimming around a coral reef. And slowly he realized that he didn't want Valentine to succeed in whatever he was planning. London was no better than Tunbridge Wheels, and this place was old, and beautiful. He wouldn't let it be smashed!

"It's Valentine!" he shouted, charging up the stairs, trying to warn the passersby of the danger. But they just stared at him without understanding, and when at last he reached the red-robed man and pulled his hood down he found the round, startled face of a pilgrim monk blinking back at him.

He looked around wildly and saw what had happened. Valentine had taken a different stairway out of the central square, leaving Tom following the wrong red robe. He went running down again. Valentine was barely visible, a red speck climbing through lantern light toward the high places of the city — and the eyrie of the great air-destroyers. "It's Valentine!" shouted Tom, pointing, but none of the people around him spoke Anglish; some thought he was mad, others thought he meant that MEDUSA was about to strike. A wave of panic spread across the square, and soon he heard warning gongs sounding in the densely packed terraces of shops and inns below.

His first thought was to find Hester, but he had no idea where to look. Then he ran to a taxi-balloon and told the pilot, "Follow that monk!" but the woman smiled and shook her head, not understanding. "Feng Hua!" Tom shouted, remembering Anna Fang's League name, and the taxi pilot nodded and smiled, casting off. He tried to calm himself as the balloon rose. He would find Miss Fang. Miss Fang would know what to do. He remembered how she had trusted him with the Jenny during the flight across the mountains, and felt ashamed for turning on her in the council meeting.

He was expecting the taxi to take him to the governor's palace, but instead it landed near the terrace where the Jenny Haniver was berthed. The pilot pointed toward an inn that clung to the underside of the terrace above like a house martin's nest. "Feng Hua!" she said helpfully. "Feng Hua!"

For a panic-stricken moment Tom thought that she had carried him to an inn with the same name as Miss Fang; then, on one of the establishment's many balconies, he caught sight of the aviatrix's blood-red coat. He thrust all the money he had at the pilot, shouting, "Keep the change!" and left her staring at the unfamiliar faces of Quirke and Crome as he raced away.

Miss Fang was sitting at a balcony table with Captain Khora and the stern young Keralan flier who had been so angry at Tom's outburst earlier. They were drinking tea and deep in discussion, but they all leaped up as Tom blundered out onto the balcony. "Where's Hester?" he demanded.

"Down on the mooring platforms, in one of her moods," said Miss Fang. "Why?"

"Valentine!" he gasped. "He's here! Dressed as a monk!"

The inn's musicians stopped playing, and the sound of the alarm gongs in the lower city came drifting through the open windows.

"Valentine, here?" sneered the Keralan girl. "It's a lie! The barbarian thinks he can frighten us!"

"Be quiet, Sathya!" Miss Fang reached across and gripped Tom by the arm. "Is he alone?"

As quickly as he could, Tom told her what he had seen. She made a hissing sound through her clenched teeth. "He has come after our Air-Fleet! He means to cripple us!"

"One man cannot destroy an Air-Fleet!" protested Khora, smiling at the notion.

"You've never seen Valentine at work!" said the aviatrix. She was already on her feet, excited at the prospect of crossing swords with London's greatest agent. "Sathya, go and rouse the guard,

228

tell them the High Eyries are in danger." She turned to Tom. "Thank you for warning us," she said gently, as if she understood the agonizing decision he'd had to make.

"I've got to tell Hester!" he protested.

"Certainly not!" she told him. "She will only get herself killed, or kill Valentine, and I want him kept alive for questioning. Stay here until it is all over." A last ferocious smile and she was gone, down the steps and out of the panicked inn with Khora at her heels. She looked grim and dangerous and very beautiful, and Tom felt himself brushed by the same fierce love that he knew Khora and the Keralan girl and the rest of the League must feel for her.

But then he thought of Hester, and what she would say when she learned that he had seen Valentine and hadn't even told her. "Great Quirke!" he shouted suddenly. "I'm going to find her!" Sathya just stared at him, not stern anymore, just frightened and very young, and as he ran toward the stairs he shouted back at her, "You heard what Miss Fang said! Raise the alarm!"

Out onto dark ladderways again, down to the mooring platform where the *Jenny Haniver* hung at anchor. "Hester! Hester!" he shouted, and there she was, coming toward him through the glow of the landing lights, tugging the red shawl up across her face. He told her everything, and she took the news with the cold, silent glare he had expected. Then it was her turn to run, and he was following her up the endless stairs.

The Wall made its own weather. As Tom and Hester neared the top the air grew thin and chill and big fluttering snowflakes brushed their faces like butterfly wings. They could see lantern-light on a broad platform ahead where a gas tanker was lifting away empty from the High Eyries. Then there was an unbelievable gout of flame shooting out of the face of the Wall, and another and another, as if it were dragons, not airships, that were stabled there. Caught in the blast, the tanker's envelope exploded, white parachutes blossoming around it as it began to fall. Hester stopped for a moment and looked back, flames shining in her eye. "He's done it! We're too late! He's fired their Air-Fleet!"

They ran on. Tom's ribs hurt him at every breath and the cold air scorched his throat, but he kept as close behind Hester as he could, crunching through snow along a narrow walkway to the platform outside the eyries. The bronze gates stood open and a crowd of men were pouring out, shielding their faces from the heat of the blaze within. Some of them were dragging wounded comrades, and near the main door Tom saw Khora being tended by two of the ground crew.

The aviator looked up as Tom and Hester ran to him. "Valentine!" he groaned. "He bluffed his way past the sentries, saying he wanted to bless our airships. He was setting his explosives when Anna and I arrived. Oh, Tom, we never imagined that even a barbarian would try something like this! We weren't prepared! Our whole Air-Fleet . . . My poor *Mokele Mbembe* . . ." He broke off, coughing blood. Valentine's sword had pierced his lung.

"What about Miss Fang?" asked Tom.

Khora shook his head. He did not know. Hester was already stalking away into the searing heat of the hangars, ignoring the men who tried to call her back. Tom ran after her.

It was like running into an oven. He had an impression of a huge cavern, with smaller caverns opening off it, the hangars where the League's warships were housed. Valentine must have gone quickly from one ship to the next, placing phosphorus bombs. Now only their buckling ribs were visible in the white-hot heart of the blaze. "Hester!" shouted Tom, his voice lost in the roar of the flames, and saw her a little way ahead of him, hurrying down a narrow tunnel that led deeper into the Wall. *I'm not following her in there!* he thought. *If she wants to get herself trapped and roasted, that's her problem. . . .* But as he turned back toward the safety of the platform, the ammunition in the gondolas of the burning airships caught, and suddenly there were rockets and bullets flying everywhere, bursting against the stone walls and howling through the air around him. The tunnel was closer than the main entrance and he scrambled into it, whispering prayers to all the gods he could think of.

Fresh air was coming from somewhere in front of him, and he realized that the passage must lead right through the Wall to one of the gun emplacements on the western face. "Hester?" he shouted. Only echoes replied, muddled with the echoing roar of the fires in the hangar. He pressed on. At a fork in the tunnel lay a huddled shape — a young airman cut down by Valentine's sword. Tom breathed a sigh of relief that it was not Hester or Miss Fang, and then felt guilty, because the poor man was dead.

He studied the branching tunnel. Which way should he go? "Hester?" he shouted nervously. Echoes. A stray bullet from the hangar came whining past and struck sparks off the stonework by his head. Choosing quickly, he ducked down the right-hand passage.

There was another sound now, closer and sharper than the dull roar of the fires, a thin, birdlike sound of metal on metal. Tom hurried down a slippery flight of steps, saw light ahead, and ran toward it. He emerged into the cold and the fluttering snow on a broad platform where a rocket battery gazed out toward the west. Flames flapped and tore in an iron brazier, lighting the ancient battlements, the sprawled bodies of the rocket crew and the wild shimmer of swords as Valentine and Miss Fang battled each other back and forth across the scrabbled snow.

Tom crouched in the shadows at the tunnel's mouth, clutching his aching ribs and staring. Valentine was fighting magnificently. He had torn off his monk's robes to reveal a white shirt, black breeches and long black boots, and he parried and thrust and ducked gracefully under the aviatrix's blows — but Tom could see that he had met his match. Holding her long sword two-handed, Miss Fang drove him back toward the rocket battery and the bodies of the men he had killed, anticipating every blow he made, feinting and swinging, jumping into the air to avoid a low backstroke, until at last she smashed the sword from his hand. He went down on his knees to reach for it, but her blade was already at his throat and Tom saw a dark rill of blood start down to stain the collar of his shirt.

"Well done!" he said, and smiled the smile that Tom remembered from that night in the Gut, a kind, amused, utterly sincere smile. "Well done, Feng Hua!"

"Quiet!" she snapped. "This isn't a game. . . ."

Valentine laughed. "On the contrary, my dear Wind-Flower, it's the greatest game of all, and my team appears to be winning. Haven't you noticed that your Air-Fleet is on fire? You really should have tightened up your security arrangements. I suppose because the League has had things its own way for a thousand years, you think you can rest on your laurels. But the world is changing. . . ."

232

He's playing for time, thought Tom. But he could not see why. Cornered on this high platform, unarmed, with no chance of escape, what did Valentine hope to gain by taunting the aviatrix? He wondered if he should go forward and pick up the fallen sword and stand by Miss Fang until help arrived, but there was something so powerful and dangerous about Valentine, even in defeat, that he dared not show himself. He listened, hoping to catch the sounds of soldiers coming down the tunnel and wondering what had become of Hester. All he could hear was the distant clamor of gongs and fire bells from the far side of the Wall, and Valentine's flirtatious, half-mocking voice.

"You should come and work for London, my dear. After all, this time tomorrow the Shield-Wall will be rubble. You will need a new employer. Your League is finished. . . ."

And light burst down from above: the harsh beam of an airship's searchlight raking across the snow. The aviatrix reeled blindly backward, and Valentine leaped up, snatching his sword, pulling her hard against him as he drove it home. For a moment the two of them stumbled together like drunken dancers at the end of a party, close enough to Tom's hiding place for him to see the bright blade push out through the back of Miss Fang's neck and hear her desperate, choking whisper: "Hester Shaw will find you. She will find you and —" Then Valentine wrenched his sword free and let her fall, turning away, leaping up onto the battlements as the 13*th Floor Elevator* came looming down out of the searchlight's glare.

29

Going Home

The black airship had been drifting in silence, riding the wind to this high rendezvous while the defenders of Batmunkh Gompa were busy with fires and explosions. Now her engines burst into life, churning the drifting snowflakes and drowning out Tom's cry of horror.

Valentine walked out along the barrel of a rocket launcher as nimbly as an athlete on a bar and sprang, spread-eagling himself for an instant on the naked air before his hands found the rope ladder that Pewsey and Gench had lowered for him. Catching it, he swung himself up into the gondola.

Tom ran forward and was plunged into sudden darkness as the searchlight snapped off. Rockets from higher batteries came sparkling down to burst against the Elevator's thick hide. One shattered some glass in the gondola, but the black airship was already powering away from the Wall. The backwash from its propellers slammed into Tom's face as he knelt over Anna Fang, shaking her in the dim hope that she might wake.

"It's not fair!" he sobbed. "He waited till you were dazzled!

You beat him!" The aviatrix said nothing, but stared past him with a look of stupid surprise, her eyes as dull as dry pebbles.

Tom sat down beside her in the reddening snow and tried to think. He supposed he would have to leave Batmunkh Gompa now, get out fast before London came, but the very thought of moving on again made him weary. He was sick of being swept to and fro across the world by other people's plans. A thin, hot anger started rising in him as he thought about Valentine, flying home to a hero's welcome. Valentine was the cause of all this! It was Valentine who had ruined his life, and Hester's, and put an end to so many more. It was Valentine who had given the Guild of Engineers MEDUSA. Hester had been right; he should have let her kill him when she had the chance. . . .

There was a noise at the far end of the platform and he looked up and saw a black mass of arms and legs and coat hurriedly untangling itself, like a big spider fallen from the ceiling. It was Hester, who had taken the wrong turn as she raced after Valentine and come out in an observation bunker high above. Now here she was, having scrambled down thirty feet of snowy wall and dropped the final ten. Her eye rested for a moment on the fallen aviatrix, then she turned and went to the battlements and stared out at the dark and the dancing snow. "It should have been me," Tom heard her say. "At least I would have made sure I took him with me."

Tom watched her. He felt tight and sick and trembly from the grief and rage inside him, and knew that this was how Hester must feel, how she had always felt, ever since Valentine killed her parents. It was a terrible feeling, and he could think of only one way to cure it.

He groped under the collar of Anna's coat and found the key on its lanyard and wrenched it free. Then he stood up and went to where Hester was and put his arms around her. It was like hugging a statue, she was so stiff and tense, but he needed to hold on to something so he hugged her anyway. Guns were still firing overhead in the vain hope of hitting the 13th *Floor Elevator*. He put his face close to Hester's ear and shouted over the noise, "Let's go home!"

She looked around at that, puzzled and a little annoyed. "Have you gone funny?"

"Don't you see?" he shouted, laughing at the crazy idea that had just come creeping into his mind. "Someone's got to make him pay! You were right; I shouldn't have stopped you before, but I'm glad I did, because the Gut Police would have killed you and then we'd never have met. Now I can help you get to him, and help you get away afterward. We'll go back to London! Now! Together!"

"You *have* gone funny," said Hester, but she came with him anyway, helping him find a way back through the Shield-Wall while soldiers came running past them, frightened, soot-stained, and far too late, crying out in woe when they saw the bodies on the rocket-platform.

The night sky over Batmunkh Gompa was full of smoke and tatters of singed envelope fabric. Fires were still burning in the High Eyries, but already the roads in the valley were clogged with constellations of small lights, the lanterns of refugees, spilling away into the mountains like water bursting from a breached dam. With the death of the Air-Fleet the Shield-Wall was finished, and its people were fleeing as fast as their feet and mules and oxcarts and freight-balloons could take them.

Down at the mooring platform, ships were already lifting into the smoky sky and turning south. The Keralan girl, Sathya, was trying to rally some panic-stricken soldiers, sobbing, "Stay and hold the Wall! The Southern Air-Fleet will reinforce us! They can be here in less than a week!" But everyone knew that Batmunkh Gompa would be gone by then, and London would be pushing south toward the League's heartlands. "Stay and hold the Wall!" she begged, but the airships kept lifting past her, lifting past her.

The *Jenny Haniver* still hung at anchor, silent, dark. The key that Tom had taken from Anna Fang's body fitted snugly into the lock on the forward hatch, and soon he was standing on the flight deck, staring at the controls. There were far more of them than he remembered.

"Are you sure we can do this?" asked Hester softly.

"Of course," said Tom. He tried a few switches. The hatch sprang open again, the cabin lights came on, the coffee machine started making a noise like a polite dog clearing its throat, and a small inflatable dinghy dropped from the roof and knocked him over.

"Quite sure?" she asked, helping him up.

Tom nodded. "I used to build model airships when I was little, so I understand the principle. And Miss Fang showed me the controls when we were in the mountains. . . . I just wish she'd labeled everything in Anglish."

He thought for a moment, then hauled on another lever, and this time the engines throbbed into life. Out on the mooring platform people turned to stare, and some made the sign against evil; they had heard of Feng Hua's death and wondered if it was her restless ghost aboard the *Jenny Haniver*. But Sathya saw Tom and Hester standing at the controls and came running toward them.

Frightened that she would stop him taking off, Tom hunted for the lever that moved the engine pods. Bearings grated as they swiveled into takeoff position. He laughed, delighted at the way the airship responded to the touch of his hands on the controls, hearing the familiar creak and huff of the gas valves somewhere overhead and the clang of the mooring-clamps disengaging. People waved their arms and shouted, and Sathya pulled out a gun, but at the last moment Captain Khora came stumbling out onto the platform, supported by one of his crewmen, and gently took it from her. He looked up at Tom, raising a hand to wish him luck, and the surprising pinkness of his palm and fingertips was what stuck in Tom's mind as the airship swayed uncertainly up into the sky and climbed through the smoke from the High Eyries. He took one last look down at Batmunkh Gompa, then swung her out over the Shield-Wall and turned her nose toward the west.

He was going home.

30

A HERO'S WELCOME

The clouds that had shed their snow on Batmunkh Gompa blew west to fall as yet more rain on London, and it was raining still when the 13th *Floor Elevator* reached home, early the following afternoon. No crowds were waiting to welcome it. The sodden lawns of Circle Park were deserted, except for some workers from the Recycling Department who were cutting down the trees, but the Guild of Engineers had been warned of Valentine's return, and as the great airship came nosing down into the wet flare of the landing beacons they ran out onto the apron with the rain beating on their bald heads and the lights making splashy reflections on their coats.

Katherine watched from her bedroom window as the ground crew winched the airship down and the excited Engineers clustered closer. Now hatches were opening in the gondola; now Magnus Crome was going forward, with a servant holding a white rubber umbrella over him, and now, now Father was coming down the gangplank, easy to recognize even at this distance by his height and his confident stride and the way his all-weather cape filled and flapped in the rising breeze.

The sight of him gave Katherine a twisting feeling deep inside, as if her heart really was about to burst with grief and anger. She remembered how much she had been looking forward to being the first to greet him when he stepped back aboard the city. Now she was not sure that she could even bring herself to speak to him.

Through the wet glass she saw him talk to Crome, nodding, laughing. A surge of white coats hid him from her for a moment, and when she saw him again he had pulled himself away from the Lord Mayor and was hurrying across the soggy lawns toward Clio House, probably wondering why she hadn't been waiting for him at the quay.

She panicked for a moment and wanted to hide, but Dog was with her, and he gave her the strength she needed. She closed the tortoiseshell shutters and waited until she heard Father's feet on the stairs, Father's knock at the door.

"Kate?" came his muffled voice. "Kate, are you in there? I want to tell you all my adventures! I am fresh from the snows of Shan Guo, with all sorts of tales to bore you with! Kate? Are you all right?"

She opened the door just a crack. He stood on the landing outside, dripping with rain, his smile fading as he saw her tearful, sleep-starved face.

"Kate, it's all right! I'm back!"

"I know," she said. "And it's not all right. I wish you'd died in the mountains."

"What?"

"I know all about you," she told him. "I've worked out what you did to Hester Shaw."

She let him into the room and shut the door, calling sharply to Dog when he ran to greet him. It was dark with the shutters closed, but she saw Father look at the heap of books spilling from the corner table, then at her. There was a freshly dressed wound on his neck, blood on his shirt. She twined a finger in her tangled hair and tried hard not to start crying again.

Valentine sat down on the unmade bed. All the way from Batmunkh Gompa, Anna Fang's last promise had been echoing in the corners of his mind: *Hester Shaw will find you.* To have the same name thrown at him here, by Katherine, was like a knife in the heart.

"Oh, you needn't worry," said Katherine bitterly. "No one else knows. I learned the girl's name, you see. And Dr. Arkengarth told me how Pandora Shaw was murdered, and I'd already found out that she died seven years ago, around the time you got back from that expedition and the Lord Mayor was so pleased with you, so I just put it all together and . . ."

She shrugged. The trail had been easy to follow once she had all the clues. She picked up a book she had been reading and showed it to him. It was *Adventures on a Dead Continent*, his own account of his journey to America. She pointed to a face in a group photograph of the expedition — an aviatrix who stood beside him, smiling. "I didn't realize at first," she said, "because her name had changed. Did you kill her yourself? Or did you get Pewsey and Gench to do it?"

Valentine hung his head, angry, despairing, ashamed. A part of Katherine had been hoping against hope that she was wrong, that he would deny it and give her proof that he was not the

Shaws' killer, but when she saw his head go down she knew that he could not and it was true.

He said, "You must understand, Kate, I did it for you. . . ."

"For *me?*"

He looked up at last, but not at her. He stared at the wall near her elbow and said, "I wanted you to have everything. I wanted you to grow up as a lady, not as an Out-Country scavenger like I had been. I had to find something that Crome needed.

"Pandora was an old comrade, from the American trip, just as you say. And yes, she was with me when I found the plans and access codes to MEDUSA. We never imagined it would be possible to reconstruct the thing. Later Pandora and I went our separate ways; she was an Anti-Tractionist and she married some clodhopping farmer and settled down on a place called Oak Island. I didn't know she was still thinking about MEDUSA. She must have made another trip to America, alone this time, and found her way into another part of the same old underground complex, a part we'd missed on the first dig. That's where she found —"

"A computer brain," said Katherine impatiently. "The key to MEDUSA."

"Yes," murmured Valentine, astonished at how much she knew. "She sent me a letter, telling me she had it. She knew it was worthless without the plans and codes, you see, and those were in London. She thought we could sell it and share the proceeds. And I knew that if I could give Crome a prize like that it would make my fortune, and your future would be secure!"

"And so you killed her for it," said Katherine.

"She wouldn't agree to sell it to Crome," said her father. "She was an Anti-Tractionist, as I said. She wanted the League to have it. I *had* to kill her, Kate."

"But what about Hester?" said Katherine numbly. "Why did you have to hurt her?"

"I didn't mean to," he said miserably. "She must have woken up and heard something. She was a pretty child. She was about your age, and she looked so like you that she might have been your sister. Perhaps she *was* your sister. Pandora and I were very close at one time."

"My sister?" gasped Katherine. "Your own daughter!"

"When I looked up from her mother's body and saw her staring at me . . . ! I had to silence her. I struck wildly at her, and I made a mess of it. I thought she was dead, but I couldn't bring myself to make sure. She escaped, vanished in a boat. I thought she must have drowned, until she tried to stab me that night in the Gut."

"And Tom . . ." Katherine said. "He learned her name, and so you had to kill him, too, because if he'd mentioned her to the Historians the truth might have come out."

Valentine looked helplessly at her. "You don't understand, Kate. If people discovered who she is and what I have done, not even Crome would be able to protect me. I would be finished, and you would be dragged down with me."

"But Crome knows, doesn't he?" asked Katherine. "That's why you're so loyal. Loyal as a dog, so long as you get paid and get to pretend that foreign daughter of yours is a High London lady."

Rain, rain on the windows and the whole room quivering as

London dragged itself across the sodden earth. Dog lay with his head on his paws, his eyes darting from his mistress to Valentine and back. He had never seen them fight before, and he hated it.

"I used to think you were wonderful," said Katherine. "I used to think that you were the best, bravest, wisest person in the world. But you're not. You're not even very clever, are you? Didn't you realize what Crome would use the thing for?"

Valentine looked sharply at her. "Of course I did! This is a town eat town world, Kate. It's a shame Panzerstadt-Bayreuth had to be destroyed, of course, but the Shield-Wall has to be breached if London is to survive. We need a new hunting ground."

"But people live there!" wailed Katherine.

"Only Anti-Tractionists, Kate, and most of them will probably get away."

"They'll stop us. They've got airships. . . ."

"No." In spite of everything, Valentine smiled, proud of himself. "Why do you think Crome sent me east? The League's Northern Air-Fleet is in ashes. Tonight MEDUSA will blast us a passage through their famous Wall." He stood up and reached for her, smiling, as if this victory that he was delivering would put right everything he had done. "Crome tells me that firing is scheduled for nine o'clock. There's to be a reception at the Guildhall beforehand: wine, nibbles, and the dawn of a new era. Will you come with me, Kate? I'd like you to. . . ."

Her last hope had been that he had not known Crome's mad plan. Now even that was gone. "You fool!" she screamed. "Don't you understand what he's doing is wrong? You've got to stop him! You've got to get rid of his horrible machine!"

"But that would leave London defenseless, in the middle of the Hunting Ground," her father pointed out.

"So? We will have to carry on as we always have, chasing and eating, and if we meet a bigger city and get eaten ourselves . . . well, even that would be better than being murderers!"

She couldn't bear to be in that room with him another second. She ran, and he did not try to stop her, or even call her back, just stood there looking pale and stunned. She left the house and ran sobbing through the rain-swept park with Dog at her heels, until the whole of High London was between her and Father. I *must do something!* was all she could think. I *must stop* MEDUSA . . .

She hurried toward the elevator station, while the Goggle-screen loops began to blare the good news of Valentine's return all over London.

31

THE EAVESDROPPER

London gathered speed, racing toward the mountains. Semi-static towns that had hidden for years on these high steppes were startled out of their torpor by its coming and went lumbering away, leaving behind them green patches of farmland and, once, a whole static suburb. The city paid no heed to any of them. The whole of London knew the Lord Mayor's plan by now. In spite of the cold, people gathered on the forward observation decks and peered through telescopes toward Shan Guo, eager for their first glimpse of the legendary Wall.

"Soon!" they told each other.

"This very night!"

"A whole new hunting ground!"

Most people at the Museum were used to Katherine and Dog by now, and nobody paid very much attention as she hastened through the lower galleries with the white wolf trotting behind her. A few noticed the frantic look in her eyes and the tears on her face, but before they could ask her what was wrong or proffer a pocket handkerchief she had swept past, heading toward Mr. Nancarrow's office at a near run.

There she found a smell of turpentine and the lingering scent of the art Historian's pipe tobacco, but no Nancarrow and no Bevis Pod. She ran back out into the hallway, where a fat Third Class Apprentice was mopping the floors. "Mr. Nancarrow's in the storerooms, Miss," he told her sullenly. "He's got that funny new bloke with him."

The funny new bloke was helping Mr. Nancarrow drag a picture out of the storage racks when Katherine burst in. It was a huge, gilt-framed painting called "*Quirke Oversees the Rebuilding of London*," by Walmart Strange, and when Bevis dropped the end he was holding it made a crash that echoed and re-echoed through the dusty storeroom like a small explosion. "I say, Pod!" complained Nancarrow angrily, but then he, too, saw Katherine's face and quickly restrained himself. "You look as if you need a nice cup of tea, Miss Valentine," he muttered, hurrying away into the maze of racks.

"Kate?" Bevis Pod took a few uncertain steps toward her. "What's happened?" He wasn't used to comforting people; it was not the sort of thing an Apprentice Engineer was trained for. He held his arms out stiffly to touch her shoulders, and looked shocked when she flung herself against him. "Er . . ." he said, "there, there . . ."

"Bevis," she sniffled, "it's up to us now. We have to do something. Tonight."

"Tonight?" He frowned, struggling to keep up with her rapid, half-sobbed explanations. "But do you mean just us alone? I thought your father was going to help us. . . ."

"He's not my father anymore," said Katherine bitterly, and realized that it was true. She clung to Bevis as tightly as she could, as if he were a raft that could carry her safely across this mire of misery and guilt. "Father's Crome's man. That's why I've got to get rid of MEDUSA, do you see? I have to make amends for the things he's done. . . ."

Nancarrow came pottering back with two tin mugs of tea. "Um! Oh! Ah!" he mumbled, embarrassed at finding his two young friends in one another's arms. "I mean . . . yes. Paperwork. Must dash. Back in an hour or two. Carry on, Pod. . . ."

As he left, he almost fell over the fat Third Class Apprentice who had been mopping the passage just outside the storeroom door. "For Quirke's sake, Melliphant!" they heard him snap. "Can't you keep out of the way?"

But Herbert Melliphant could not keep out of the way. Ever since his demotion he had been looking for a handhold that would help him claw his way back up to First Class. This Pod person had caught his eye a few days ago — this stranger who seemed so friendly with the old Guildsmen; who went about with the Head Historian's daughter; who dressed as an apprentice but who didn't sleep with the others in the dormitory or join them for lessons. He had heard on the Goggle-screens that the Guild of Engineers were still hunting the people who had infiltrated their secret meeting, and he was starting to suspect that Dr. Vambrace might be very interested in Nancarrow's little helper. As soon as the old man was out of sight he put down his mop and pail and stepped back to the door.

" . . . the Anti-Traction League can't defend themselves," Katherine was saying. "That's what Father has been doing: spying out their cities and blowing up their Air-Fleet. That's why it's up to us."

"What about the Historians?" asked Bevis.

Katherine shrugged. "They're too scared to help us. But I can do it alone, I know I can. Father's invited me to the Lord Mayor's reception. I'm going to go. I'm going to find Father and tell him I've forgiven him, and we'll go to Crome's party like a happy little family; but while the others are all telling Crome how clever he's been and eating sausages on sticks I'll slip away and find MEDUSA and smash it. Do you think a hammer would do the trick? I know where Dr. Arkengarth keeps the keys to the caretaker's stores. There's bound to be a hammer in there. Or a crowbar. Would a crowbar be better?"

She laughed, and saw Bevis flinch at the mad, brittle sound. For a moment she feared that he was about to say something like "Calm down," or "It can't possibly work." She touched his face, his blushing ears, and felt the quick pulse beating in his throat and the muscles flexing as he swallowed.

"A bomb," he said.

"What?"

"MEDUSA must be huge — it probably fills half of St. Paul's. If you really want to smash it you need explosives." He looked excited and scared. "The cleaning stuff the Museum caretakers use has nitrogen in it, and if I mix it with some of Dr. Nancarrow's picture-restoring fluids and make a timer . . ."

"How do you know all this?" asked Katherine, shocked, because even she had not thought as far as bombs.

"Basic chemistry," said Bevis with a shrug. "I did a course, in the Learning Labs. . . ."

."Is that all they think about, your lot?" she whispered. "Making bombs and blowing things up?"

"No, no!" he replied. "But science is like that. You can use it to do whatever you want. Kate, if you really want to do this I'll make you a bomb you can put in a satchel. If you can get to MEDUSA, leave it near the computer brain and set the timer and run away. Half an hour later . . ."

Outside, Melliphant's ear flattened itself against the wood of the door like a pale slug.

❋

Faster and faster and faster. It is as if the Lord Mayor's eagerness has infected the very fabric of his city; the pistons in the engine rooms beat as eagerly as his heart, the wheels and tracks race like his thoughts, rushing toward the Wall and the next chapter in London's great story.

All afternoon Valentine has hunted for Katherine through the park, startling his friends from their suppers by suddenly looming up at the French windows, a dripping wraith in bloodstained clothes, demanding, *Is my daughter here? Have you seen her?* Now he strides to and fro across the drawing room at Clio House, his boots dribbling water onto the muddy carpet as he tries to walk the wet cold of the park out of his bones, the fear out of his mind.

At last he hears footsteps on the gravel drive, footsteps in the entrance hall, and Pewsey bursts in, looking as wet and miserable as his master. "I tracked her down, Chief! She's at the Museum. Been spending a lot of time there lately, according to old Creaber at the front desk. . . ."

"Take me there!" shouts Valentine.

"You sure, Chief?" Pewsey studies his own feet rather than

250

look at his master's feverish, tear-streaked face. "I think it might be better if you let her alone for a bit. She's safe at the Museum, ain't she, and I reckon she needs a chance to think things over. She'll come back in her own time."

Valentine slumps down in a chair, and the old aviator moves quietly around the room, lighting the lamps. Outside, the daylight is fading. "I've polished your sword, and laid out your best robes in the dressing room," says Pewsey gently. "It's the Lord Mayor's reception, sir, remember? Wouldn't do to miss it."

Valentine nods, staring at his hands, his long fingers. "Why did I go along with his schemes, all these years, Pewsey? Why did I give him MEDUSA?"

"I couldn't rightly say, sir. . . ."

He stands up with a sigh and heads for the dressing room. He wishes he had Kate's sharpness to know so easily what's right, what's wrong. He wishes he had the courage to stand up to Crome the way she wants him to, but it is too late for that, too late, too late.

❈

And Crome himself looks up from his dinner (a puree of vegetables and meat-substitute, with just the right amounts of proteins, carbohydrates, vitamins, et cetera), looks up at the shivering Apprentice Historian whom Vambrace has just thrust into his office and says, "So, Apprentice Melliphant, I gather you have something to tell us?"

CHUDLEIGH POMEROY
SEES IT THROUGH

She found that she could cope. Earlier she had wanted to curl up in a corner and die of grief, but now she was all right. It made her remember the way she had felt when her mother died; flattened by the great numb blow of it and faintly surprised at the way life kept going on. And at least this time she had Dog to help her, and Bevis.

"Kate, I need another bolt, like this one but longer. . . ."

She had come to think of Bevis Pod as a sweet, clumsy, rather useless person, someone who needed her to look after him, and she suspected that was how the Historians all thought of him as well. But that afternoon she had begun to understand that he was really much cleverer than her. She watched him work, hunched under a portable argon globe in a corner of the Transport gallery, carefully measuring out the right amounts of scrubbing powder and picture-cleaning fluid. Now he was building a timing mechanism out of lengths of copper picture wire and parts from the dashboard of a centuries-old bug, fitting it all into the satchel she had found for him.

"A bolt, Kate?"

"Oh, yes . . ." She ratched quickly through the pile of spare parts on the floor beside him and found what he wanted. Handed it to him. Checked her watch. It was eight o'clock. Soon she would have to go back to Clio House and fit a smile onto her face and say to Father, "I'm sorry I was so silly earlier — welcome home — please can I come with you to the Lord Mayor's party?"

"There," said Bevis, holding up the satchel. "It's done."

"It doesn't look like a bomb."

"That's the idea, silly! Look." He opened it up and showed her the package nestling inside, the red button that she had to push to arm it and the timing mechanism. "It won't make a very big bang," he admitted, "but if you can get it close enough to the computer-brain . . ."

"I'll find a way," she promised, taking it from him. "I'm Valentine's daughter. If anybody can get to MEDUSA, it's me." He looked rueful, she thought, and she wondered if he was thinking of all that wonderful old-world computing power, an Engineer's dream, about to be sacrificed. "I've got to do it," she said.

"I know. I wish I could come with you, though."

She hugged him, pressing her face against his face, her mouth against his mouth, feeling him shiver as his hands came up nervously to stroke and stroke her hair. Dog gave a soft growl, jealous perhaps, afraid that he was losing Katherine's love and would soon be abandoned, like the poor old soft toys on the shelves in her bedroom. "Oh, Bevis," she whispered, pulling back, trembling. "What's to become of us?"

The sound of distant shouting reached them, echoing up the

stairwell from the lower floors. It was too faint to make out any words, but they both knew at once that something must be wrong; nobody ever shouted in the Museum.

Dog's growl grew louder. He went running to the door and they both followed him, pushing their way quietly out onto the darkened landing. A cool breeze touched their faces as they peered over the handrail and down, the long spiral of stairs dwindling into darkness below with the bronze handrails gleaming. More shouts, then the bang and clatter of something dropped. Flashlight beams stabbed a lower landing and they heard the shouting voice quite clear: Chudleigh Pomeroy's, saying, "This is an outrage! An outrage! You are trespassing on the property of the Guild of Historians!"

The Engineer security team came up the stairs in a slapping rush of rubber-soled boots, flashlights sliding over their coats and their shiny, complicated guns. They slowed as they reached the top and saw Dog's eyes flashing, his ears flattening backward as he growled and growled and crouched to spring. Guns flicked toward him, and Katherine grabbed him by the collar and shouted, "He won't hurt you, he's just frightened. Don't shoot. . . ."

But they shot him anyway, the guns giving sharp little cracks and the impact of the bullets wrenching Dog away from her and slamming him back against the wall with a yelp; then silence, and the whispering sound of the big body falling. In the dancing flashlights the blood looked black. Katherine gasped for breath. Her arms and legs were shaking with a quick, helpless shudder that she couldn't stop. She could not have moved if she had wanted to, but just in case, a sharp voice barked, "Stay where you are, Miss Valentine."

"Dog . . ." she managed to whine.

"Stay where you are. The brute is dead."

Dr. Vambrace came up the stairs through the thin, shifting smoke. "You, too, Pod," he added, seeing the boy make a twitching move toward the body. He stood on the top step and smiled at them. "We've been looking everywhere for you, Apprentice. I hope you're ashamed of yourself. Give me that satchel."

Bevis held it out and the tall Engineer snatched it from him and opened it. "Just as Melliphant warned us: a bomb."

Two of his men stepped forward and hauled the prisoners after him as he turned and started down the stairs. "No!" wailed Katherine, struggling to keep hold of Bevis's hand as they were dragged apart. "No!" Her voice bounced shrilly back at her from the ceiling and went echoing away down the stairwell, and she thought it sounded frail and helpless, like a child having a tantrum, a child caught playing some stupid, naughty trick and protesting at its punishment. She kicked at the shins of the man who held her, but he was a big man, and booted, and didn't even wince. "Where are you taking us?"

"You are coming with me to Top Tier, Miss Valentine," said Vambrace. "You will be quite the talking point of the Lord Mayor's little party. As for your sweetheart here, he'll be taken to the Deep Gut." He grinned at the little noise Bevis made, a helpless gulped-back squeak of fear. "Oh, yes, Apprentice Pod, some very interesting experiences await you in the Deep Gut."

"It wasn't his fault!" Katherine protested. She could feel things unraveling, her foolish plan running out of control and lashing backward to entrap her and Bevis and poor Dog. "I *made* him help me!" she shrieked. "It's nothing to do with Bevis!" But Vambrace had already turned away, and her captor clamped a chemical-tasting hand across her mouth to stop her noise.

❋

Valentine's bug pulls up outside the Guildhall, where the bugs of most of the Guild heads are already parked. Gench gets out and holds the lid open for his master, then fusses over him like a mother sending her child off to school, brushing his hair off his face and straightening the collar of his best black robe, buffing the hilt of his sword.

Valentine looks absently up at the sky. High, feathery clouds, lit by the fast-sinking sun. The wind is still blowing from the east, and it brings a smell of snow that cuts through his thoughts of Katherine for a moment, making him think again of Shan Guo. "*Hester Shaw will find you*," the Wind-Flower had whispered, dying. But how could she have known about Hester? She could not have met the girl, could she? Could she? Is Hester still alive? Has she made her way somehow to Batmunkh Gompa? And is she waiting in those mountains now, ready to climb back aboard London and try again to kill him — or, worse, to harm his daughter?

Pushing Gench's big hands away, he says, "If you don't mind missing the party, boys, it might be worth taking the 13th *Floor Elevator* up for a spin tonight. Just in case those poor brave fools from the League try anything."

"Right you are, Chief!" The two old airmen have not been looking forward to the Lord Mayor's reception — all that finger food and posh chat. Nothing could cheer them up better than the prospect of a good fight. Gench climbs in next to Pewsey and the bug veers away, startling Engineers and Beefeaters out of its path. Valentine straightens his own tie and walks quickly up the steps into the Guildhall.

❀

The Engineers marched their prisoners through the lower galleries of the Museum to the Main Hall. There was nobody around. Katherine had never seen the Museum as empty as this. Where were the Historians? She knew they couldn't help her, but she wanted to see them, to know that somebody knew what had become of her. She kept listening for the pattering feet of Dog on the floor behind her, and being surprised when she couldn't hear them, and then remembering. Bevis was marching next to her, but he wouldn't look at her, just stared straight ahead as if he could already see the chambers of the Deep Gut and the things that would happen to him there.

Then, at the top of the steps that led down to the main entrance, the Engineers halted.

Down in the foyer, their backs to the big glass doors, the Historians were waiting. While Vambrace's men were busy upstairs they had raided the display cases in the Weapons & Warfare gallery, arming themselves with ancient pikes and muskets, rusty swords and tin helmets. Some had strapped breastplates over their black robes, and others carried shields. They looked like a chorus of brigands in an amateur pantomime.

"What is the meaning of this?" barked Dr. Vambrace.

Chudleigh Pomeroy stepped forward, holding a blunderbuss with a brass muzzle as broad as a tuba's. Katherine started to realize that other Historians were watching from the shadows at the edges of the hall, lurking behind display cases, pointing steam-powered rifles through the articulated ribs of dinosaurs.

"Gentlemen," said Pomeroy nervously, "you are on the property of the Guild of Historians. I suggest that you unhand those young people immediately."

"Immediately!" agreed Dr. Karuna, training her dusty musket on the red wheel between Vambrace's eyebrows.

The Engineer began to laugh. "You old fools! Do you think you can defy us? Your Guild will be disbanded because of what you've done here today. Your silly trifles and trinkets will be fed to the furnaces, and your bodies will be broken on engines of pain in the Deep Gut. We'll make you history, since history is all you care about! We are the Guild of Engineers! We are the future!"

There was a heartbeat pause, near-silent, just the echo of Vambrace's voice hanging on the musty air and the faint sounds of men reaching for guns and arthritic fingers tightening on ancient triggers. Then the foyer vanished into smoke and stabbing darts of fire, and the noise bounced from the high-domed roof and came slamming down again, a ragged crackle split by the deep boom of Pomeroy's blunderbuss and the shrieking roar of an old cannon concealed in a niche behind the ticket office, which went off with a great jet of flame as Dr. Nancarrow set his lighter to the touchhole. Katherine saw Vambrace and the two men next to him swiped aside; Dr. Arkengarth fall backward with his arms windmilling; felt the man who held her jerk and stumble and the thick slap as a musket ball went through his rubber coat.

He fell away from her, and she dropped to her knees, wondering where to hide. Nothing remained of Vambrace but his smoldering boots, which would have been cartoony and almost funny except that his feet were still inside them. Half his men were down, but the rest were rallying, and they had better weapons than the Historians. They sprayed the foyer with gunfire, striking sparks from the marble floor and flinging splinters of dinosaur bone high into the air. Display cases came apart in bright cataracts of powdered glass, and the Historians who were cowering behind them went scrambling back to other hiding places, or fell among the fallen exhibits and lay still. Above them, argon globes smashed and guttered until the hall was dark, stuttering like cine-film in the migraine flicker of gun light, and the Engineers pushed forward through it toward the doors.

Behind them, forgotten, Bevis Pod reached for an abandoned gun and swung it up, his long hands feeling their way across the shiny metal for catches and triggers. Katherine watched him. The air around her was thick with wailing shot and whirling chips of marble and moaning Battle Frisbees, but she could not tear her eyes or her mind away from Bevis long enough to think about finding cover. She watched him unfold the gun's spindly armrest and wedge it into the crook of his elbow, and saw the small blue holes it made in the backs of the Engineers' coats. They flung up their arms and dropped their guns and spun around and fell, and Bevis Pod watched them through the bucking sights with a calm, serious look, not her gentle Bevis anymore but someone who could kill quite coldly, as if the Engineer in him really did have no regard for human life, or maybe he had just seen so much death in the Deep Gut that he thought it was a little thing and did not mind dealing it out.

And when he stopped shooting it was very quiet, just the rubbery lisp of the corpses settling and a quick bony rattle that

Katherine slowly recognized as the sound of her own teeth chattering.

From the corners of the hall Historians came creeping. There were more of them than Katherine had feared. In the flicker of battle she had thought she saw all of them shot, but, although some were wounded, the only ones dead were a man called Weymouth, whom she had never spoken to, and Dr. Arkengarth. The old curator of ceramics lay near the door, looking indignant, as if death was a silly modern fad that he rather disapproved of.

Bevis Pod knelt staring at the gun in his hands, and his hands were shaking, and blue smoke unraveled from the mouth of the gun and drifted up in scrolls and curlicues toward the roof.

Pomeroy came stumping up the stairs. His wig had been blown off and he was nursing a wound on his arm where a splinter of bone had cut him. "Look at that!" he said. "I must be the first person to be harmed by a dinosaur for millions of years!" He blinked at Katherine and Bevis, then at the fallen Engineers. None of them were laughing at his little joke. "Well!" he said. "Well, eh? Gosh! We showed them! As soon as I told the others what was going on we all agreed it wouldn't do. Well, most of us did. The rest are locked in the canteen, along with any apprentices we thought might support Crome's men. You should have seen us, Kate! 'We won't let them take Miss Valentine!' we all said, and we didn't. It goes to show, you know. An Engineer is no match for a Historian with his dander up!"

"Or *her* dander, CP!" chirped Moira Plym, hurrying up the steps to stand beside him. "Oh, that'll teach them to fiddle with my furniture, all right! That'll show them what happens to —"

The visor of the helmet she was wearing snapped shut, muffling the rest.

Katherine found the fallen satchel, lying in the muck and blood on the stairs. It seemed to be undamaged, except for some unpleasant stains. "I've got to go to Top Tier. Stop MEDUSA. It's the only way. I'll go to the elevator station and . . ."

"No!" Clytie Potts came bounding up the steps from the front entrance. "A couple of Engineers who were stationed outside got away," she said. "They'll have raised the alarm. There'll be a guard on the elevators, and more security men here at any minute. Stalkers, too, probably." She met Pomeroy's worried gaze and dipped her head as if it was all her fault. "Sorry, CP."

"That's all right, Miss Potts." Pomeroy slapped her kindly on the shoulder, almost knocking her over. "Don't worry, Katherine. We'll keep the devils busy here, and you can sneak up to Top Tier by the Cat's Creep."

"What's that?" asked Katherine.

"It's the sort of thing Historians know about and everybody else has forgotten," said Pomeroy, beaming. "An old stairway, left over from the first days of London when the elevator system couldn't always be relied on. It goes up from Tier Three to Top Tier, passing through the Museum on the way. Are you ready to travel?"

She wasn't, but she nodded.

"I'm going with her," said Bevis.

"No!"

"It's all right, Kate. I want to." He was turning dead Engineers over, looking for a coat without too many holes in it. When he

261

found one he began to fumble with the rubber buttons. "If the Engineers see you walking about alone up there they'll guess what happened," he explained. "But if I'm with you, they'll think you're a prisoner."

"He's right, Kate," said Pomeroy, nodding, as Clytie Potts helped the young Engineer into the coat and wiped away the worst of the blood with the hem of her robe. He checked his watch. "Eight-thirty. MEDUSA goes off at nine, according to the Goggle-screens. That should give you plenty of time to do whatever you're planning to do. But we'd better start you on your way, before those Engineers get back with reinforcements."

33

WINE AND NIBBLES AND THE DAWN OF A NEW ERA

The *Jenny Haniver* was filled with memories of Anna Fang: the mark of her mouth on a dirty mug, the print of her body on the unmade bunk, a half-read book on the flight deck, marked with a ribbon at page 205. In one of the lockers Hester found a chest full of money — not just bronze coins but silver taels and golden sovereigns, more money than she or Tom had ever seen in their lives.

"She was rich!" she whispered.

Tom turned around in the pilot's seat and stared at the money. All through their long flight from Shan Guo he had not thought twice about taking the airship; he felt as if they were just borrowing her to finish a job that Miss Fang would have wanted done. Now, watching Hester lift the tinkling handfuls of coin, he felt like a thief.

"Well," said Hester, snapping the treasure chest shut, "it's no use to her where she's gone. And no use to us, since I expect we'll soon be joining her there." She glanced up at him. "Unless you've changed your mind?"

He shook his head, although the truth was that the anger he had felt earlier had drained away during his struggles to master the airship and steer it westward through the fickle mountain weather. He was starting to feel afraid, and starting to remember Katherine and wonder what would become of her when her father was dead. But he still wanted to make Valentine pay for all the misery he had caused. He started scanning the radio frequencies for London's homing beacon while Hester hunted through the lockers until she found what she needed: a heavy black pistol and a long, thin-bladed knife.

❀

For one night only, London's great council chamber has been decked out with lights and banners and turned into a party venue. The heads of the greater and lesser Guilds mingle happily among the green leather benches and sit on the speaker's dais, chattering excitedly about the new hunting ground, glancing at their watches from time to time as the hour for firing MEDUSA draws closer. Apprentice Engineers tack to and fro among the revelers, handing out experimental snacks prepared by Supervisor Nimmo's department. The snacks are brown and taste rather peculiar, but at least they are cut into perfectly geometrical shapes.

Valentine pushes his way through the crowd until he finds Crome and his aides, a wedge of white rubber surrounded by the tall black shapes of Stalker security guards. He wants to ask the Lord Mayor what became of the agent he sent after Hester Shaw. He wades toward them, elbowing well-upholstered Councillors aside and catching quick snatches of their conversation: "There's Valentine, look, back from Shan Guo!"

"Blew up the League's whole Air-Fleet, so I heard!"

"What charming snacks!"

"Valentine!" cries the Lord Mayor when the explorer finally reaches him. "Just the man we've been waiting for!"

He sounds almost jolly. Beside him stand the geniuses who have made MEDUSA work again: Dr. Chandra, Dr. Chubb, and Dr. Wismer Splay, along with Dr. Twix, who simpers and bobs a curtsy, congratulating Valentine on his trip to Shan Guo. Behind her the black-clad guards stand still as statues, and Valentine nods at them. "I see you've been making good use of the old Stalker parts I brought you, Crome. . . ."

"Indeed," agrees the Lord Mayor with a chilly smile. "A whole new race of Resurrected Men. They will be our servants and our soldiers in the new world that we are about to build. Some are in action even as we speak, down at the Museum."

"The Museum?"

"Yes." Crome watches him slyly, gauging his reactions. "Some of your Historians are traitors, Valentine. Armed traitors."

"You mean there is fighting? But Kate's there! I must go to her!"

"Impossible," the Lord Mayor snaps, gripping his arm as he turns to leave. "Tier Two is out of bounds. The Museum is surrounded by Stalkers and security teams. But don't worry. They have strict instructions not to harm your daughter. She will be brought up to join us as soon as possible. I particularly want her to watch MEDUSA in action. And I want you here, too, Valentine. Stay."

Valentine stares at him, past the frozen faces of the other partygoers, in the sudden silence.

"Where does your real loyalty lie, I wonder," muses Crome. "With London, or with your daughter? Stay."

"Stay." As if he's a dog. Valentine's hand curls for a moment on his sword hilt but he knows he will not draw it. The truth is that he is afraid, and all his adventures and expeditions have only been attempts to hide himself from this truth: He is a coward.

He stretches a smile across his trembling face, and bows.

"Your obedient servant, Lord Mayor."

❇

There was a door in the wall near Natural History, a door that Katherine must have passed hundreds of times without even seeing it. Now, as Pomeroy unlocked it and heaved it open, they heard the strange, echoing moan of wind in a long shaft, mingled with the rumble of the city's engines. He handed Bevis the key and a flashlight. "Good luck, Mr. Pod. Kate, good luck. . . ."

From somewhere behind him came a great dull boom that set the glass rattling in the display cases. "They're here," said Pomeroy. "I'm needed at my post. . . ."

"Come with us!" Katherine begged him. "You'll be safer on Top Tier, among the crowds."

"This is my Museum, Miss Valentine," he reminded her, "and this is where I'll stay. I'd only get in your way up there."

She hugged him, pressing her face into his robe and savoring its smell of mothballs and pipe tobacco. "Your poor Museum!"

Pomeroy shrugged. "I don't think the Engineers would have let us keep hold of our relics much longer. At least this way we'll go down fighting."

"And you might win. . . ."

"Oh yes." The old Historian gave a rueful chuckle. "We used to thrash them regularly in the inter-guild soccer cup, you know. Of course, they didn't have machine guns and Stalkers to help them." He lifted her face and looked into her eyes, very serious. "Stop them, Katherine. Stick a spanner in the works."

"I'll try," she promised.

"We'll meet again soon," said Pomeroy firmly, hefting his blunderbuss as he turned away. "You've got your father's gift, Kate: People follow you. Look at the way you stirred us up!"

They heard the cannon roar again as he closed the door on them, and then the clatter of small arms, closer now and tangled with faint screams.

❈

"There!" said Tom.

They were flying high through thin drifts of clouds, and he was looking down at London, far ahead.

"There!"

It was bigger than he remembered, and much uglier. Strange, how when he lived there he had believed everything the Goggle-screens told him about the city's elegant lines, its perfect beauty. Now he saw that it was ugly; no better than any other town, just bigger: a storm front of smoke and belching chimneys, a wave of darkness rolling toward the mountains with the white villas of High London surfing on its crest like some delicate ship. It didn't look like home.

"There . . ." he said again.

"I see it," said Hester, beside him. "Something's going on on Top Tier. It's lit up like a fairground. Tom, that's where Valentine will be! They must be getting ready to use MEDUSA!"

Tom nodded, feeling guilty at the mention of MEDUSA. He knew that if Miss Fang were here she would be coming up with a plan to stop the Ancient weapon, but he did not see what he could do about it. It was too big, too terrible, too hard to think about. Better to concentrate on what mattered to him and Hester, and let the rest of the world look after itself.

"He's down there," whispered the girl. "I can feel him."

Tom didn't want to go too close, in case the Lord Mayor had set men to watch the skies, or sent up a screen of spotter-ships. He tugged on the controls and felt the big, slow movement as the airship responded. She rose, and London faded to a smudge of speeding light beneath the clouds as he steered her southward and began to circle around.

❀

They climbed out of darkness into darkness, Bevis Pod's flashlight flittering on stair after identical metal stair. Their big shadows slid up the walls of the shaft. They didn't speak much, but each listened to the other's steady breathing, glad of the company. Katherine kept looking back, expecting to see Dog at her heels.

"Five hundred steps," whispered Bevis, stopping on a narrow landing and shining his flashlight upward. The stairs spiraled up forever. "This must be Tier One. Halfway."

Katherine nodded, too out of breath to speak, too on edge to rest. Above them the Lord Mayor's reception must be in full swing. She climbed on, her knees growing stiff, each intake of breath a cold hard ache in the back of her throat, the too-heavy satchel banging against her hip.

Through the windows of the airship Hester could see the Out-Country streaming past, only a hundred or so feet below, scarred with the same ruler-straight trenches that she and Tom had stumbled along on the days after they first met. And there was London, red taillights in the darkness, dimming as Tom brought the airship up into the thick poison-fog of the city's exhaust. He was good at this, she realized, and thought what a pity it was that his plan was not going to work.

The radio crackled into life: London Docks and Harbor Board, demanding their identity codes.

Tom looked back at her, scared, but she knew how to handle this. She went to the radio and flipped the "transmit" switch up and down quickly, garbling her message as if the communications system was shot. "London Airship GE47," she said, remembering the code name that had come crackling over the inn's loudspeakers in Airhaven all those weeks before. "We're taking Shrike back to the Engineerium."

The radio said something, but she snapped it off. Black smog pressed against the windows, and water droplets condensed on the glass and went quivering off this way and that, leaving wriggly trails.

"I'll circle the city for twenty minutes and then come in and pick you up," Tom was saying. "That should give you time to find Valentine and . . ."

"I'll be dead in twenty minutes, Tom," she said. "Just get yourself safe away. Forget about me."

"I'll circle back. . . ."

"I'll be dead."

"I'll circle back anyway. . . ."

"There's no point, Tom."

"I'll circle back and pick you up."

She looked at him and saw tears shining in his eyes. He was crying. He was crying for her, because she was going into danger and he would not see her again, and she thought it was strange that he cared about her that much, and very sweet. She said, "Tom, I wish . . ." and, "Tom, if I . . ." and other little broken bits of sentences that petered out in silence, because she didn't even know herself what she was trying to say, only that she wanted him to know that he was the best thing that had happened to her.

A light loomed out of the swirling dark, then another. They were rising past Tier Three, and very close. Tier Two slid by, with people staring up from an observation deck, and then Circle Park with lanterns strung between the last remaining trees. Tom fumbled with the controls and the *Jenny* went powering forward, low over the rooftops of Knightsbridge and up toward the aft edge of Top Tier. He glanced quickly at Hester. She wanted to hug him, kiss him, something, but there was no time now, and she just gasped, "Tom, don't get yourself killed," slammed the hatch controls to "open," and ran to it and jumped as the airship swung in a shuddery arc over the rim of Top Tier.

She hit the deck-plate hard and rolled over and over. The *Jenny Haniver* was pulling away fast, lit by the sparkling trails of rockets from an air-defense battery on the Engineerium. The rockets missed, darkness swallowed the airship, and she was alone, scrambling into the shadows.

"A single airship, Lord Mayor." It is a nervous-looking Engineer, a shell-like radio clipped to his ear. "It has pulled clear, but we believe it may have landed a boarding party."

"Anti-Tractionists on Top Tier?" The Lord Mayor nods, as if this is the sort of little problem that crops up every day. "Well, well. Dr. Twix, I think this might be a good opportunity to test your new models."

"Oh, goody!" trills the woman, dropping a plate of canapés in her excitement. "Come along, my chicks! Come along!"

Her Stalkers turn with a single movement and form up behind her, striding through thrilled partygoers to the exits.

"Bring me the boarders alive!" Crome calls after her. "It would be a pity if they missed the big event."

34

IDEA FOR A FIREWORKS DISPLAY

Tom wiped at his eyes with the heel of one hand and concentrated on his flying, steering the *Jenny* away from London and up. He wasn't frightened now. It felt good to be doing something at last, and good to be in charge of this huge, wonderful machine. He turned her eastward, pointing her nose toward the last faint gleam of day on the summit of Zhan Shan. He would circle for twenty minutes. It felt as if half that time had passed already, but when he checked the chronometers he saw that it was less than two minutes since Hester jumped down into London and —

A rushing, brilliant thing slammed into the gondola, and the blast plucked him out of his seat. He clung to a stanchion and saw papers and instrument panels and sputtering lengths of cable and the shrine with its photographs and ribbons and Miss Fang's half-read book all rushing out through a jagged hole in the fuselage, tumbling into the sky like ungainly birds. The big windows shattered and the air turned sharp and shimmery with flying glass.

He craned his neck, peering up through the empty windows,

trying to see if the envelope was burning. There were no flames, but overhead a great dark shape slid past, moonlight slithering along its armored envelope. It was the 13th Floor Elevator, pulling past the Jenny and performing a lazy victory-roll far over the foothills of Shan Guo before it came sweeping back to finish him.

✳

Magnus Crome watches his guests crowd out into the square, gazing up at the glare and flicker of the battle taking place above the clouds. He checks his wristwatch. "Dr. Chandra, Dr. Chubb, Dr. Splay; it is time to deploy MEDUSA. Valentine, come with us. I'm sure you are keen to see what we've made of your machine."

"Crome," says the explorer, blocking his path, "there is something I must say. . . ."

The Lord Mayor raises an eyebrow, intrigued.

Valentine hesitates. He has been planning this speech all evening, knowing that it is what Katherine would want him to say. Now, faced with the Lord Mayor's arctic eyes, he falters, stammering a moment. "Is it worth it, Crome?" he says at last. "Destroying the Shield-Wall will not destroy the League. There will be other strongholds to defeat, hundreds of fortresses, thousands of lives. Is it really worth so much, your new hunting ground?"

There is a ripple of amazement among the bystanders. Crome says calmly, "You have left it rather late to have doubts, Valentine. You worry too much. Dr. Twix can build whole armies of Stalkers, more than enough to crush any resistance from Anti-Tractionist savages."

He starts to push past, but Valentine is in front of him again. "Think, Lord Mayor. How long will a new hunting ground

273

support us? A thousand years? Two thousand? One day there will be no more prey left anywhere, and London will have to stop moving. Perhaps we should accept it; stop now, before any more innocent people are killed; take what you have learned from MEDUSA and use it for peaceful purposes. . . ."

Crome smiles. "Do you really think I am so shortsighted?" he asks. "The Guild of Engineers plans further ahead than you suspect. London will never stop moving. Movement is life. When we have devoured the last wandering city and demolished the last static settlement we will begin digging. We will build great engines, powered by the heat of the earth's core, and steer our planet from its orbit. We will devour Mars, Venus, and the asteroids. We shall devour the sun itself, and then sail on across the gulf of space. A million years from now our city will still be traveling, no longer hunting towns to eat, but whole new worlds!"

Valentine follows him to the door and out across the square toward St. Paul's. *Katherine is right*, he keeps thinking. *He's as mad as a spoon! Why didn't I put a stop to his schemes when I had the chance?* Above the clouds, the rockets flare and bang, and the light of an exploding airship washes across the upturned faces of the crowd, who murmur, "Oooooooooh!"

❋

And Hester Shaw crouched at the Tier's edge as the Resurrected Men stalked by, green eyes sweeping the walls and deckplates, steel claws unsheathed and twitching.

❋

The Cat's Creep ended in a small circular chamber with stenciled numbers on the sweaty walls and a single metal door. Bevis slipped the key into the lock, and Katherine heard it turn. A crack of light appeared around the door's edge, and she heard voices outside, a long, tremulous, "Ooooh!"

"We're in an alley off Paternoster Square," Bevis said. "I wonder why they sound so excited?"

Katherine pulled out her watch and held it in the thin sliver of light from the door. "Ten to nine," she said. "They're waiting for MEDUSA."

He hugged her one last time and whispered quickly, shyly, "I love you!" Then he pushed her past him through the door and stepped out after her, trying to look like her captor, not her friend, and wondering if any other Engineer had ever said what he had just said, or felt the way he felt when he was with Katherine.

❋

Tom scrambled through the debris in the listing wreck of the *Jenny's* gondola. The lights were out and blood was streaming into his eyes from a cut on his forehead, blinding him. The pain of his broken ribs washed through him in sick, giddy waves and all he wanted to do was lie down and close his eyes and rest, but he knew he mustn't. He fumbled for the rocket controls, praying to all the gods he had ever heard of that they had not been blown away. And sure enough, at the flick of the right switch a viewing scope rose out of the main instrument panel, and he wiped his eyes and saw the dim upside-down ghost of the 13th *Floor Elevator* framed in the crosshairs, growing bigger every minute.

He heaved as hard as he could on the firing controls, and felt the deck shift under him as the rockets went shrieking out of their nests beneath the gondola. Dazzling light blossomed as they hit their target, but when he blinked the bright afterimages away and peered out the black airship was still there, and he realized that he had barely dented the great armored envelope, and that he was going to die.

But he had bought himself a few more moments, at least, for the *Elevator's* starboard rocket projectors were damaged and she was pulling past him and turning to bring her port array to bear. He tried to calm himself. He tried to think of Katherine, so that the memory of her would be what he took down with him to the Sunless Country, but it was a long time since he had dreamed of her, and he couldn't really remember what she looked like anymore. The only face that he could call to mind was Hester's, and so he thought of her and the things that they had gone through together, and how it had felt to hold her on the Shield-Wall last night, the smell of her hair and the warmth of her stiff, bony body through the ragged coat.

And from some corner of his memory came the echo of the League rockets that had battered at the 13th *Floor Elevator* as she banked away from Batmunkh Gompa, the thick crump of the explosions and the small, bright, prickling noise of broken glass.

Her envelope was armored, but the windows could be broken.

He lurched back to the rocket controls and retargeted them so that the crosshairs on the little screen were centered not on the *Elevator's* looming gasbags, but on her windows. The gauge beside the viewscope told him he had three rockets left, and he fired them all together, the shattered gondola shivering and groaning as they sprang away toward their target.

For a fraction of a second he saw Pewsey and Gench on their flight deck, staring at him, faces wide with silent terror. Then they vanished into brightness as the rockets tore in through their viewing windows and their gondola filled with fire. A geyser of flame went tearing up the companion-ladders between the gasbags and blew out the top of the envelope. By the time Tom could see again the huge wreck was veering away from him, fire in her ruined gondola and the hatches of her hold, fire flapping from her steering vanes, fire unraveling from shattered engine-pods, fire lapping inside her envelope until it looked like a vast Chinese lantern tumbling down toward the lights of London.

❋

Katherine stepped out of the alley's mouth into a running crowd, people all around her looking up, some still clutching drinks and nibbles, their eyes and mouths wide open. She looked at St. Paul's. The dome had not yet opened, so it couldn't be that they were staring at. And what was this light, this swelling orange glow that outshone the argon lamps and made the shadows dance?

At that moment the blazing wreckage of an airship came barreling out of the sky and crashed against the façade of the Engineerium in a storm of fire and glass and outflung scythes of blackened metal. A whole engine broke free of the wreck and came cartwheeling across the square toward her, red-hot and spraying blazing fuel. Bevis pushed her aside and down. She saw him standing over her, his mouth open, shouting something, and saw a blue eye on the blistered engine cowling as it tore him away, a whirl of limbs, a flap of a torn white coat, his scream lost in the bellow of twisting metal as the wreckage smashed against the Top Tier elevator station.

A blue eye on the cowling. She knew it should mean something, but she could not think what.

She stood up slowly, shaking. There were small fires on the deck all around her, and one great fire in the Engineerium that cast Hallowe'en light across the whole tier. She stumbled to where the blazing engine lay, its huge propeller blades jutting out of the deck-plate like megaliths. Raising her hand to shield her face against the belching heat, she looked for Bevis.

He was lying broken in a steep angle of the debris, twisted in such impossible ways that Katherine knew at once there was no point even calling out his name. The flames were rising, making his coat bubble and drip like melting cheese, heat pressing against her face, turning her tears to puffs of steam, driving her backward over wreckage and bodies and pieces of bodies.

"Miss Katherine?"

A blue eye on the engine cowling. She could still see the outline, the paint peeling under the tongues of the fire. Father's ship.

"Miss Katherine?"

She turned and found one of the men from the elevator station standing with her, trying to be kind. He took her by the arm and led her gently away, gesturing toward the main part of the wreck, the scorching firestorm in the Engineerium. "He wasn't in it, Miss."

She stared at his smile. She didn't understand. Of course he had been in it! She had seen him there, his dead, gaping face and the flames rising around him. Bevis, whom she had led here, who had loved her. What was there to smile about?

But the man kept smiling. "He wasn't aboard, Miss. Your dad, I mean. I saw him not five minutes ago, going into St. Paul's with the Lord Mayor."

She felt the sinister weight of the satchel still hanging from her shoulder, and remembered that she had a job to do.

"Come on, Miss," said the man. "You've had a nasty shock. Come and have a sit-down and a nice cup of tea. . . ."

"No," she said. "I have to find my father."

She left him there and turned away, stumbling across the square, through panicked crowds in smoke-stained robes and party frocks, through the long, shivering bray of sirens to St. Paul's.

❋

Hester was darting toward the Guildhall when the explosion lifted her off her feet and flung her out of the shadows and into the harsh spill of light from the blazing Engineerium. She rolled over and over on the quaking deck-plate, stunned, her pistol skittering away, her veil torn off. There was a moment of silence, then noises came crowding in: screams, sirens. She shuffled through her memories of the moments before the blast, trying to put them in some sort of order. That light above the rooftops, that burning thing sliding down the sky, had been an airship. The *Jenny Haniver*. "Tom," she said, whispering his name to the hot pavement, and felt smaller and more alone than ever before.

She pushed herself up on all fours. Nearby, one of the new Stalkers had been caught by the blast and cut in half, and its legs were stamping aimlessly about and bumping into things. The shawl that Tom had given her blew past. She caught it, knotted it around her neck, and turned to look for the fallen gun, only to find another squad of Stalkers, quite unharmed, closing in upon

279

her from behind. Their claws were fire-colored slashes in the darkness, and firelight lit their long, dead faces, and she realized with a hollow stab of disappointment that this was the end of her.

And above the black, silhouetted rooftops of the Guildhall, beyond the smoke and the dancing sparks, the dome of St. Paul's was starting to open.

35

THE CATHEDRAL

The *Jenny Haniver's* shattered gondola moaned like a flute as the west wind blew through it, carrying it swiftly away from London.

Tom slumped exhausted at the controls, crumbs of broken glass clinging like grit to his face and hands. He tried to ignore the wild spinning of the pressure gauges as hydrogen leaked from the damaged envelope. He tried not to think about Pewsey and Gench, burning inside their burning gondola, but every time he closed his eyes he saw their screaming faces, as if the black zeroes of their open mouths were etched forever onto his eyeballs.

When he raised his head he saw London, far to the east. Something was happening to the cathedral, and torrents of pink and green fire were gushing from the Engineerium. Slowly he started to understand what had happened. It was his fault! People must be dead down there, not just Pewsey and Gench but lots of people, and if he had not shot down the 13th *Floor Elevator* they would still be alive. He wished he had never fired those rockets. It would be better to be dead himself than to sit here watching Top Tier burn and know that it was all his fault.

Then he thought, *Hester!*

He had promised her he would go back. She would be waiting, down there among the fires. He couldn't let her down. He took a deep breath and leaned on the controls. The engines choked back into life. The *Jenny Haniver* turned sluggishly into the wind and started inching back toward the city.

❀

Katherine moved like a sleepwalker through Paternoster Square, drawn toward the transformed cathedral. Around her the fires were spreading, but she barely noticed. Her eyes were fixed on the terrible beauty above her — that white cowl unfolding against the night sky, turning toward the east. She no longer felt afraid. She knew Clio was watching over her, keeping her safe so that she could atone for the dreadful things Father had done.

The guards on the cathedral door were too distracted by the fires to pay much attention to a schoolgirl with a satchel. At first they told her to clear off, but when she insisted that her father was inside and flashed her crumpled gold pass at them they simply shrugged and let her through.

She had never been inside St. Paul's before, but she had seen pictures. They hadn't looked anything like *this*.

The pillared aisles and the high, vaulted ceilings were still where they had always been, but the Guild of Engineers had sheathed the walls in white metal and hung argon globes in wire cages from the ceilings. Fat electric cables snaked up the nave, feeding power toward something at the heart of the cathedral.

Katherine walked slowly forward, keeping to the shadows under the pillars, out of the way of the scores of Engineers who were scurrying about checking power linkages and making notes on clipboards. Ahead of her, the dais under the great dome was filled with strange machinery. A mass of girders and hydraulics supported the weight of the huge cobra hood that towered up into the night, and around its base stood a forest of tall metal coils, all humming and crackling in a slowly rising surge of power. Engineers were hurrying between them, and going up and down the central tower on metal stairways, and many more were clustered around a nearby console like priests at the altar of a machine god, talking in hushed, excited voices. Among them she saw the Lord Mayor, and beside him, looking grim, was Father.

She froze, safe in the shadows. She could see his face quite clearly. He was watching Crome, and frowning, and she knew he would rather be outside helping with the rescue work and only the Lord Mayor's orders kept him here. She forgot for a moment that he was a murderer; she wanted to rush over and hug him. But she was in Clio's hands now, the agent of History, and she had work to do.

She edged closer, until she was standing in the shelter of an old font at the bottom of the dais steps. From there she had a good view of what Crome and the others were doing. Their console was a cat's cradle of wires and flexes and rubberized ducts, and in the middle of it sat a little sphere no bigger than a soccer ball. Katherine could guess what that was. Pandora Shaw had found it in a deep laboratory of lost America and brought it back with her to Oak Island, and Father had stolen it the night he murdered her. The Engineers had cleaned and repaired it as best they could, replacing damaged circuits with primitive machines that they had cobbled together from Stalkers' brains. Now Dr.

Splay sat in front of it, his fingers spidering over an ivory keyboard, typing up green, glowing sequences of numbers on a portable Goggle-screen. A second screen showed a murky image of the view ahead of London, crosshairs centered on the distant Shield-Wall.

"The accumulators are charged," somebody said.

"There, Valentine!" said Crome, resting a bony hand on her father's arm. "We are ready to make history."

"But the fires, Crome . . ."

"You can play at fireman later," snapped the Lord Mayor. "We must destroy the Shield-Wall *now*, in case MEDUSA is damaged by the blaze."

Splay's fingers kept clattering on the keyboard, but the other sounds of the cathedral faded away. The Engineers were staring in awe at the coil-forest, where weird, rippling wraiths of light were forming, drifting upward toward the sky above the open dome with a faint, insectile buzz. Katherine began to suspect that they didn't really understand this technology that her father had dug up for them; they were almost as awed by it as she.

If she had run forward then, primed her bomb, and flung it at the Ancient computer, she might have changed everything. But how could she? Father was standing right beside the thing, and even when she told herself that he was *not* her father anymore and tried to weigh his life against the thousands about to die in Batmunkh Gompa, she still could not bring herself to harm him. She had failed. She turned her face to the vaulted roof and asked, *What do you want me to do? Why have you brought me here?*

But Clio didn't answer.

Crome stepped toward the keyboard. "Give MEDUSA its target coordinates," he ordered.

Splay's fingers rattled over the keys, typing in the latitude and longitude of Batmunkh Gompa.

"*Target acquired,*" announced a mechanical voice, booming from fluted speakers above Splay's station. "*Range: 130 miles and closing. Input clearance code Omega.*"

Dr. Chubb produced a sheaf of thick plastic sheets, the laminated fragments of Ancient documents. Faint lists of numerals showed through the plastic, like insects trapped in amber, as he flipped through the sheets until he found the one he wanted and held it up for Splay to read.

But before Splay could begin typing in the code numbers there was a confused babble of voices down by the main entrance. Dr. Twix was there, with some of her Stalkers close behind her. "Hello, everybody!" she chirped, hurrying up the aisle and beckoning for her creations to follow. "Just look what my clever babies have found for you, Lord Mayor! A real live Anti-Tractionist, just as you asked. Though I'm afraid she's rather ugly. . . ."

"*Input clearance code Omega,*" repeated MEDUSA. The mechanical voice had not really changed, but to Katherine it sounded slightly impatient.

"Shut up, Twix!" barked Magnus Crome, staring at his instruments, but the others all turned to look as one of the Stalkers lurched up onto the dais and dumped its burden at the Lord Mayor's feet.

It was Hester Shaw, her hands tied in front of her, helpless and sullen and still wondering why the Stalkers had not killed her straight away. At the sight of her ruined face the men on the dais froze, as if her gaze had turned them all to stone.

"Oh, *great Clio!*" whispered Katherine, seeing for the first time what Father's sword had done. And then she looked from Hester's face to his, and what she saw there shocked her even more. The expression had drained from his features, leaving a gray mask, less human and more horrible than the girl's. This was how he must have looked when he killed Pandora Shaw and turned around to find Hester watching him. She knew what would happen next, even before his sword came singing from its sheath.

"No!" she screamed, seeing what he meant to do, but her mouth was dry, her voice a whisper. Suddenly she understood why the goddess had brought her here, and knew what she must do to make amends for Father's crime. She dropped the useless satchel and ran up the steps. Hester was stumbling backward, lifting her bound hands to ward off Father's blow, and Katherine flung herself between them so that suddenly it was *she* who was in his path, and his sword slid easily through her and she felt the hilt jar hard against her ribs.

The Engineers gasped. Dr. Twix gave a frightened little squeak. Even Crome looked alarmed.

"*Input clearance code Omega,*" snapped MEDUSA, as if nothing at all had happened.

Valentine was saying "No!" and shaking his head as if he couldn't understand how she came to be here with his sword through her. "Kate, no!" He stepped back, pulling the blade free.

Katherine watched it slither out of her. It looked ridiculous, like a practical joke. There was no pain at all, but bright blood was throbbing out of a hole in her tunic and splashing on the floor. She felt giddy. Hester Shaw clutched at her but Katherine shook her off. "Father, don't hurt her," she said, and took two faltering steps forward and fell against Dr. Splay's keyboard. Meaningless green letters spattered the little Goggle-screen as her head hit the keys, and as Father lifted her and laid her gently down she heard the voice of MEDUSA boom, "*Incorrect code entered.*"

New sequences of numbers spilled across the screens. Something exploded with a sharp crack amongst the looping webs of cable.

"What's happening?" whimpered Dr. Chubb. "What's it doing?"

"It has rejected our target coordinates," gasped Dr. Chandra. "But the power is still building. . . ."

Engineers rushed back to their posts, stumbling over Katherine where she lay on the floor, her head on Father's lap. She ignored them, staring at Hester's face. It was like looking at her own reflection in a shattered mirror, and she smiled, pleased that she had met her half sister at last, and wondering if they were going to be friends. She started to hiccup, and with each hiccup blood came up her throat into her mouth. A numb chill was spreading through her body, and she could feel herself beginning to drift away, the sounds of the cathedral growing fainter and fainter. *Am I going to die?* she thought. *I can't, not yet, I'm not ready!*

"Help me!" Valentine bellowed at the Engineers — but they were only interested in MEDUSA. It was the girl who came to his side and lifted Katherine while he ripped a strip from his robe and tried to stanch the bleeding. He looked up into her one gray eye and whispered, "Hester . . . thank you!"

Hester stared back at him. She had come all this way to kill him, through all these years, and now that he was at her mercy she felt nothing at all. His sword lay on the ground where he had dropped it. No one was watching her. Even with her wrists bound she could have snatched it up and stuck it through his heart. But it didn't seem to matter now. Dazed, she watched his tears fall, plopping into the astounding lake of blood that was spreading out from his daughter's body. Confused thoughts chased each other through her head. *He loves her! She saved my life! I can't let her die!*

She reached out and touched him, and said, "She needs a doctor, Valentine."

He looked at the Engineers, clustering around their machine in a frantic scrum. There would be no help from them. Outside the cathedral doors curtains of golden fire swung across Paternoster Square. He looked up, and saw something red catch the firelight beyond the high windows of the starboard transept.

"It's the *Jenny Haniver!*" shouted Hester, scrambling to her feet. "Oh, it's Tom! And there's a medical bay aboard. . . ." But she knew the *Jenny* couldn't land amid the flames of Top Tier. "Valentine, can we get onto the roof somehow?"

Valentine picked up his sword and cut the cords on her wrists. Then, flinging it aside, he lifted Katherine and started to carry her between the spitting coils to where the metal stairway zigzagged up into the dome. Stalkers reached out for Hester as she scurried after him, but Valentine ordered them back. To a startled Beefeater he shouted, "Captain! That airship is not to be fired upon!"

Magnus Crome came running to clutch at his sleeve. "The

machine has gone mad!" he wailed. "Quirke alone knows what commands your daughter fed it! We can't fire it and we can't stop the energy buildup! Do something, Valentine! You discovered the damned thing! Make it stop!"

Valentine shoved him aside and started up the steps, through the rising veils of light, the crackling static, through air that smelled like burning tin.

"I only wanted to help London!" the old man sobbed. "I only wanted to make London *strong!*"

36

THE SHADOW OF BONES

Hester took the lead, climbing up through the open top of the dome into smoky firelight and the shadow of the great weapon. Off to her right, the charred skeleton of the *13th Floor Elevator* lay draped over the ruins of the Engineerium like a derelict roller coaster. The fire had spread to the Guildhall, and the Planning Department and the Hall of Records were blazing, hurling out firefly-swarms of sparks and millions of pink and white official forms. St. Paul's was an island in a sea of fire, with the *Jenny Haniver* swinging above it like a low-budget moon, scorched and listing, veering drunkenly in the updrafts from the burning buildings.

She climbed higher, out onto the cobra hood of MEDUSA. Valentine came after her; she could hear him whispering to Katherine, his eyes fixed on the struggling airship.

"What idiot is flying that thing?" he shouted, working his way across the cowl to join her.

"It's Tom!" Hester called back, and stood up, waving both arms and shouting, "Tom! Tom!"

❁

It was the shawl that Tom saw first, the one he had bought for her in Peripatetiapolis. Knotted around her neck now, streaming on the wind, it made a sudden flash of red, and he saw it from the corner of his eye and looked down and saw her there, waving. Then a black wing of smoke came down over her and he wondered if he had only imagined that tiny figure inching out onto the cobra's hood, because it seemed impossible that anyone could survive in this huge fire that he had caused. He made the *Jenny Haniver* swoop closer. The smoke lifted, and there she was, flapping her arms, with her long black coat and her long-legged stride and her ugly, wonderful face.

✻

Katherine opened her eyes. The cold inside her was growing, spreading from the place where the sword had gone in. She was still hiccuping, and she thought how stupid it would be to die with hiccups, how undignified. She wished Dog was with her. "Tom! Tom!" somebody kept shouting. She turned her head and saw an airship coming down out of the smoke, closer and closer until the side of the gondola scraped against MEDUSA's cowl and she felt the downdraft from its battered engine pods. Father was carrying her toward it, and she could see Tom peering out at her through the broken windscreen, Tom who had been there when it all began, whom she had thought was dead. But here he was, alive, looking shocked and soot-stained, with a V-shaped wound on his forehead like the mark of some unknown Guild.

The gondola was much bigger inside than she expected. In fact, it was a lot like Clio House, and Dog and Bevis were both waiting for her there, and her hiccups had stopped, and her wound wasn't as bad as everyone had thought, it was just a scratch. Sunlight streamed in through the windows as Tom flew them all up and up into a sky of the most perfect crystal blue, and she relaxed gratefully into her father's arms.

Hester reached the airship first, hauling herself aboard through its shattered flank. But when she looked back, holding out her hand to Valentine, she saw that he had fallen to his knees, and realized Katherine was dead.

She stayed there, still with her hand outstretched, not quite knowing why. There was an electric shimmer in the air above the white metal hood. She shouted, "Valentine! Be quick!"

He lifted his eyes from his daughter's face just long enough to say, "Hester! Tom! Fly! Save yourselves!"

Behind her, Tom was cupping his hands to his ears and shouting, "What did he say? Is that Katherine? What's happened?"

"Just go!" she yelled, and, clambering past him, started switching all the engines that still worked to full power. When she looked down again Valentine was dwindling away below, a dark shape cradled in his arms, a pale hand trailing. She felt like Katherine's ghost, rising into the sky. There was a terrible pain inside her and her breath came in sobs and something wet and hot was spilling down her cheek. She wondered if she could have been wounded without noticing it, but when she put her hands to her face her fingers came away wet, and she understood that she was crying, crying for her mum and dad, and Shrike, and Katherine, and even for Valentine as the crackling light around the cathedral grew brighter and Tom steered the *Jenny Haniver* away into the dark.

❀

Down in the Gut, London's enormous motors suddenly cut out, without warning and all at once, doused by the strange radiations that were starting to sleet through the city's fabric. For the first time since it crossed the land bridge the great Traction City started to slow.

In a hastily barricaded gallery in the London Museum, Chudleigh Pomeroy peered cautiously over the replica of the blue whale and saw that the squads of Stalkers advancing on his last redoubt had all stopped in their tracks, pale clouds of sparks coiling around their metal skulls like barbed wire. "Great Quirke!" he said, turning to his surviving handful of Historians. "We've won!"

❁

Valentine watches the red airship fly away, lit by the flames of Top Tier and by the spitting forks of light that are beginning to flare around St. Paul's. He can hear hopeless fire bells jangling somewhere below, and the panic-stricken shouts of fleeing Engineers. A halo of St. Elmo's fire flares around Katherine's face and her hair sparks and cracks as he strokes it. He gently moves a stray strand that has blown into her mouth, and holds her close, and waits — and the storm-light breaks over them and they are a knot of fire, a rush of blazing gas, and gone: the shadows of their bones scattering into the brilliant sky.

37

THE BIRD ROADS

London wore a wreath of lightning. It was as if the ray that should have reached out across a hundred miles to sear the stones of Batmunkh Gompa had tangled around the upper tiers instead, sending cataracts of molten metal splashing down the city's flanks. Explosions surged through the Gut, heaving vast fragments of wreckage end over end into the sky like dead leaves in a gale. A few airships rose with them, seeking to escape, but their envelopes ignited and they shriveled and fell, small bright flakes of fire amid the greater burning.

Only the *Jenny Haniver* survived, riding on the fringes of the storm, spinning and pitching as the shock waves battered her, streamers of rainbow light spilling from her rigging and rotor blades. Her engines had all failed together in that first great pulse of energy, and nothing that Tom knew how to do would make them start again. He slumped down in what was left of the pilot's seat, weeping, watching helplessly as the night wind carried him farther and farther from his dying city.

"It's my fault," was all he could think to say. "It's all my fault. . . ."

Hester was watching, too, staring back at the place where St. Paul's had been as if she could still see the afterimages of Katherine and her father lost in the brightness there. "Oh, Tom, no," she said. "It was an accident. Something went wrong with their machine. It was Valentine's fault, and Crome's. It was the Engineers' fault for getting the thing to work and my mum's fault for digging it up in the first place. It was the Ancients' fault for inventing it. It was Pewsey's and Gench's fault for trying to kill you, and Katherine's for saving my life. . . ."

She sat down beside him, wanting to comfort him but afraid to touch him, while her reflections sneered at her from fractured dials and blades of window glass, more monstrous than ever in the fluttering glare of MEDUSA. Then she thought, *Silly, he came back, didn't he? He came back for you.* Trembling, she put her arms around him and pulled him close, nuzzling the top of his head, shyly kissing away the blood from the fresh wound between his eyebrows, hugging him tight until the dying weapon had spent itself and the first gray daylight crept across the plain.

"It's all right, Tom," she kept telling him. "It's all right. . . ."

London was far away, motionless under banners of smoke. Tom found Miss Fang's old field glasses and focused them on the city. "*Someone* must have survived," he said, hoping that saying it would make it true. "I bet Mr. Pomeroy and Clytie Potts are down there, organizing rescue parties and handing out cups of tea. . . ." But through the smoke, the steam, the pall of hanging ash he could see nothing, nothing, nothing, and although he swung the binoculars to and fro, growing increasingly desperate, all they showed him were the bony shapes of blackened girders, and the scorched earth littered with torn-off wheels and blazing lakes of fuel and broken tracks lying tangled on themselves like the cast-off skins of enormous snakes.

"Tom?" Hester had been trying the controls, and had found to her surprise that the rudder levers still worked. The *Jenny Haniver* responded to her touch, turning this way and that on the wind. She said gently, "Tom, we could try and reach Batmunkh Gompa. We'll be welcome there. They'll probably think you're a hero."

But Tom shook his head: Behind his eyes the 13*th Floor Elevator* was still spiraling toward Top Tier, and Pewsey and Gench were riding their black, silent screams into the fire. He didn't know what he was, but he knew he was no hero.

"All right," said Hester, understanding. It took time to get over things sometimes, she knew that. She would be patient with him. She said, "We'll head for the Black Island. We can repair the *Jenny* at the air-caravanserai. And then we'll take the Bird Roads and go somewhere far away. The Hundred Islands, or the Tannhäuser Mountains, or the Southern Ice Waste. I don't mind where. As long as I can come, too."

She knelt beside him, resting her arms on his knees and her head on her arms, and Tom found that he was smiling in spite of himself at her crooked smile. "You aren't a hero, and I'm not beautiful, and we probably won't live happily ever after," she said. "But we're alive, and together, and we're going to be all right."

Acknowledgments

I am gratefully indebted to Leon Robinson and Brian Mitchell, who provided me with inspiration, encouragement, and good ideas; to Mike Grant, who published my early efforts in his late lamented small-press magazine *The Heliograph*; and to Liz Cross, Kirsten Skidmore, and Holly Skeet, without whose patience, enthusiasm, and sound advice this book would have ended its days in my fireplace as a lot of very neatly typed kindling.

PHILIP REEVE lives in Dartmoor, England, with his wife and son. His first novel, *Mortal Engines*, was published in the UK in 2001. Three sequels followed, the last of which, *A Darkling Plain*, won both the Guardian Children's Fiction Prize and the Los Angeles Times Book Award. Philip later wrote three prequels to the Mortal Engines Quartet—*Fever Crumb*, *A Web of Air*, and *Scrivener's Moon*. He has also written a novel set in dark age Britain called *Here Lies Arthur*, which won the Carnegie Medal; a stand-alone novel for younger readers called *No Such Thing as Dragons*; as well as an illustrated younger fiction series with illustrator Sarah McIntyre; and a young-adult trilogy, RailHead. He is the coauthor, with Brian Mitchell, of a stage musical, *The Ministry of Biscuits*. His most recent book, *Night Flights*, returns to the world of Mortal Engines with three short stories about the character Anna Fang.

From the "wildly imaginative mind" of

PHILIP REEVE

comes a gripping tale that soars and astonishes.

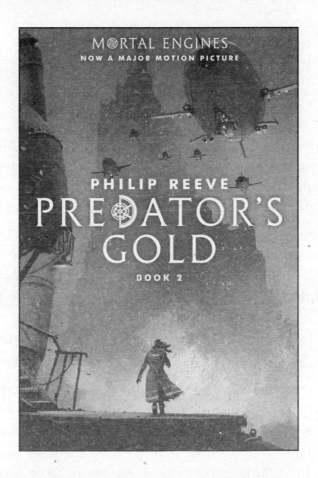

Hester and Tom's adventure continues…

*School Library Journal

HESTER AND TOM

Hester Shaw was starting to get used to being happy. After all her muddy, starveling years in the ditches and scavengervilles of the Great Hunting Ground she had finally found herself a place in the world. She had her own airship, the *Jenny Haniver* (if she craned her neck she could just see the upper curve of her red envelope, behind that Zanzibar spice-freighter at strut seventeen) and she had Tom: gentle, handsome, clever Tom, whom she loved with her whole heart and who, in spite of everything, seemed to love her, too.

For a long time she had felt sure it wouldn't last. They were so different, and Hester was hardly anyone's idea of beautiful: a tall, graceless scarecrow of a girl, her coppery hair done up in tootight plaits, her face split in half by an old sword blow that had robbed her of one eye and most of her nose and twisted her mouth into a snaggletoothed sneer. *It won't last,* she had kept telling herself, all the time they were waiting on the Black Island for the shipwrights to repair the poor battered *Jenny Haniver.* *He only stays with me out of pity,* she had decided, as they flew down to Africa, then crossed to South America. *What can he see in me?* she wondered, while they grew rich ferrying supplies to the great oil-drilling cities of Antarctica and then suddenly poor again, jettisoning cargo to outrun air-pirates over Tierra del Fuego. Flying back across the blue Atlantic with a merchant convoy she whispered to herself, *It cannot possibly last.*

And yet it had lasted; it had lasted for more than two years now. Sitting in September sunshine on this balcony outside the Crumple Zone, one of the many coffeehouses on Airhaven High Street, Hester found herself beginning to believe that it might last forever. She squeezed Tom's hand beneath the table and smiled her crooked smile, and he looked at her with just as much love as when she first kissed him, in the fluttering light of MEDUSA on the night his city died.

Airhaven had flown north this autumn and now hung a few thousand feet above the Frost Barrens, while small scavenger towns that had been up on the ice during the months of the midnight sun clustered below it to trade. Balloon after balloon rose to moor at the docking struts of the flying free-port, disgorging colorful Old-Tech traders who started shouting their wares the instant their boots touched its lightweight deckplates. The frozen north was a good hunting ground for diggers-up of lost technology, and these gentlemen were selling Stalker parts, Tesla Gun accumulators, nameless odds and ends of machinery left over from half a dozen different civilizations, even some pieces of an Ancient flying machine which had lain undisturbed in the High Ice since the Sixty Minute War.

Below them to the south, the east, and west, the Frost Barrens stretched away into the haze: cold, stony country where the Ice Gods ruled for eight months of the year, and where patches of snow already lay in the shady bottoms of the crisscross town-tracks. Northwards rose the black basalt wall of the Tannhäuser Mountains, the chain of volcanoes that marked the northernmost limit of the Great Hunting Ground. Several were erupting, their plumes of gray smokelike pillars holding up the sky. Between them, faint behind a veil of ash, Hester and Tom could just make out the worldwide white of the Ice Wastes, and something moving there, vast, dirty and implacable, like a mountain gone rogue.

Hester pulled a telescope from one of the pockets of her coat and put it to her eye, twizzling the focusing ring until the blurry view came suddenly sharp. She was looking at a city: eight tiers of factories and slave-barracks and soot-spewing chimneys, a sky-train riding the slipstream, parasite airships sifting the exhaust plume for waste minerals, and down below, ghostly through veils of snow and powdered rock, the big wheels rolling.

"Arkangel!"

Tom took the telescope from her. "You're right. It keeps to the northern foothills of the Tannhäusers in summer, eating up scavenger towns as they come through the passes. The polar ice cap is much thicker now than it was in olden days, but there are still parts that are too thin to take Arkangel's weight till summer's end."

Hester laughed. "Know-all."

"I can't help it," Tom said. "I was an apprentice historian, remember? We had to memorize a list of the World's Great Traction Cities, and Arkangel was right near the top, so I'm not likely to forget it."

"Show off," grumbled Hester. "I wish it had been Zimbra, or Xanne-Sandansky. You wouldn't look so clever then."

Tom was peering through the telescope again. "Any day now it'll lift up its tracks and lower its iron runners and go skating off in search of ice cities and Snowmad scavenger towns to gobble up. . . ."

For the present, however, Arkangel seemed content to trade. It was too vast to haul itself through the narrow passes of the Tannhäusers, but airships were lifting from its harbors and flying south through the haze towards Airhaven. The first of them cut an arrogant swath through the swirl of balloons around the floating town and swooped in to dock at strut six, just below Tom and Hester's perch; they felt the faint vibration as its docking clamps gripped the quay. It was a lean, short-range attack ship with a red wolf painted on its sable envelope and its name underneath in Gothic script: the *Clear Air Turbulence*.

Men swaggered out of the armored gondola, stomping along the quay and up the stairways that led to the High Street. Big, burly men with fur cloaks and fur hats and a chilly glitter of chain mail under their tunics. One wore a steel helmet from which sprouted two huge, flaring gramophone horns. A cord led from the helmet to a brass microphone, clamped in the fist of another man, whose amplified voice boomed out across Airhaven as he climbed the stairs.

"Greetings, airlings! From Great Arkangel, Hammer of the High Ice, Scourge of the North, Devourer of the Spitzbergen Static, greetings! We have gold to exchange for anything you can tell us about the locations of ice cities! Thirty sovereigns for information leading to a capture!"

He started to push his way between the Crumple Zone's tables, still booming out his offer, while all about him aviators shook their heads and made sour faces and turned away. Now that prey was in such short supply everywhere several of the big predators had begun to offer finder's fees, but few did it this openly. Honest air-traders were starting to fear that they might soon be barred altogether from the smaller ice cities, for what mayor would risk giving docking permits to a ship that might fly off the next day and sell his course to a greedy great urbivore like Arkangel? Yet there were always others, smugglers and demi-pirates and merchants whose ships were not bringing in the profits they had hoped for, who were ready to accept predator's gold.

"Come and find me at the Gasbag and Gondola if you have traded this summer aboard Kivitoo or Breidhavik or Anchorage and know where they plan to overwinter!" urged the newcomer. He was a young man, and he looked stupid and rich and well-fed. "Thirty in gold, my friends: enough to keep your ships in fuel and *luftgaz* for a year . . ."

"That is Piotr Masgard," Hester heard a Dinka aviatrix at a neighboring table tell her friends. "He's the youngest son of the Direktor of Arkangel. Calls that gang of his the Huntsmen. They don't just advertise for snoops; I've heard they land that ship of theirs on peaceful little cities too fast for Arkangel to catch and force them to stop, or turn around — force them at sword-point to steer straight into Arkangel's jaws!"

"But that's not fair!" cried Tom, who had also been listening, and unluckily his words fell loudly into a momentary gap in Masgard's speech. The Huntsman swung around, and his big, lazy, handsome face grinned down at Tom.

"Not fair, airling? What's not fair? This is a town eat town world, you know."

Hester tensed. One thing she could never understand about Tom was why he always expected everything to be fair. She supposed it was his upbringing. A few years living by his wits in a scavenger-ville would have knocked it out of him, but he'd grown up with all the rules and customs of the Guild of Historians to keep real life at bay and, despite all he'd seen since, he could still be shocked by people like Masgard.

."I just mean, it's against all the rules of Municipal Darwinism," Tom explained, looking up at the big man. He got to his feet, but found that he was still looking up, for the towering Huntsman was at least a foot taller. "Fast cities eat slow ones, and strong cities eat weak ones. That's the way it's meant to work, just like in nature. Offering finder's fees and hijacking prey upsets the balance," he went on, as though Masgard was just an opponent at the Apprentice Historians' Debating Society.

Masgard's grin grew broader. He flicked his fur cloak aside and drew his sword. There were gasps and cries and a clatter of falling chairs as everyone in the vicinity tried to get as far back as possible. Hester grabbed hold of Tom and began pulling him away, always keeping her eye on that gleaming blade. "Tom, you idiot, leave it!"

Masgard stared at her a moment, then let out a roaring laugh and sheathed his sword. "Look! The airling has a pretty girlie to keep him from harm!"

His crew laughed with him, and Hester blushed patchily and tugged up her old red scarf to hide her face.

"Come and find me later, girl!" Masgard shouted. "I'm always at home to a pretty lady! And remember, if you have a city's course to tell me of, I'll give you thirty in gold! You can buy yourself a new nose!"

"I'll remember," promised Hester, pushing Tom quickly away. Anger flapped inside her like a trapped crow. She wanted to turn and fight. She was willing to bet Masgard didn't know how to use that sword he was so proud of. . . . But the dark, murderous, revengeful part of her was something she tried to keep hidden these days, so she contented herself with slipping out her knife and quietly severing the lead of Masgard's microphone as she passed. The next time he tried to make an announcement the laughter would be directed at him.

"Sorry," Tom said bashfully, as they hurried down to the docking ring, which was crowded now with traders and sightseers fresh in from Arkangel. "I didn't mean — I just thought —"

"It's all right," said Hester. She wanted to tell him that if he didn't do brave, foolish things like that from time to time he wouldn't be Tom, and she might not love him so. But she couldn't put all that into words, so she pushed him into the space under a tier-support and, after making sure that nobody was looking, wrapped her skinny arms around his neck and pulled her veil down and kissed him. "Let's leave."

"But we don't have cargo yet. We were going to look for a fur trader or —"

"There are no fur traders here, only old-tech, and we don't want to start carrying that sort of stuff, do we?" He looked uncertain, so she kissed him again before he could say anything. "I'm tired of Airhaven. I want to be back on the Bird Roads."

"All right," said Tom. He smiled, stroking her mouth, her cheek, the kink in her eyebrow where the scar cut through. "All right. We've seen enough of northern skies. Let's go."

But it was not to be so simple. When they reached strut seventeen there was a man waiting beside the *Jenny Haniver*, sitting on a big leather pack. Hester, still smarting a little from Masgard's mockery, hid her face again. Tom let go her hand and hurried to meet the stranger.

"Good day!" cried the man, standing up. "Mr. Natsworthy? Miss Shaw? I gather you are the owners of this splendid little ship? Golly, they told me at the harbor office you were young, but I didn't realize quite how young! You're barely more than children!"

"I'm almost eighteen," said Tom defensively.

"Never mind, never mind!" beamed the stranger. "Age makes no difference if the heart is great, and I'm sure you have a great heart. 'Who's that handsome young chap?' I asked my friend the harbormaster, and he told me, 'That's Tom Natsworthy, pilot of the *Jenny Haniver*.' 'Pennyroyal,' I said to myself, 'that young man may be just the fellow you're looking for!' So here I am!"

Here he was. He was a smallish man, balding and slightly overweight, and he wore a trim white beard. His clothes were the typical outfit of a northern scavenger — a long fur coat, a tunic with many pockets, thick breeches and fur-lined boots — but they looked too expensive, as if they'd been run up for him by a fashionable tailor as a costume for a play set in the Ice Wastes.

"Well?" he asked.

"Well what?" asked Hester, who had taken an instant dislike to this posturing stranger.

"I'm sorry, sir," said Tom, much more politely. "We don't really understand what you want. . . ."

"Oh, I do apologize, I beg your pardon," the stranger babbled. "Permit me to elucidate! My name is Pennyroyal: Nimrod Beauregard Pennyroyal. I have been exploring a little among these great horrible towering fire-mountains, and now I am on my way home. I should like to book passage aboard your charming airship."

EXPLORE THE WORLD OF
MORTAL ENGINES!

THE ORIGINAL SERIES!

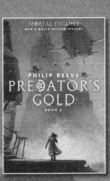

THE PREQUEL SERIES!

RETURN TO THE WORLD OF MORTAL ENGINES...

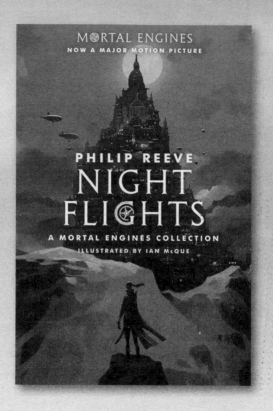

Follow the rebellious young aviatrix, Anna Fang, through three gripping short stories: her childhood as a slave aboard the moving city Arkangel, a showdown against a robotic Stalker that is terrifyingly out of control, and her free life as an intelligence agent for the Anti-Traction league that might not be quite as free as she hoped . . .

IReadYA.com

NIGHTFLIGHTS